Readers love
ROWAN MCALLISTER

We Met in Dreams

"There are layers of this story. When you finish it, you will ponder ~~~~~~~~~~~~ discovering nuances in the story as it h   pproach

"Ms. Mc   riguing, emotional   historical rom   nce here and I completely loved it."

—Gay Book Reviews

Power Bottom?

"I was smiling and happy throughout the read. Highly entertained."

—Badass Book Reviews

"*Power Bottom?* was nothing like I thought it would be—it turned out even better!"

—Alpha Book Club

Water and Fire

"Rowan McAllister has become one of my go-for-comfort authors. Her writing, stories, and characters just click with me."

—Boys in Our Books

By ROWAN MCALLISTER

Published by DREAMSPINNER PRESS
www.dreamspinnerpress.com

ROWAN McALLISTER

THE SECOND TIME AROUND

DREAMSPINNER
PRESS

Published by
DREAMSPINNER PRESS

5032 Capital Circle SW, Suite 2, PMB# 279,
Tallahassee, FL 32305-7886 USA
www.dreamspinnerpress.com

The Second Time Around
© 2018 Rowan McAllister.

Cover Art
© 2018 Adrian Nicholas.
adrian.nicholas177@gmail.com
Cover content is for illustrative purposes only and any person depicted on the cover is a model.

Mass Market Paperback ISBN: 978-1-64108-014-9
Trade Paperback ISBN: 978-1-64080-522-4
Digital ISBN: 978-1-64080-481-4
Library of Congress Control Number: 2017916215
Mass Market Paperback published September 2018
v. 1.0

Printed in the United States of America
∞
This paper meets the requirements of
ANSI/NISO Z39.48-1992 (Permanence of Paper).

To all those who open their hearts and their homes to the abused and unwanted, giving them that second chance at a better life.

CHAPTER ONE

"OH SHIT!"

Tires squealed and gravel ricocheted off the under-carriage. The back end of his pretty red BMW 4 series convertible kicked up a cloud of dirt and rocks, fishtail-ing toward the drop-off. His hands locked on the steer-ing wheel, and his foot tried to slam the brake pedal through the floor as he spun out and his heart lodged itself firmly in his throat.

His life could be ending—right there, right then—and the best he could come up with was "oh shit"?

When the car finally rocked to a stop, the pounding of his heart was almost deafening in the sudden quiet. The whole terrifying ordeal had taken only a few sec-onds at most, but it felt like years had been shaved from his life.

Cracking open one tightly clamped eyelid, he half expected to find himself teetering over the edge, sec-onds away from toppling down the side of one of the foothills he'd been speeding through. But no, all four tires were safely supported by an extra-wide gravel shoulder, apparently designed to save assholes like him who weren't paying attention and took that last turn way too fast.

Drama queen.

The voice in his head was his father's, though Jordan was pretty sure William Alexander Thorndike II had never actually spoken that particular phrase aloud in his life.

With a grimace, he pried his cramped fingers off the leather-wrapped steering wheel and flexed them a few times before shutting off the engine with one shaking hand. Closing his eyes again, he tossed the keys on the passenger seat, let his head flop back against the headrest, and just breathed. He needed to calm down. He needed to get his head together before he got back on the road, or he really would end up killing himself.

He could see the headline now: Millionaire Banker's Son Killed in Tragic Crash!

His father would probably be overjoyed. Tragic death in the family would beat out disinheriting gay son scandal any day of the week. Both his parents would get all kinds of sympathy from their country club friends without being tainted by the ugly truth. Win-win.

Except Jordan wouldn't give them the satisfaction.

"Fuck them." And because he liked the way that sounded, he lifted his head and shouted it to the hills and trees and birds. "Fuck them!"

Fuck them all. They could keep their perfect first-born and their darling baby girl. The middle kid always got the shaft anyway, didn't they? He'd been doomed from the start.

Once his heart slowed to something approaching normal, he climbed out of the car on stiff, shaking legs, rested his palms on the uncomfortably warm glossy red hood, and hung his head. He was being unfair to his siblings. Will Jr. couldn't help that he was so god-damned perfect, and Gemma would probably be stuck as the baby her entire life. They all had issues, though none of them had ever fucked things up quite as much as Jordan had this time.

He was good at that, if nothing else.

"Don't say another word. I don't want to hear it."

His father had stood ramrod straight in his study, his back to Jordan with his hands clasped behind him, staring out the window behind his desk. Jordan's mom sniffled from the chair she'd collapsed into behind him, but Jordan couldn't take his eyes off his father.

"Father, I—"

"No. Not one more word. You're going to go take a walk, Jordan. When you come back, you're going to apologize to your mother for upsetting her with this sick joke. You're going to tell us you're more than hap-py to escort Madson's daughter, Sheila, to the dressage festival dinner, and anything else she wants you to go to this summer before you return to school in the fall and finish your degree. I won't hear anything else."

Wincing at the memory, Jordan sank to the ground and slumped against the side of his car. After twen-ty-four years of trying, and mostly failing, to live up to their expectations, he'd done it. He'd finally plucked up the courage to tell them the truth. He would never—*could* never—be who they wanted him to be.

He should feel relieved. The soul-crushing weight of all those expectations was gone. He wouldn't have to pretend to date girls he had no interest in anymore. He wouldn't have to smile and flirt and flatter the parade of pampered princesses his parents foisted on him in hopes he'd find a good Christian girl who'd settle his wild ways. He wouldn't have to act as if getting his degree and passing the bar was all he'd ever wanted out of life. He was free.

Instead, he hurt. The center of his chest ached as if he'd been punched, only the pain hadn't faded even a tiny bit in the hours since he'd taken his parents aside and done the deed. It just kept burning on and on.

He'd prepared himself for yelling. He'd prepared himself for his mom's tears and his father's disapproval and disappointment. The latter was something he was intimately familiar with. But he hadn't been prepared to be so completely, coldly, and utterly shut out. His mom had barely uttered a half-hearted "Maybe it's just a phase" before his father had cut her off with the ultimatum: go back to pretending to be the son they wanted him to be or he was no longer their son at all—no discussion, no room for debate. He'd packed up his things in a daze, hoping the whole time someone would come and offer him a thread of hope, some hint that the door wasn't shut for good, but no one came.

A trickle of sweat slid down his back, breaking in on the useless playback that had been stuck on repeat since he'd sped away from Thorndike Farms. He needed to think, not dwell. Pushing the memories aside, he got to his feet, dusted off his linen shorts, and scanned his surroundings. He was on a lonely stretch of winding road, headed up into the mountains, and he had no idea where he was going. Dark green summer leaves rustled in the weak breeze, cicadas chirped in the trees, and a haze shimmered off the nearby pavement. The air was as heavy and wet as Virginia in July could get, and he didn't relish the thought of melting into a puddle on the side of the road, with his father's voice still ringing in his ears.

Now that the adrenaline had worn off, he was drained, which did nothing to help his mood or his ability to function. Slipping back into the driver's seat, he started the car again and cranked the air conditioning. The top was still down, but the cool air blasting on his face helped wake him up a bit. He turned the radio on loud enough to drown out the voices in his head and pulled back onto the road, hoping inspiration would strike as he went. He wasn't exactly in any shape to make decisions right now, but sitting still somewhere, alone with his thoughts, was not really an option either. He had to *do* something.

As the signs for I-81 became more frequent, he went with his gut and followed the arrows. Over the mountains and out of Virginia seemed like a fantastic idea. He'd put horse-country snobbery and Lynchburg's rigid narrow-mindedness in the rearview for a while, at least until he figured out what the hell he was going to do with himself.

The problem was, he'd never really been able to plan much beyond the coming-out part. Maybe if he'd had some idea of who he wanted to be, instead of who he didn't, the talk with his father might have gone better. He'd have been able to stand up to the old man, instead of slinking away like a kicked dog… not that the end result would have been much different probably. But he might not have felt so lost in the aftermath. He would have had somewhere to go at least.

Near the on-ramp for 81-S, he pulled into a gas station to fill up and grab some coffee. His onboard computer couldn't find a Starbucks close enough, so he'd have to make do with whatever the gas station had. At the pump, he slid his card into the machine and it beeped at him. Frowning, he tipped his polarized sunglasses down and tried again, but it did the same thing. See Cashier flashed across the screen.

Inside, he handed his card to the cashier as the ache in his chest grew stronger. "Hi. There's something wrong with the pump. It won't take my card."

"How much do you want to put in?"

"Thirty."

The bored-looking woman behind the counter swiped the card in her machine. "Sorry, sir. It says declined."

A slightly sharper pain lanced through him as he took the card back and schooled his expression to bland confusion. Sweat prickled under his collar, and he felt like everyone was looking at him, judging. "Oh, sorry, must be something wrong with the account. Here, try this one."

He wasn't willing to risk any more humiliation, so he gave her the debit card to his personal bank account, the one only he had access to. He'd check the other accounts on his phone as soon as he was somewhere private, but a sinking dread filled his stomach.

"It went through."

Struggling to breathe, he nodded and smiled for the woman before taking his card and heading back to his car, skipping the coffee. As he filled the tank, he pulled up his credit card accounts and the bank account his father put his allowance into, one by one, only to be denied access or find zero balances.

"Well, that was quick," he murmured numbly.

The numbers on the screen made his situation somehow more real, and the vise on his chest tightened another crank.

The gas nozzle *thunked* loudly next to him, startling him out of his daze. On autopilot, he returned it to the pump, twisted the cap on his tank, and climbed behind the wheel, gripping it with sweaty palms.

Now he had no family, no job, and no money beyond a couple grand in the only account his father didn't have access to—the account he'd created so he could go to gay clubs and hook up in hotels without leaving a paper trail his father could find.

At least he still had his car. He could sell that if things really got desperate. The thought pained him, but it was only a drop in the bucket at this point.

From everything to nothing with just a few little words.

Who knew "I'm gay and I don't want to be a lawyer" could have such power?

Weird.

But he'd known, at least to some extent. Otherwise he would have said them a decade ago, instead of chickening out year after year.

"But isn't love supposed to conquer all?" His words were snatched away by the wind as he put his foot down and sped past eighteen-wheelers and cars and SUVs packed with camping gear and loaded down with bike racks.

The funny thing was, the whole reason he'd finally gotten the balls to do it was that he'd been thinking it was time to settle down... or at least *think* about settling down and having a future—no more wild child, no more frat parties or crazy stunts. He'd been thinking it was time to try a real relationship with someone for once, actual dating and not just fucking around, and to find a career path that he could stomach without wanting to off himself every day when he got out of bed. That was everything his father always said he wanted from his son, wasn't it? Just not quite how he wanted it.

How stupid was that?

CHAPTER TWO

AROUND KNOXVILLE, TN, he decided to stop. He was drained, physically and emotionally. He didn't have anything even approaching a plan. He wasn't really paying attention to where he was going, and he would probably get someone killed, driving seventy down the interstate, if he pushed himself to go any farther.

With a few commands, the onboard computer found him a Motel 6 off I-40, and he went for it. Despite his upbringing, he'd seen the inside of more than a few cheap motels on the hunt for some D, although he'd never actually stayed a full night in one. He'd have to get used to it from now on, it seemed.

The bedspreads were slippery polyester and the carpet was gross, but the sheets were stiff enough to have been well bleached, and all he needed was a flat surface to collapse onto as soon as he got drunk enough to pass out. That was the sum total of the plan he'd been able to come up with so far... well, that and getting a pizza delivered so he wouldn't starve. He'd have to pay for that bit of cheating at the gym later, but he didn't have the energy to find someplace with a decent salad, and what better way to drown his sorrows than to glut?

Luckily, he'd had enough sense to grab his laptop and tablet when he'd packed up his things, and his Netflix and Prime memberships were already paid for, so he didn't have to rely on the dubious television choices available through the hotel. The Wi-Fi was weak at best, but he was able to find something distracting until the Jameson he'd picked up at the liquor store across from the hotel kicked in.

"To my glorious future," he said to his reflection in the mirror across from the bed, before downing another big swallow from the bottle.

He didn't remember much after that.

SUNLIGHT RHYTHMICALLY stabbed through his eyelids from the gaps in the swaying vertical blinds over the air conditioner. With a groan, he rolled to an upright position and braced himself for the pain. Racing to the bathroom, he emptied his stomach until all he could do was dry heave, but he was grateful for the hangover. Vomiting up the pizza meant he wouldn't have to worry as much about that trip to the gym— when he found a gym he could afford. And the hammering in his skull meant he couldn't think about much of anything beyond coffee, Tylenol, and a long shower.

Win-win.

The shower had to come first because he wasn't so bad off that he was willing to settle for the tiny coffeepot and sachet of Maxwell House in the room. He might be poor now, but he still had standards. He had to go out for the Tylenol anyway.

This time he found a Starbuck's and splurged on a Venti Caramel Macchiato, although with half the syrup. He hadn't completely lost his mind.

Sitting in the parking lot, watching people come and go, he tried not to think about anything until he'd drained the last drop from the paper cup. But all too soon, it was empty, and he couldn't put it off any longer. He had to come up with some sort of plan, and the idea of "The Rest of His Life!" was almost overwhelming.

The problem was, he'd been pretending to be someone else for so long, he didn't even know who he was anymore—if he ever had. He was free now, but free to do what? It wasn't as if he'd ever been really good at anything, not good enough anyway. Having a rich father had opened a lot of doors for him that he never would've been able to open on his own. Could he survive on his own merits?

A little flutter of panic started in his belly as people with places to go and things to do continued to pass by him.

Oh God.

He might've just thrown his whole life away for nothing. He'd stood in his dad's office and demanded they accept him for who he was when he didn't even know himself. What was he thinking?

Drama queen.

The words caught him up short before he headed toward a total freak-out in a public place where everyone could see. Clenching his jaw, he lifted his chin and forced the panic down with a few carefully controlled breaths.

He'd made the right choice. His planning and execution could have used some work, but the decision was right. He had to believe that. His old life, all those expectations, had been crushing him. He never would have been able to keep it up without losing his shit entirely.

"So what do I do now?"

He didn't expect an answer from his reflection in the rearview, but some sort of sign would've been helpful.

About to give up and just hit the road again without a plan—hoping inspiration would strike somewhere along the way—he jumped when his phone vibrated in his pocket. Frowning, he fished it out. He could've sworn he'd turned off notifications for pretty much everything last night. The usual barrage from Instagram and Snapchat, plus texts from friends who'd never really been friends, had been compounded by numerous texts from his siblings, until he just couldn't take it anymore and shut everything off—especially since none of the texts from his family were from his mother or father or included any words like *come home* or *we love you*.

"What the hell did you do now?" pretty much summed up all the messages from his older brother, Will Jr., and *"What's going on? Why doesn't anybody tell me anything?"* was about all his little sister, Gemma, had to contribute.

This time the notification on the screen was a calendar reminder he'd put in months ago.

July 16: Call mom re: B STAR trip

Today he was supposed to give his mom an answer about whether he'd be joining her for a week at the rescue ranch that was one of his family's pet charities for as long as he could remember. She'd planned the trip during one of her empty-nest moments, now that Gemma had started college, as a bonding experience for the two of them. He'd kind of blown her off at the time and then totally forgotten about it.

Staring at the screen, he choked up a little, despite being pissed at his mom for not even trying to stand up for him. He wouldn't be making that call. They wouldn't be bonding over anything anytime soon... maybe not ever.

"Fuck!"

He threw his phone on the passenger seat and thumped his head on the steering wheel. He would not cry in public. He would *not* cry in public.

He took deep breaths until the need faded. Then he grabbed the phone again and worried his lower lip.

Some of his happiest memories from childhood were from the B STAR. It was one of the few actual "family" vacations they took together. He couldn't remember why his parents had stopped going, especially given the size of the check they still wrote the place every year and the fundraising his mother did on their behalf. Maybe the "kids" had just gotten too old for it.

The name stood for Better the Second Time Around Rescue, and as he stared at the letters on the screen, his lips began to curve up for the first time in days.

He'd asked for a sign. What better place to go to figure things out than a home for the unloved and unwanted... his very own island of misfit toys?

It wasn't a permanent solution, but it was a place to start. He'd been around horses his whole life. He knew his way around a stable, at least enough to be useful. Texas was a long drive, but he could feel the weight on his chest lifting the more he thought about it. He had a plan, somewhere to go, somewhere with nothing but fond memories and plenty of work to keep him out of his head for a while. It was like fate had thrown him a lifeline.

"Perfect."

Scanning through his phone until he found the address, he started the engine again. After putting it into the navigation system, his phone connected to Bluetooth, and he cranked up his road-trip playlist. With a deep breath and a silent prayer, he joined the stream of bustling humanity and headed for the highway.

CHAPTER THREE

THE BUTTERFLIES started a mosh pit in his stomach as soon as he pulled off the main road and drove under the rusted-metal scrolling B and five-pointed star mounted between weathered wood posts. Much of the place was the same as he remembered from fourteen years ago, like the rows of fences and pens filled with animals and the big red barn next to the house. But a lot had changed too. The main house had been repainted a deep green with white trim and shutters. There were new outbuildings and shelters scattered among the old. And llamas, alpacas, a camel, and an ostrich had joined the horses, donkeys, goats, and cows beyond the fences.

His little red convertible stuck out like a sore thumb among the dusty, beat-up trucks and SUVs in the gravel lot. Fixing his gaze straight forward, toward his goal, he ignored the men and women he passed as they turned to mark his approach, so his nerves wouldn't get the better of him. As messed-up as he was right now, his mask was going to be fragile enough. He couldn't afford any distractions.

He parked in front of the main house, next to a white pickup with the B STAR logo on the side. The two people sitting in rockers on the front porch stood up as he pulled in, and an involuntary "Helllloooo cowboy" escaped his lips before he could rein it in, momentarily distracting him from his nervousness.

Although she was a bit older, he recognized the silver-haired woman from his childhood and the ranch's promotional materials—Phyllis Wharton. She'd started the rescue with her husband thirty years ago. But the cowboy next to her was all new, and all beefcake. Older than Jordan usually went for, maybe in his late thirties, the man was still damned fine, so exceptions could be made. Tall and lean, with worn jeans and a thin T-shirt that hugged him in all the right places and showed off tanned muscled arms, Jordan could almost imagine those hard hands, lips, and stubbled jaw on every inch of his body.

Damn.

He really should've found somewhere to sow his oats before driving into the middle of nowhere, even deeper into the heart of the Bible Belt, for a prolonged stay. More poor planning on his part. But to be fair, he'd had other things on his mind right up until this very moment.

Luckily, Jordan was still wearing his sunglasses, so his ogling wasn't quite so obvious. He'd hate to get punched before he'd even gotten a chance to plead his case.

Focus, Thorndike. You've got a little old lady to charm.

He got out of his car, and Phyllis's weathered face split into a welcoming smile as she descended the steps to greet him.

"Hey there! Welcome to B STAR rescue!"

In her crisp plaid short-sleeved pink blouse, jeans, and boots, she looked almost exactly how Jordan remembered, though her hair had gone from washed-out blonde to silver. Her open smile and cheerful voice eased some of the ache in his chest, and the broad smile he gave her in return was only partially forced.

"Hi. I'm sure you don't recognize me, but my family used to come here all the time when I was a kid. I'm Jordan Thorndike. My mother might have talked to you about coming out this summer?"

Phyllis's eyes widened a bit, and Jordan held his most winning smile. Just because his family had disowned him didn't mean he couldn't use their name to get what he wanted. He wouldn't abuse it to get special treatment. He didn't want special. He wanted to be worked into exhaustion every day so he didn't have to feel anything at all for a while. But he wasn't above using his family to get his foot in the door.

"Oh my word, Jordan! I haven't seen you since you were a little thing, tagging after your big brother and spending so much time with the horses we thought we should set you up a bed in the barn."

More tension leeched from his shoulders. Phyllis was a saleswoman. She had to be to keep the donations flowing, but genuine caring lurked beneath her mask, unlike most of the people in his parents' circles. She was a good person. She had to be to give her whole life to the rescue, and it was nice to be remembered.

"That was me," he replied, shifting so he stopped catching the hottie on the porch out of the corner of his eye. The man hadn't moved or said anything yet, and Jordan was still finding him a little too distracting for his own good.

"Your momma did send us word she was thinking of coming down for a spell, but she said she'd prefer to wait 'til fall when it's not quite so hot," Phyllis continued, her smile undimmed.

"Yeah. I know. I'm not exactly sure if she's still going to make the trip at all, but I decided to come down anyway." He shifted and shot a nervous glance toward the man on the porch before lifting his sunglasses and holding Phyllis's gaze. "I'd actually like to talk to you about maybe staying on here for a little while… volunteering with the animals, if possible."

Her smile slipped, and her silver eyebrows lifted, stark against the brown of her skin. "You want to volunteer?"

"Yes. I'm not looking for any special treatment or tours of the facilities like before. I want to work, just like the rest of the volunteers, and maybe stay in one of the bunkhouses or something. I don't need anything fancy, just a roof and maybe some meals," he said, upping the wattage on his smile.

Her eyebrows drew down in confusion, and she pursed her lips. After shooting a quick glance at the man behind her, she said, "I'll be honest with you, Jordan, you surprised me. But… why don't you come inside for a drink and we'll talk?"

She lifted her arm, indicating he precede her, but he shook his head.

"Ladies first."

At the top of the stairs, she stopped in front of the hottie in the straw cowboy hat and said, "Jordan, this is Russ Niles, my foreman and right-hand man. Russ, this is Jordan Thorndike. His family has been a very generous contributor to our little operation here for forever, and longtime friends."

Russ's hand was warm, hard, and calloused as he shook Jordan's, and damned if Jordan didn't feel it all the way to his cock. The man was even yummier up close. Thick brown hair peeked out from under his hat, and chocolate-brown eyes held his for far too short a time before turning back to Phyllis.

"Nice to meet you," Russ replied shortly.

Not a single spark of interest had lit the man's eyes, crushing any fantasies Jordan might have dreamed up.

The good ones are always straight.

Even as wounded and fragile as Jordan was, the man's lack of interest only stung a little. Straight was straight, and trying to change that was a waste of time. Besides, he wasn't there for sex. He could find a club or bar within driving distance if he really needed to scratch an itch. Houston was less than two hours away, and he'd never had trouble getting picked up. He spent countless hours grooming himself and sweating at the gym to make sure of that.

His loss.

He still smoothed a nervous hand over his flat stomach and tugged at the waistband of his shorts to make sure nothing was out of place. But he needn't have bothered, because the man only turned on his heel and headed down the stairs without another word.

Alrightee, then. I didn't want to talk to you anyway.

Jordan still watched him go, enjoying the view, until Phyllis cleared her throat, offered a slightly more forced smile, and said, "Come on in out of the heat, and I'll get you somethin' to wet your whistle."

At the enormous wood-plank kitchen table, Phyllis served him a tall glass of lemonade before taking a seat on the bench across from him.

"How's your mama doin' these days?"

"She's well... busy with all her charities as usual," Jordan answered automatically.

"Yeah, I remember. She's got a good heart, and we're grateful for all her hard work. So, you want to come work with us for a while?" she asked, studying his face with faded blue-gray eyes.

"Yes. Like I said, I'm not a complete novice. I've worked in your stables before, and others as well. I know how to handle horses, and I'm not afraid to get my hands dirty or learn how to help the other animals too. I want to work."

A trickle of sweat slid down his side, and he shifted uncomfortably before downing a gulp of lemonade. He felt like he was on a job interview instead of offering to be a volunteer, but if they wouldn't let him stay, he had no idea where he'd go.

"Oh, I know that, darlin'. If I remember right, you had quite a way with the horses. I guess I'm just not sure why you're here now exactly. Your mama sends us the Christmas letter every year, catching us up on the family, and she's right proud of how you're doing in college. You're gonna be a lawyer, right? Is this a summer break before you go back to school?"

He stifled a wince and gave the woman a wry grin. "Something like that."

"I don't know much about becomin' a lawyer myself, but I woulda thought you'd want to be doing some sort of apprenticeship or internship or something, now that you're getting so close to finishin'."

Jordan shrugged as his stomach twisted around the syrupy-sweet drink. Telling the woman to mind her own business wouldn't exactly win him any friends, so he said, "I'm just taking a little break before the final plunge, you know? A chance to do some real work out in the open air before I get stuck behind a desk."

She nodded sagely, but Jordan wasn't completely sure she believed him. He was racking his brain for something more convincing to say, when she thumped her palm on the table and grinned. "Well then, Jordan, welcome to the B STAR. After you finish up that lemonade, go get your gear, and I'll show you a room upstairs where you can bunk down."

He was so startled by the sudden change that he just blinked at her for a few seconds before smiling his relief. "That's great! Thank you. But are you sure about upstairs? Like I said, I don't need special treatment. I can stay out in a bunkhouse or something, if that's more convenient."

She waved a dismissive hand, her smile just a little sad. "We got plenty of room upstairs. It's just me and Russ rattling around in the old house now. There are only a couple of other full-timers, and they have their own places in town. The part-timers and weekenders don't stay overnight too often, so we converted the old bunk into kind of a hospital area for some of the newest additions. Guests of the ranch stay here, upstairs, like a real-life B and B, now that my Sean's gone and Lacey's moved out. We keep changing with the times, so it's no bother."

After he finished his lemonade in a few gulps he'd probably regret later, Phyllis led the way out to the porch again so he could grab his stuff. Russ, the hottie, was nowhere in sight, but Jordan paused at the top of the steps anyway as ingrained Southern manners pushed their way past his nervousness and self-involvement. "I was sorry to hear about your husband's passing. I remember Sean was a good man, always patient with an annoying kid who wanted to know everything there was to know about horses."

Her smile was a little sad, but her eyes shone with pride. "He liked you too. The flowers and wishes your family sent were much appreciated."

With a nod, he continued to his car, closed the roof and windows to keep out some of the dust, and grabbed his bags. Once upstairs, Phyllis showed him to a room at the end of the hall.

"Like I said, it's only us now, so you can have your privacy down here. But if you need anything in the night, I'm downstairs, down the hall past the kitchen, and Russ's right there," she said, pointing to a blue door three down from where they stood.

"Thank you. Let me get cleaned up a little and changed, and I'll be ready for you to put me to work."

She smiled and shook her head. "Nonsense. Not tonight. You look a little worn out from your trip, and we're really almost done for the day. Get yourself some rest. Supper's at five, and I'll introduce you around to whoever stays for it. Then we'll get you going in the morning, okay?"

He didn't exactly relish the idea of being left alone again with his thoughts, but it didn't look like he had much of a choice. "Sounds good. Thanks, Phyllis."

"Thank you for coming to help out. See ya at supper."

After she'd left, Jordon kicked off his shoes and stretched out on the green-and-white quilted cotton bedspread with a groan. The lacy curtains on either side of the windows swayed softly in the steady breeze from the floor vents, and every once in a while, the muffled call of an animal outside broke the silence. He hadn't intended to fall asleep, but the nerves and the long hours of driving must've suddenly caught up to him, because he didn't even remember closing his eyes.

CHAPTER FOUR

AFTER RUBBING a few proffered noses as he walked past the line of stalls in the barn, Russ settled on a bench halfway down the aisle and kicked his feet up on a straw bale to wait. Phyllis would be coming after him, once she'd dealt with the trust-fund brat, sure as God made little green apples.

Everybody knew she was grooming him to take over the place someday, but the one area she despaired of ever getting him ready was in groveling for the patrons, and she was right. If the spoiled baby had come to him, throwing his name around and expecting special treatment, Russ would've laughed in his face and sent him packing. The last thing they needed was a whiny little princess to coddle night and day when they had real work to do.

"Russ!"

He winced. The woman might be small and pushing seventy, but she had a voice like a bullhorn when she wanted.

"Here."

With a sigh, he rose to receive his tongue-lashing. He'd be damned if he took it sitting down, even if he knew she was right.

"Got anything to say for yourself?" she challenged with her hands propped on her denim-clad hips.

"Nope." Best not to give her any more ammunition.

"You're gonna have to do better than that if you want to keep this place running for more than a year after I'm gone," she scolded.

"You're not going anywhere. You'll outlive all of us," he sent back with a wink and a smile.

"Bull hockey," she snorted, but a smile crept across her face no matter how hard she tried to fight it.

"So, what'd you do with him?" he asked to distract her.

"He's in the green room, close enough he can find you if he needs something."

He groaned and rolled his eyes.

"Don't you roll your eyes at me, mister. You know as well as I do his parents have donated more to this place over the years than any other single donor. You've seen the checks. Plus, they happen to be friends of mine."

"Friends?"

She glared at him a second before rolling her eyes too. "Of a sort. They've always been kind and real generous. What they give helps us keep doing what we do here, and if that ain't a friend, I don't know what is."

"But they're not really friends," he pressed. "They're rich people who chose us as their pet project, somewhere to throw their money to feel good about themselves. That doesn't make them friends... not real ones anyway... not like us, and Jon and Ernie."

She sighed and threw up her hands. "One of these days you're going to realize not everything in this world has to be all or nothin'. You can care about somebody, call 'em friend, but not have your heart crushed to pieces just 'cause they don't give as much as you. Without us to do the work, the animals would suffer, but without them to pay the bills, they'd suffer just as much. Both are necessary. That young man upstairs is necessary. Besides, I should think you'd be pleased to see one of them pitching in and doing the dirty work. Isn't that what you're always preachin'?"

He grunted. "What's he doing here anyway?"

She shrugged. "Wouldn't really say. I have a feeling there's a story there."

"Oh God," he groaned. "Not another wounded bird, Phyl, please. We've got enough of them as it is."

"At the B STAR, there's always room for a second chance," Phyllis intoned, and Russ groaned even louder. "Quit your grousing. You care about these wounded creatures here as much as I do... even the human kind. Otherwise you never would've stayed on, you big softie."

"I'm not that soft," he grumbled.

She grinned and patted his bicep. "I noticed... and by the by, I think our newest volunteer noticed too... and he ain't too shabby neither."

With a grin and a wink, she spun on her booted heel and strode away, patting a few hopeful muzzles on her way.

"Great."

Just what he needed, a spoiled pretty boy complicating his peaceful, ordered existence. Luckily, "Jordan Thorndike of the Virginia Thorndikes" probably wouldn't last the week, and Russ would get his peace and quiet again sooner rather than later. He could hold on to his temper for a week.

A COUPLE of hours later, Russ plunked down on the bench at the kitchen table with a gusty sigh of relief. After cracking his neck and rolling some of the stiffness from his shoulders, he breathed in a deep lungful of chili-and-cornbread-scented air and smiled for the first time in hours.

Phyl's heaven in a bowl just about made up for the day he'd had.

Ernesto slumped onto the bench beside him with a groan of his own. "How's our pretty bird, Calliope, today?" he asked, his characteristic grin widening.

The ranch's one and only ostrich might be a big draw for the tourists, but she was the bane of Russ's existence too.

Throwing a scowl at Ernie, he growled, "Maybe I'll let you find out for yourself tomorrow. Let her use your head for target practice this time."

"Oh no, Boss, she's all yours," he replied, throwing up his hands and laughing. "I already been bit once, and that's enough for me. I'll do my part and clean her water when it's my turn again, but beyond that, I'll stick to the llamas and alpacas. They let me keep in touch with my South American roots."

Ernie always used that excuse to keep away from most of their problem children, but he was good with the camelids, including Ralph, the one actual dromedary camel they'd rescued from a traveling circus last year, so no one really called him on it.

"Rosa leave you to fend for yourself tonight?"

"Sí. She and her Tía Angela are headed to Dallas for the long weekend, wedding dress shopping for her sobrina, Sofia."

"So we'll be seeing a lot of you this weekend," Russ teased.

Ernie rolled his eyes. "Are you kidding? I have a date with my couch, a pizza, and a six-pack. The kids are with their abuela. Nothing but quiet and solitude for me. Besides, the weekenders will be here. You don't need me to come in on my days off."

Russ opened his mouth to say he'd take Ernie over a dozen weekenders any day, when Jon Parks, the other full-timer, plunked down across from them with a relieved sigh of his own. "A little birdie told me we had fresh meat come in today," he said, pointing a finger at the ceiling before reaching for the basket of rolls on the table.

He didn't get within five inches of it before a wooden spoon came out of nowhere and smacked him on the back of the hand.

"Ow!"

"Serves you right," Russ snickered.

Phyl might be getting up there in years, but she could move like a ninja in that kitchen.

"You'll wait with the rest of us until dinner's ready," she huffed, wagging the spoon at him to make her point.

Jon grimaced and nodded. "Yes, ma'am."

Russ grinned. "You shoulda known better."

"I'm hungry," Jon whisper-whined back, keeping a wary eye on Phyl's retreating form.

"Aren't you supposed to be on your way home to your own kitchen anyway?" Ernie chimed in with a smirk.

Jon scowled at him and crossed his arms. "It's chili day," he said, as if the answer should have been obvious, and Russ had to agree. No one could beat Phyl's chili.

Jon's wife, Cylla, was a gorgeous woman with a full-time job at the bank that let Jon do what he loved on the somewhat meager salary the ranch could afford to pay him, but a gourmet chef she was not. Still, she insisted, since she sat behind a desk all day while he toiled in the sun and her commute was only a five-minute walk, meals were her responsibility, and Jon kept his mouth shut, like any smart man would, and ate what he was given. That didn't stop him from sneaking some grub at the ranch whenever he thought he could get away with it.

"So what's with the new guy in the fancy convertible?" Jon tried again.

Both men looked to Russ.

With a wary eye on Phyl across the room—the woman had selective super hearing when she wanted to—Russ gave them a shrug. "Don't know much. Says he wants to come on and help us for a while. He's the kid of our biggest donor, so Phyl rolled out the welcome mat."

"Great," Ernie said, rolling his eyes. "Another greenhorn to train."

Phyl banged her wooden spoon on the edge of the pot. "No complaints. You'll give him the work no one else wants, just like you do with all the new volunteers, until he's caught up—"

"If he stays that long," Russ muttered under his breath.

"—and you'll be *nice* while you're at it," Phyl finished, giving Russ the full weight of her glare.

"Yes, ma'am," the three men said in unison.

Before anyone could add anything, the object of their discussion sauntered through the door to the kitchen, clean and shiny as a new penny, in slightly wrinkled linen khakis and a blue-striped polo that brought out the color of his eyes, not an expertly highlighted hair out of place. Ten or fifteen years ago, a young Russ wouldn't have been able to take his eyes off him, but now all he saw was trouble with a capital *T*. No one looked that good after being on the road all day without spending way too much time in front of a mirror. And vanity was not a quality Russ greatly admired.

"Hey! I hope I'm not late," Jordan said, flashing a smile at them that probably broke hearts wherever he went.

Phyl rushed over, smiling broadly, and waved him to a seat. "Not a bit. We haven't even set the table yet."

After a pointed look from her, the three men currently seated at the table sprang up to get the dishes and silverware, practically tumbling over each other in the process.

Russ lagged behind the others, coming back as Phyl made the introductions.

"You met Russ earlier, but this is Ernesto Ruiz and Jon Parks, the other two full-timers here. We'd be lost without them. Jon, Ernie, this is Jordan Thorndike, and he'll be staying on for a while to help out."

They shook hands and exchanged greetings before Jordan said, "So you guys volunteer full-time?"

"Would that we could, but no. We're not independently wealthy, so we gotta take a paycheck to help cover the mortgage," Jon answered, then winced when Phyl shot him a look.

"We can't quite pay 'em what they're worth, but we give 'em what we can," Phyl cut in smoothly with a smile. "The ranch is a big operation, and the animals need looking after 24-7-365, plus the home inspections and interviews and training, so a few experienced paid employees are necessary to manage the volunteers, as well as care for our babies. We could always use more help, but we make do with the budget we have."

Russ knew the speech, in one form or another, by heart after all these years, but thank God, he hadn't had to make it himself yet. Phyl was the master at getting money out of people to keep the B STAR alive. Russ didn't know what they'd ever do without her. He cringed just thinking about having to deal with all those people on his own.

"Well, I hope I can be of some help too, while I'm here. I'm ready to work as hard as you need me," Jordan answered with another of those smiles that probably got him everything he ever wanted, and damned if Phyl's eyes didn't go all soft and motherly in response.

Russ's palm itched to give her a little tap on the back of the head to knock some sense into her, but he ignored it in the interests of self-preservation and slapped the silverware on the table.

Jordan cast a searching glance in his direction before smoothing a hand over his perfect hair and clearing his throat. "Whatever that is in the pot, it smells delicious. Is that cornbread in the oven? My mouth's watering already."

He shot doe eyes at Phyl, looking like butter wouldn't melt in his mouth, and Phyl beamed at him. "Why, ain't you sweet. That's my world-famous chili and jalapeno cornbread supper. And I whipped up a little side salad in honor of your first night with us."

"You cooked all this yourself?" Jordan asked.

"Yep. When we have guests for the tours and fundraisers and such, I hire a sweet gal from town, but most of the time, there's only a few of us to feed, and since I can't do as much of the hauling and lifting as I used to, I try to make sure them that do, get a good meal in 'em."

As she talked, Phyl went back to the stove and pulled the trays of cornbread out of the oven.

"Can I help with anything?" Jordan replied.

Phyl shook her head. "Don't you worry, we'll put you to work plenty in the morning. You just sit down and enjoy your supper tonight."

She filled bowls and handed them to Jon and Ernie to carry to the table, which left Russ to bring the salad. Once the cornbread and salad had been passed around, they waited for Phyl to say grace before digging in.

Russ stayed silent while Ernie and Jon satisfied their curiosity about Jordan, peppering him with questions about Ivy League schools, his flashy car, and East Coast horse country. Russ got a few strange looks from his friends, but they soon ignored him in favor of the something new and shiny. Russ didn't pay much attention to what was said. All he really heard was Jordan's friendly, warm, and smooth delivery wash over the room like honey. Jordan had the other three eating out of his palm without even breaking a sweat, but Russ didn't plan on being taken in. He knew the type. He'd gotten his heart ripped out and stomped on in his twenties by a man who could've probably been Jordan's clone, and he wasn't dumb enough to fall for it twice.

Because he was outside the conversation, he was able to see something the others missed. Jordan wasn't actually eating the food in front of him. For all the show he put on, praising Phyl's cooking to the skies, he barely ate half the bowl of chili. He picked around the croutons and shredded cheese on the salad and only ate the lettuce and tomato. He barely made a dent in the cornbread, other than to crumble it up a bit to make like he'd eaten more.

Russ scowled as he carried his dishes to the sink. Phyl was a damned fine cook, best cook Russ had ever had the pleasure of enjoying, but somehow that wasn't good enough for Mr. Ivy League. Maybe it was because there weren't any radish rosettes or artfully arranged tidbits drizzled in au jus on a great big white plate for him to nibble daintily on.

"Here, let me."

Russ jolted and looked up to find pretty blue eyes smiling at him as Jordan set his own dishes on the counter next to the sink. "You've worked hard all day. I think I can manage to clean a few dishes."

With a shrug, Russ swept his arm in a grand flourish to show he was more than willing to accept the offer. Jordan's killer smile drooped a little, which actually made Russ crack the beginnings of a grin himself. If Jordan thought Russ was going to treat him with kid gloves and refuse because of his family's generous donations to the ranch, he had another think coming.

Phyl frowned at him while she helped clear the table, but she didn't offer to take Jordan's place either.

"Good night, everybody. I think I'll go up and read for a while. See you in the morning," Russ called as he headed for the door.

Jon and Ernie waved at him, and Phyl nodded and said, "Good night, sweetie."

Jordan gave him a nod and a considerably less brilliant smile from the sink before turning back to his work. Unable to stop himself, Russ did take a quick glance at Jordan's admittedly outstanding ass in his perfectly fitted slacks before he moved out of sight. He had absolutely no intentions of going there, but he wasn't dead either. The brat came in a fine package, that was for sure. It was a shame, really.

CHAPTER FIVE

THE KITCHEN emptied not long after Russ left. The other two men, Jon and Ernesto, said their good-byes and headed home, and Phyllis went to her own bedroom as soon as she'd helped him dry a few dishes, showed him where everything went, and told him to make himself at home.

Now that he was alone, the house was almost pain-fully quiet. Jordan had forgotten how early everyone went to bed on a ranch. The sun wasn't even down yet and everyone had disappeared. Of course, the last time he'd been there, he'd been barely ten and had run him-self into exhaustion every day before the adults went to bed, so he'd never really paid much attention.

Phyllis might actually be going to her room to sleep, given her age and how early they had to get up in the morning. But he'd lay odds that Russ was a long way from going to bed. If the looks he'd gotten were any indication, he just didn't want to get stuck alone with Jordan. No one at the ranch knew why he was there, so it couldn't be the gay thing. Even people who prided themselves on their gaydar told him he didn't set it off unless he chose to, so maybe it was just the outsider thing.

Was he being too sensitive?

Maybe Russ was just an asshole... except he'd seemed friendly enough with everyone else.

Such a waste of a gorgeous piece of manflesh.

After putting the last dish away, Jordan let out a heavy sigh and smoothed the wrinkles in his shirt. He wandered out of the kitchen and into what had to be the family room. Worn, mismatched furniture sat on a braided blue-and-cream rug, crowding the center of the room. Pictures lined the bookcases and TV stand, as well as the wall along the staircase, from floor to ceiling. There was even an old one of him and his family on the ranch from forever ago, all five Thorndikes smiling and looking happy. He'd quickly averted his gaze when he'd spotted it earlier, and he tried hard to avoid looking at it again now.

The house had obviously never seen a decorator, and much of the décor was trapped in the last century, but it seemed like the definition of what people would call homey. By contrast, the same could not be said for any room in his parents' houses. His mother had excellent taste, the rooms were always beautiful, but like a museum, not a home—look but don't touch. He might actually prefer this place, even though it was all alien to him.

On impulse, he flopped into a recliner in the corner and popped the footrest up. His dad had a leather recliner in his office, but Jordan couldn't actually remember ever seeing him kicked back in it, relaxing. Of course, that might have been because his father had hardly been in a mood to relax on any of the many occasions Jordan had been summoned to his office.

Never good enough, even before I nuked my life.

His stomach twisted, and tension returned to his neck and shoulders. He was beginning to regret the spicy chili he'd eaten earlier, but it had been really good. If he wasn't careful, he'd gain ten pounds in no time with Phyllis's cooking. Still, even without a gym, he imagined he'd get a decent workout every day on the ranch. They'd probably have him shoveling shit to start. That was what the stable manager at home had done that first week before he'd let Jordan on his very first pony, as some sort of sacred equestrian initiation or something. Phyllis's husband had done it on the ranch too, until Jordan's parents had objected to the manure he'd tracked into their rooms at night.

He was the newbie, after all, and if they thought he couldn't handle a little shit work—literally—they had another think coming. Hard, back-breaking, mind-numbing labor was exactly why he was there. He wanted to go until he collapsed, just like he did at the gym, to exorcise his demons. He wanted to barely be able to lift his arms by the end of the day so he could collapse into oblivion at eight o'clock at night like the rest of them, instead of being left alone, tortured by his thoughts.

Hopping up, he prowled that room a little more before wandering through the rest of the downstairs. Unfortunately, nothing held his attention for long. He thought about getting drunk, but the only alcohol he could find was a couple of beers in the refrigerator and a couple of bottles of wine in the pantry, and he wasn't comfortable opening any of it without asking. He still had what was left of the bottle of bourbon stashed in his bag, but just thinking about it made him a little queasy. It wasn't as if he needed the calories, and starting his first day of work hungover wouldn't exactly win him any brownie points either.

Too keyed up to sleep or even sit still for a movie or show on his tablet, he stepped out into the slowly fading light and headed for the barn. As soon as he crossed the threshold and the smells of horse and hay enveloped him, his shoulders slumped and the ache in his chest eased again.

Yes. This *is what I needed.*

After his last horse, Wiley, had been put down, his parents hadn't bothered getting him another, since he was away at school for most of the year. He'd avoided going home as much as humanly possible in the last couple of years, which meant he hadn't been in a stable in months. He'd almost forgotten the Zen he felt just from being around horses, he'd been so caught up with everything else going on in his life.

The horses had obviously been settled in for the night, but in the light from the open door, as well as the dim glow from a dozen or so small lights set along the floor down the main aisle, he could see a few curious heads had popped out of the stalls at his approach. Wishing he'd thought to bring apples or some other treat from the kitchen by way of introduction, Jordan held out his palm a safe distance from the nearest animal.

"Hey there," he murmured encouragingly, "I think we're going to be working together for a while."

The B STAR was a rescue ranch, so even though it had been quite a few years, Jordan still remembered Sean and Phyllis's warnings. He didn't know the history of any of these animals, so he had to stay alert, but he also shouldn't broadcast any nervousness they could pick up on. Whatever the reason the large black in front of him had come to the ranch, it didn't appear to have been abused, because the animal nuzzled and lipped his palm, looking for treats with no hesitation before bumping Jordan's hand with his muzzle, begging for scratches when it didn't find anything edible.

Jordan chuckled and another knot in his chest eased. "You're a friendly one, aren't you?"

The black gazed at him with big dark eyes that reflected the fading sunlight from the door, and nudged him with its graying muzzle again, eliciting another chuckle. "And bossy too. That's okay. I don't mind bossy."

He kept up a litany of nonsense as he petted and praised the animal. He didn't go so far as to enter the stall, but the horse didn't seem to mind. It closed its eyes and lifted its head to give him better access.

Happiness and peace spread through him as he petted the warm sleek coat and the horse made happy little chuffing noises. This was a good idea, coming to the ranch. This was exactly what he needed.

The black whickered when Jordan stepped away, but he kept going down the line, surveying each occupied stall as big eyes studied him in return. He took his time, moving slowly and quietly, but even so, several of the other horses shied away and whickered nervously if he got within even a few feet of them. None were quite as puppyish and friendly as the black in the front, but Jordan didn't mind.

"You guys are going to get used to me. You'll see."

At the end of the row, separated by a few empty stalls from the others, a head poked out. The area was mostly dark, so he only caught a glimpse of a horse several hands shorter than the others. He moved a little closer to get a better look, but it ducked back inside and neighed nervously before kicking at the door a couple of times.

"Okay, sweetie. I get the message. I'm backing up now. No worries. We'll make proper introductions another time."

"What are you doing in here?"

He nearly jumped out of his skin at the gruff demand barked at him from somewhere near the door.

"You shouldn't be out here before we've had a chance to walk you through. These aren't your show ponies and pampered pets. The B STAR can't afford the hit to our insurance if you get hurt," Russ continued when Jordan didn't answer.

Russ had barely spoken two words to him before then, but Jordan had a feeling he'd know that voice anywhere.

Jordan closed the distance between them, and when he was about ten feet away, he squared off with the man. "I've been around horses my whole life, and for your information, I've been here before. Sean and Phyllis have both given me 'the speech' enough times that I'm pretty sure I can remember it, verbatim, even if it has been a few years."

Russ's eyes narrowed and his jaw worked a second before he said, "Well, maybe you should hear it again before you go strolling through the barn like you own the place."

"I didn't—"

"And anyway," Russ cut him off, "these animals have been through enough in their lives. The last thing they need is someone pestering them when they're trying to get a little shut-eye. They get enough of that bullshit on the weekends, when the well-meaning but useless come down from town to do their good deed for the month."

"I know what I'm doing in a stable. I wasn't pestering anyone," Jordan gritted out through clenched teeth. "I was only saying hello."

"How the hell would I know if you know what you're doing?"

"Phyllis does. She knows me."

"Phyl ain't in charge of the horses anymore. I am. And you won't get anywhere near 'em unless I say so. Got it?"

Jordan opened his mouth to tell the asshole just where he could shove his attitude, but snapped it shut again. Restless rustling behind him, accompanied by a few nervous snorts, reminded him they were doing exactly the opposite of what he was trying to convince Russ. It wasn't exactly his fault. Russ was the one being a dick, but Jordan obviously wasn't going to get anywhere arguing, and he really didn't want to get into a fight with the foreman his first night there. He'd talk to Phyllis in the morning. She'd understand.

Without another word, Jordan swept around him and headed for the house. He didn't run. He didn't stomp. He calmly returned to his room and quietly shut the door behind him before leaning against it and flipping both middle fingers in the direction of the barn.

Apparently, Russ was going to be a bit of an obstacle to Jordan's search for the Zen he needed to figure out his next step. Russ might have decided not to like him, for some unknown reason, but Jordan needed this place too badly to let some super-hot asshole get in his way.

After closing his eyes and taking a few breaths, he rolled his shoulders, kicked off his shoes, and got undressed. On the bed, he propped himself on a pile of pillows and stared up at the ceiling for a while until his temper cooled.

He could do this. He wasn't so fragile that one jerk would send him running. Besides, he didn't have anywhere else to go.

He'd been caught off guard. He wasn't himself these days—whoever that was—so he hadn't even tried to turn on the charm. He'd do better tomorrow. He'd figure out how to win Russ over eventually, if it killed him. No one withstood the Thorndike charm forever.

CHAPTER SIX

RUSS LEANED against the barn door and followed Jordan's progress as he returned to the house. Watching that boy walk away was probably the best part of his night... for a number of reasons. And because of those reasons, he looked forward to seeing the back of him for good when the brat got tired of real work and headed home to Mommy and Daddy.

Dallas whickered hopefully at him from his stall at the front of the barn, and Russ smiled. "No more for you tonight, greedy Gus. Go to sleep."

He pushed away from the door and headed back to the house. The light in Jordan's window came on when he was halfway across the yard, and Russ felt the slightest twinge of guilt for yelling at him. Jordan hadn't actually done anything wrong, except jumping the gun a bit. When Russ had spotted him headed for the barn on the security camera feed, he'd been equal parts irritated and worried, which had translated to all irritated when he'd spotted the guy charming the horses like he did everyone else.

"Too goddamned slick," he muttered under his breath.

Still, unfair or not, it was best to set some ground rules. Jordan probably wouldn't be around long enough for it to matter, but Russ wasn't going to pussyfoot around the brat, no matter what Phyl said.

LIKE CLOCKWORK, before dawn, Russ was showered, dressed, and enjoying a cup of coffee on the front porch in the quiet of the morning. This was his favorite time of day. As a few sleepy crickets gave half-hearted chirps on their way to bed, the soft purple twilight spread across the sky. Mist clung heavy and still in the air as if the world held its breath, waiting for the sun to paint the horizon bright orange and stir the whole place to life for another day.

This was home, the first real home he'd ever had, and he couldn't have asked for a better one.

The screen door creaked and Phyl joined him in the second rocking chair, where they sat in silence, sipping their coffee as the sky steadily brightened. When Sean was still alive, he'd been the one in the other rocker while Phyl puttered in the kitchen or her office, too antsy to sit still before the day's work started in earnest. But after Sean's death, she'd slowed down a bit. For a few months, she'd taken to sitting in that chair and rocking the days away. Until one morning, she'd hopped up and put herself back to work again, just like that. But she still came out and spent the mornings with him most days, which helped him start the day off right and made missing Sean a little easier—probably for both of them.

"You're going to be nice to him, right?" Phyl asked as the sun finally broke the horizon and Ralph, the camel, let out one of his lowing grunts.

Russ grimaced. "Put him with Ernie."

"Ernie's herd doesn't need as much attention as yours. People around here aren't going to be trying to ride his llamas and alpacas if they take them. The horses need more gentling and training if we're ever going to find them good forever homes. Besides, Jordan knows what he's doing with the horses. Even as a kid, he was always great with them. I doubt that's changed."

Russ scowled and sipped at the last lukewarm dregs in his mug, but refrained from comment, and Phyl gave him a light slap to his bicep. "Quit being an ass. I don't know what's gotten into you, but you need to put a lid on it. Quit your bellyachin' and put a civil tongue in your head, 'cause he ain't goin' nowhere for the time being. Got it?"

Despite his best efforts, the huff she expelled as she pushed herself out of the chair and headed back inside made him crack a smile.

"I've gotta go check on the bacon before it burns," she muttered.

Apparently he'd already gotten on her last nerve, and the day had barely begun. If he wasn't careful, she might send him to bed without his supper tonight or, God forbid, make him fend for himself.

"So, are you going to wake sleeping beauty or wait for him to roll out of bed when he feels like it?" he asked as he strolled into the kitchen to pour himself another cup a few minutes later.

Phyl frowned at him from her place by the stove, but Russ only raised his eyebrows and smiled blandly, contriving to look as innocent as possible.

Rolling her eyes, she turned back to the eggs in the pan. "He's already up. I heard the shower kick on upstairs before I went outside."

As if to prove her point, they heard footsteps on the stairs a moment before Jordan entered the kitchen, looking fresh as a daisy, his perfectly sculpted, blond-highlighted hair still wet.

"Looks like I'm late," he said with an apologetic, self-deprecating smile that had Phyl's grin widening and her eyes softening in seconds.

Russ would have rolled his, but he was already skating on thin ice and wasn't willing to risk starvation or food poisoning by his own hand.

"Not late at all, darlin'," Phyl cooed. "Breakfast is just about ready. We'll get you filled up, and then Russ here'll take you on a tour before settin' you to work."

Jordan threw him a tentative smile, his blue eyes wide and disingenuous. Russ couldn't find a lick of the fire from the night before anywhere in his face, even when Phyl turned her back on them.

What's he playin' at?

Jordan continued to regard him with that bland, expectant expression until Russ shifted uncomfortably and looked away.

"Here we are," Phyl said, carrying a bowl of eggs and a plate of bacon to the table. "I hope you don't mind scrambled, Jordan."

"No. That's wonderful. Thank you."

Phyl's smile widened. "Russ, will you get us some plates?"

Jon and Ernie arrived as they were eating. Jon snuck a piece of toast and some bacon while everyone but Russ exchanged small talk... and everyone but Russ hung on Jordan's every word.

It was disgusting.

After they were done eating, Jordan offered to clean up again, but Phyl wouldn't hear of it. "You go on out with Russ and the others, and I'll take care of this. It's one of the few things I can still do on the ranch that isn't paperwork and fundraising."

"She likes to put on a show, but the truth is, she can run any one of us into the ground, any day of the week," Jon cut in conspiratorially.

Phyl chuckled and rolled her eyes. "Yeah, and 'in the ground' is where I'd stay if I tried. Go on. Get out of here. Don't you have work to do?"

"Yes, ma'am," Jon, Ernie, and Russ said in unison.

Outside, Jordan hung back a little, and with a resigned sigh, Russ motioned him to follow. "Come on. I'm supposed to give you a tour before I put you to work."

"You don't have to do that. I mean, not that much has changed. I can find my way around if you've got things you'd rather be doing," Jordan chimed in as he hurried to catch up.

Russ grunted and kept walking.

At the doors to the barn, he stopped and reluctantly turned to his ball-and-chain for the foreseeable future. "Like I said last night, you'll need to know a bit about the animals before you can be left alone with them. I don't care how much experience you've got with horses."

Jordan's smile fell just a fraction before resuming its earlier blinding brilliance. "Of course. Is that where I'm working today, in the barn?"

"Phyl says you're good with our equine friends here, so here's where she wants you." He made sure his tone made it clear that this wasn't his idea and he wasn't exactly happy about it, but Jordan's smile and expectant expression didn't falter again.

"All right, then," Jordan replied, clapping his hands together briskly, "lead the way."

Russ's scowl deepened. The brat was too god-damned cheerful. He didn't like it. But he had plenty of work to wipe that smile off Jordan's face.

Pursing his lips so they wouldn't split into an evil grin, he gave Jordan an obvious once-over. "Your boots look sturdy enough, so that's at least something. Although you may regret the shiny new jeans and T-shirt you're wearing."

Jordan let out a chuckle that might have been charming, if Russ had been in any kind of mood to be won over. "Yeah, when I decided to come down, I realized I didn't really have any clothes with me that could be considered work clothes, so I stopped at a Walmart on the way. Luckily, I grabbed my steel-toed hiking boots and my riding boots before I left home. Those would've been harder to replace."

Which tells me this visit wasn't exactly planned. Interesting.

Without comment, Russ turned and led the way to the first stall, and a great black head poked greedily out into the aisle. "This is Dallas, the attention whore I'm sure you met last night. He's as sweet-tempered as they come and kind of a grandpa to the herd. He spent his younger years being run into the ground on the racing circuit, so all four legs have foundered. He'll never be ridden again, but he's real good with the visitors and kids, and he holds a special place here at the ranch. He's earned his retirement, and he's not going anywhere but here where we can take care of him." His voice softened and his shoulders relaxed as he rubbed Dallas's muzzle while he talked. When he glanced over his shoulder, Jordan had gone a little doe-eyed too, so he cleared his throat and moved down the aisle. "Most of the horses that we keep in the barn are either new and need to be evaluated, sick or injured, or don't get along with the rest of the herd that we allow to stay out in the pasture. Dallas gets his stall whenever he wants it, because he's special."

Continuing down the line, he gave histories, general temperaments, and lists of injuries etcetera for the rest of the seven horses in the barn, taking particular time to point out the more dangerous of his charges. He'd given this speech or one like it to dozens of volunteers, so by the end he was running on autopilot. Jordan didn't interrupt with questions until they reached Marina's stall at the very end of the row.

"Is she pregnant?"

"You noticed, huh?" Russ sneered.

Jordan grimaced and rolled his eyes, his Pollyanna routine slipping for the first time that day, but only for a second. Russ blinked, and Jordan's face had smoothed out again. "She's very skinny."

Russ turned away from Jordan and rested his gaze on the little bay mare in the stall instead. "She was worse when we got her, barely a two on the Henneke scale. In two weeks, we've managed to put thirty pounds on her, but she's got a long way to go. The other horse we found with her died before we could get to them."

"That's awful. How could anyone do that, just let their horses starve?"

Russ actually agreed with him, but things were rarely ever black-and-white in the real world, and having a man who'd probably never had to worry about money a day in his life passing judgment on people he didn't even know, got Russ's back up. "Not everyone in this world has millions to fall back on," he snapped.

"Times are hard, and a lot of folks can't keep up. If it comes to feeding themselves or feeding their stock, the choice is made. Don't always make 'em bad people, just hard up."

He'd seen more than his fair share of tearful good-byes as people gave up their beloved animals to the rescue.

"Still," Jordan argued, "they should've brought them to you before it came to this point."

He was right, but damned if Russ was going to admit it. Instead, he said, "Just steer clear of her for the time being. She's scared, weak, and we've got to take our time. Between the rain rot on her back, the state of her hooves, and everything else that comes with malnutrition, she's a mess, but we can only do what she'll let us, a little at a time. She's my project for now, separate from the others for a reason." He moved back up the aisle without checking if Jordan followed.

Outside, he waved a hand at the wheelbarrow, shovel, and rake. "Should I assume you know how to properly clean a stall?"

"Yeah."

Surprised by the laughter in Jordan's voice, Russ shot him a look. When Jordan only grinned back, Russ's eyebrows drew together. "All right, then. I'll trust Phyl's judgment and leave you to it. I'll let the ones out who can be with the herd. Take care of their stalls first, then come and get me, and I'll lead the others out, one by one, into a pen, until you're done there. We keep fresh straw in the empty stalls on the right, and you can find gloves in the tack room."

"Okay."

A little suspicious of Jordan's easy acceptance— *everyone* groaned at least a little when given mucking duty—Russ left him with the wheelbarrow, moved to the fence beyond the barn, and whistled. About a dozen heads lifted in the distance, and Daisy and Missy broke into a trot coming toward him. They were the biggest suckers for a bit of apple or a sugar cube, and always first in line at feeding time. They were also the most likely to be adopted soon, given their age, level of training, and temperaments.

The rest of the herd moved in at a slightly slower pace, so by the time he'd let Dallas and a couple of others out of their stalls and into the paddock, the rest of the herd had lined up at or near the fence hoping for treats.

"All right, kids. I think I might have a little something to make you happy."

He grabbed a bucket of pellets from the feed shed and took a few minutes to coax each horse over for a little hand feeding and a pat or two. Most of the group had been gentled enough by now that they needed little coaxing, but a few of the newer additions required a bit more effort. The greedier ones jockeying for position didn't always make things easy either, but he got the job done.

Once or twice he caught Jordan just standing around watching him, but a pointed scowl helped put the brat back to work soon enough. Russ had a feeling he'd have to ride Jordan's lazy, entitled ass to get a decent day's work out of him, but maybe if Jordan complained, Phyl would dump him on someone else.

One can only hope.

Much sooner than Russ expected, Jordan showed up at his elbow.

"I'm ready for you to lead the others out, unless you want me to do it," Jordan said.

Russ frowned and led the way back to the barn to inspect Jordan's work, but the stalls were clean and strewn with a blanket of fresh straw. Unreasonably irritated, Russ moved to the next occupied stall, clipped a lead to Bannock's halter after coaxing the injured horse forward, and led it out into a pen for some sunshine and fresh air.

From what the police could gather, Bannock had been used for target practice by a "person or person's unknown" on his previous owner's farm. The wounds had been left untreated until the owner was forced to surrender the gelded draft horse to the ranch. He was a big beast, but mostly gentle, just a bit touchy about his healing wounds. He'd make a gorgeous addition to the right family, once he'd had time to heal and a little more training.

While Jordan cleaned up the massive beast's equally massive mess, Russ checked out each of the healing wounds, slowly and carefully.

"You're looking good, big guy," he murmured. "You'll be out with the others pretty soon, and we'll be able to put your pretty mug on the website for adoption before you know it."

His shoulders itched like he was being watched, and sure enough, when he glanced over his shoulder, Jordan was there.

"Don't you have work to do?" he grumbled as he patted Bannock's shoulder.

"I'm done. I was just waiting for you to finish."

With a huff, Russ led Bannock back into the freshly cleaned stall.

"You know, you won't win any brownie points if you've shot your wad before noon," he grouched as he shoved the latch home and moved on to the next stall.

As the day passed, Russ kept waiting for Jordan to cry uncle, but the man kept chugging away like a machine, giving Russ nothing to gripe about... which irritated him no end, particularly when Phyl brought them sandwiches, bottles of water, and glasses of lemonade, and went on and on about how great a job Jordan was doing.

"I gotta go soon, or Jon and Ernie'll pass out from starvation. But I think the two of you should saddle up the girls, Daisy and Missy, and go for a ride," Phyl said cheerily.

Russ tried to hide his scowl, but he wasn't completely successful, judging by Phyl's pointed glare.

"We still have Marina's stall and a few other things to do round here."

"That won't take more'n an hour," Phyl countered, waving a dismissive hand. "You got plenty of time, and with the weekend coming up, I need those two well-exercised and on their best behavior, in case they catch someone's eye."

She was right, of course. The girls needed the practice, and if Jordan rode, Russ wouldn't have to make two trips. That didn't mean he had to like it.

"Yeah, okay. After we finish up, we'll go."

Jordan's smile this time was nothing like the ones Russ had seen so far. There was no hint of practiced perfection, only delight. It lit up his whole face, making an already pretty man goddamned luminous.

Experiencing an all too familiar tug in his gut, Russ shoved off the straw bale he'd been sitting on and charged down the aisle. "I'll go get Marina moved," he threw over his shoulder as he went.

CHAPTER SEVEN

JORDAN WAS soaked with sweat and filthy by the time the barn met Russ's standards for cleanliness. Lugging horseshit and straw around all day long was a distinctly different kind of workout from a couple of hours hitting the machines at the gym, but he'd been mentally prepared for it, and quite frankly looking forward to it ever since he'd come up with this crazy plan. Anything that kept him out of his own head for a while was a good thing. And despite Russ being an asshole for no reason, he was easy on the eyes, making him a nice added distraction from the wreck of Jordan's life.

In the fantasies that filled his head as he shoveled shit, Russ never said a word beyond "yes" and "more." Unfortunately, he had to deal with the reality far too often to truly enjoy those daydreams.

He hadn't given up on winning over the hot bastard yet, though. Russ might be a harder sell than Jordan was used to, but today was only his first real day on the ranch. He'd have time to work on the problem.

"You get Missy," Russ bit out as he passed by, leading Jordan to the tack room.

"Anything I should know about her?" Jordan asked, hurrying to collect the saddle, pad, and hackamore he'd been directed to before rushing after Russ again.

Russ slowed his stride slightly. "She isn't one of our hard cases. Both girls are from a farm that had to downsize due to an illness in the family. They'd asked around, tried to sell 'em, but couldn't find buyers quick enough. The horses had a spot of the flu, and the family couldn't afford the vet bills on top of everything else. They'd already been saddle broke, just didn't have much training beyond that. We nursed 'em back to health and gave 'em a bit of training, but that's pretty much it." He eyed Jordan appraisingly for a second, the severe line of his lips never changing. "All I'd say is, Missy's young, a little high-spirited, but mostly sweet and eager to please. She won't be as disciplined as what you're probably used to, that and obviously she's Western saddle broke, which you're also probably not used to."

"I've done both."

Russ grunted, turned away, and kept moving.

I'm going to impress you, cowboy. You're going to like me, whether you like it or not.

Jordan smoothed a hand down his T-shirt, only realizing how ridiculous the gesture was when his hand came back even grimier than before. His looks wouldn't be winning him any brownie points at the moment, but Russ hadn't seemed to give a damn even when Jordan had been clean, pressed, and freshly gelled.

Maybe the guy liked it a little dirty and rumpled.

Jordan bit his lip and shook that thought right out of his head. The last thing he needed was to sport wood in front of Russ, or climb into a saddle for a long ride with a boner, come to think of it. He stifled a laugh and dropped his gaze to his boots when Russ shot him a look over his shoulder.

Even Russ's attitude wouldn't spoil this day for him. Jordan wouldn't let it. He'd exceeded Russ's expectations at every turn. He knew it, no matter what Russ's face said. And now he was going for a ride in the open air on a pretty little mare. He'd show the cranky cowboy how good a rider he was, and then maybe Russ would let him do more than mucking from now on, without bitching about it.

Ahead of him, Russ lifted a leg to the bottom rail of the fence, rested his saddle on the top, and whistled. The two young mares were the first to the fence, and Russ let them into a small separate corral before closing the gate behind them.

"Do you think you can handle the saddle on your own?"

Jordan managed to not roll his eyes by only the slimmest of margins. "I can do it."

"Well, get to it, then." Russ turned his back on Jordan and set to readying his own mount.

Before approaching Missy, Jordan took a deep breath in and let it out, shaking the tension from his limbs at the same time. Missy didn't know him, and the last thing he wanted was to let any of his irritation with Russ spill over to their first meeting.

"Hey there, sweet girl. I'm Jordan. You ready to go for a little ride today with your friend?"

Keeping his voice low and soft, Jordan studied Missy's body language for any signs of tension as he approached. Missy stepped up, eagerly nuzzling his hands, looking for treats, probably.

"Sorry, sweetie, you got your treats earlier. Now you get a little workout."

Russ already had the halter and pad on his mount, but Jordan didn't care. Russ could wait.

"We're going to get to know each other a little first," he murmured as he stroked Missy's smooth neck and shoulder. Her gleaming auburn coat was warm from the hot Texas sun, sleek and gorgeous, and Jordan felt a weight lift from his chest just touching her. "We're going to do each other some good," he whispered for her ears only.

In all honesty, he didn't need to be so slow and careful. Missy was a pussycat, as eager to please and ready for a ride as they'd said. If Russ had been the one training them, he'd done an even better job than he'd said.

Hot and humble, damn, he's sexy.

Such a shame.

"Are you two gonna cuddle all day, or are we going for a ride?" the man in question groused from the other side of the paddock.

Jordan did roll his eyes this time, but he didn't utter a peep as he slid the halter and hackamore in place and moved on to the pad and saddle. The breast collar gave him a bit of trouble, especially since Missy was eager to join Russ and Daisy, but eventually he got everything buckled in and tightened down. He could feel Russ's eyes on him the whole time, but Russ said nothing, so Jordan did his best to ignore him.

Once Missy was all saddled and ready to ride, Russ opened the gate at the other end of the paddock, led Daisy out, and waited to close the gate after Jordan and

Missy had passed through. They mounted in silence, and Russ nudged Daisy into a canter without looking to see if Jordan followed.

As soon as Missy got moving under him, the rest of Jordan's aching muscles relaxed into the familiar movements. He didn't care if his riding companion was a grumpy bastard. He didn't care that he probably wouldn't be able to move tomorrow. He didn't even care where they were going, as long as they kept riding.

Despite the heat, the sweat on his skin dried quickly as the horses picked up speed. Jordan really didn't have to do much directing. Missy followed right on Daisy's heels with seemingly no interest in wandering off, so Jordan could relax and enjoy the landscape.

Still packed with plenty of grasses, wildflowers, and shrubs, and dotted with trees, the central Texas hill country was a stark contrast to the lush and overgrown greens of Virginia he was used to, but beautiful in its own way. Away from the ranch proper, the land rose steadily as the hot sun beat on his head and back. He'd need to find a hat sometime soon or his forehead and nose would be red as a lobster before the week was out.

At the top of the first hill, he had a great view of the main house, barns, and outbuildings. The dark and light shapes of horses, donkeys, llama, alpaca, goats, and some cattle dotted white-fenced pens and yellow-green-and-brown splotched pastures. Many of the animals seemed to prefer the dubious shade of the few scrubby live oaks, though some braver souls were venturing out, now that the sun was lower in the sky.

"It all looks so much bigger than I remember," Jordan said.

For the first time that day, Russ actually slowed his horse and cracked a half smile as he gazed down on the ranch. "We've done pretty well, despite the times. Each year we try to save more animals than the last. Sometimes we succeed."

As if he suddenly remembered who he spoke to, Russ's smile fell away and he nudged Daisy into a trot, down the hill and on to the next one.

Guess we're done having our moment.

Jordan sighed as he watched Russ's straight broad shoulders, tight ass, and hard thighs for a few seconds before nudging Missy after them.

Such a damn, damn *shame.*

The rest of the ride, they barely exchanged a word. Ordinarily, Jordan would have chafed at the silence, but he was enjoying his time in the saddle too much to complain about his less-than-satisfactory company. The Western saddle was a lot bigger than he was used to, so some of his muscles would definitely be complaining later at the unaccustomed stretch. Still, if it helped him sleep through the night without pounding shots of bourbon, he'd count every single exhausted muscle, ache, and pain a win.

Russ turned and headed back toward the house long before Jordan was ready, but he didn't have much say in the matter, at least for now. The man was as taciturn on the way back as he'd been riding out, and before Jordan knew it, the ranch was in sight and his lovely sojourn was over.

With a sigh of regret, Jordan dismounted in the yard and led Missy into the paddock. After removing most of her gear, Russ told him to fetch the grooming supplies, and they took some time to curry and brush away the trail dust and sweat before removing the hackamores and releasing them back into the pasture with the others.

Outside the barn, Jordan waited for some word of approval for a day's work well done, but the best Russ could come up with was apparently a brisk nod on his way past as he headed for the house. When Russ reached the bottom step, Phyllis stepped out onto the porch. With a smile and a wave for Jordan, she moved to the edge of the porch and rang the brass bell mounted to a post.

"Time to get washed up for supper, Jordan," she called as he approached the house.

Jordan smiled his relief and gratitude, and he dragged his aching body up the steps. Now that he was done for the day, the aches and stiffness were definitely settling in. The set of stairs up to the bedrooms gave him pause, but he pushed through and climbed. He would not sit down to dinner covered in everything he was currently covered in.

After a quick shower, he pulled on the second pair of jeans he'd bought on the drive down and one of his polo shirts, figuring the skinny jeans, silk slacks, and linen shorts wouldn't make him anyone's favorite at the dinner table. He hadn't really planned ahead very well. Everything he'd packed from home was useless on the ranch. He was going to need more than two pairs of work pants, or he'd be doing laundry several times a week.

Did Phyllis do the laundry? If not, he was going to need to figure out how to ask for instructions without humiliating himself. He'd never done a load of laundry in his life.

Did Amazon deliver way out there? How much could he afford to spend? The credit card attached to his account had probably been canceled with the rest of them, so that only left his debit card, and—

Flinching away from those thoughts, Jordan fussed with his hair in the mirror above the scarred antique dresser in his room and smoothed a hand down his shirt. He'd worked his ass off today so he wouldn't have to think, but reality had a way of butting back in, no matter how hard he tried to ignore it.

Russ stepped into the hall from the bathroom at the same time Jordan left his room, and they nearly collided in the hall. Apparently Russ had also showered, because he was running a white towel over his damp brown hair and he'd replaced his chambray work shirt from earlier with a stark white undershirt that stretched across his muscled chest and hugged the outlines of his nipples.

Jordan stifled a groan.

Such a shame, a tragedy really.

Flashing a smile, he said, "I forgot to thank you for taking me out with you this afternoon. Missy really is a sweetheart, and it was great to be back in a saddle again. It's been far too long for me."

"You can thank Phyl. It was her idea, not mine."

Persevering, Jordan took a step back and held his smile. "Still, you were the one out there, so thanks."

Russ pursed his lips and gave a terse nod before stepping through the door to his room and closing it in Jordan's face.

With an aggrieved sigh, Jordan turned and headed downstairs. Russ was Phyl's right-hand man, he reminded himself. They were obviously close. Jordan needed his approval if he was going to stay on the ranch for… well, for however long he needed to. Charming him was just going to take a little longer than he'd hoped.

CHAPTER EIGHT

FOUR DAYS.

Four days of slaving away, of shoveling shit from dawn until dusk, never complaining even once, and did he get a single "good job" or an "atta boy" from Russ?

Nope. Not one.

Phyllis and Jon and Ernie all showed appropriate amounts of approbation and gratitude, stroking his ever-more-brittle ego, but not Russ.

It was a little like working for his father, except his father threw in an occasional "nice work," even though the words were usually followed by a "but."

He still shied away from thoughts like that just as fast as they came up, but who else was he going to compare Russ to? He just hadn't had that many assholes in his life up until that point, at least not ones he couldn't ignore or tell to fuck off.

Bracing a foot on the fence, he rested his arms on the top rail and watched the herd in the pale light of the full moon. Crickets chirped in a constant drone broken by an occasional sleepy snort from a horse or bray of a donkey as an owl hooted somewhere off in the distance. The air was heavy and damp from a passing thunderstorm earlier in the day, and heat still radiated from the ground, despite the sun having set a couple of hours ago.

He was bone tired from another hard day and should have been in bed like the rest of them, but his mind wouldn't stop working. He'd been pushing himself hard, punishing his body with work for days, but it wasn't enough.

What did he want from his life?

Where did he go next?

Did he have to call the school to let them know he wouldn't be coming back?

Did his father cancel the lease on his apartment near campus?

How long was his car insured for before he'd have to take over the payments?

Would his therapist even answer if he called?

Did he still have health insurance to pay for the therapist or a doctor if he got hurt?

All these questions and more lapped at his ankles, warning of the impending flood. His heart raced with a sudden need to be moving, to run until he collapsed, but it wouldn't do any good, and he could barely lift his legs as it was. He felt sick. What he'd been able to eat of Phyllis's fine but heavy cooking sat like a stone in his stomach.

Instead of running, he abandoned his post by the fence and moved into the barn. In the dim closeness, Dallas greeted him first as always. With a small smile, Jordan accepted his invitation and continued down the aisle, scratching each proffered neck, until he reached the end. Marina eyed him from just beyond the door to her stall, and Jordan smiled as he settled on the pile of straw bales a few feet away. He'd taken to coming out here each night and sitting quietly with the skittish mommy to be. He was calmer in the barn, the smells and sounds of the horses working their magic on him. Marina was used to him by now and had even taken a smuggled treat or two from his hand that morning, when Russ wasn't looking.

"You and me, we're going to be okay," he murmured. "We're a little broken now, but nothing that can't be mended, right?"

She snorted and one big eye glittered at him from the shadows of her stall, and he smiled, closed his eyes, and tipped his head back against the rough woodplanked wall.

God, I hope so anyway.

"HEY."

He jerked awake at the nudge to his boot and found Russ looming over him, silhouetted against the pale indigo of predawn beyond the barn doors.

"Hope you managed to get your beauty sleep, 'cause sleeping in the barn ain't an excuse to call in sick on a Saturday."

Stifling a groan, Jordan tried to get his stiff muscles to cooperate. He felt about eighty years old and was pretty sure he looked it too. Thank God the barn was still dark back where he was.

Showing not even a hint of pity, Russ made shooing motions toward the house. "Phyl's got breakfast in the works. Go inside and eat something for a change.

You're gonna need your strength for babysitting the weekenders."

Jordan stumbled out of the barn and over to the house like a zombie, not processing Russ's words until he reached the steps up to the porch.

"What the hell is that supposed to mean, 'eat something for a change'?"

He scowled back at the barn, but Russ was nowhere in sight.

"Mornin', sunshine," Phyllis greeted him with far too much cheer as Jordan stepped into the kitchen.

"Isn't it a little early for breakfast?" he groused as he shuffled to the coffeepot.

"It's Saturday, busy day for us. Weekenders, tourists, potential adoptions."

"Weekenders?" he managed between gulps from his cup.

"It's what we call the well-meaning patrons who bring their families out to *volunteer* on the weekends." Her grin faltered a little as she seemed to realize who she was talking to. "Not that we don't appreciate all the help we can get, but some of the less regular helpers actually make more work for us instead of less, if you know what I mean." She paused and stirred the eggs in the pan before turning back to him. "But it's all to a good cause. And the more people who see what we do here, and raise their kids to respect animals and give of themselves, the better the world will be in the end," she finished, using what Jordan had come to recognize as her fundraising voice.

"Makes sense," he mumbled between sips from his second cup.

She eyed him critically. "Are you feeling all right?"

"Yeah, just a little tired."

"Russ has really put you through it this week, hasn't he?"

Yes.

"Not really. Besides, hard work builds character, right?" He flashed his best smile at her, and her face softened.

"Well, you don't have to worry about any of that today. We'll have plenty of hands to help out." She paused, pursed her lips, and eyed him speculatively. "You know what? I think that's a great idea."

"Huh? Did I miss something?"

She smiled wide. "Sorry. My thoughts tend to run away sometimes. I think you should spend the day with me, talking to folks. You got a knack for it. People like you."

"Not everyone," Jordan grumbled into his mug.

"Enough, though," she said with a dismissive wave. "The work we do is necessary. Taking care of the animals is why we're here, after all, but we wouldn't be able to do it without the donors, without the people who support us. That part of the job is as important, if not more so than mucking stalls… even if I can't seem to knock that into *some* people's heads." She harrumphed. "Without the donations of those lovely people that come here for a family day out every once in a while, we wouldn't be here. And without them people coming out and falling in love with some of our animals and taking 'em home, we wouldn't be able to rescue any more. The people matter."

Jordan nodded, and her eyes lit up.

"See? I knew you'd get it."

Instead of asking him to set the table, she dished him up a plate from the stove and told him to sit down.

"Is it just us?" he asked, confused.

"Yep, I'll leave some out if Russ wants to come back to get it, but Jon and Ernie have the day off. We usually have plenty of help, particularly in the summer when the kids aren't in school. This week has been pretty quiet, but we get Girl Scout troops, 4-H, church youth groups, summer camps, etcetera, coming in at least for a day most weeks. I do my bit and give 'em a tour and then put 'em to work mucking, giving baths, or hauling feed… simple stuff. All we have to do is keep an eye on 'em."

"Babysitting," Jordan sighed.

She chuckled. "It ain't so bad. You get to sit down from time to time, and you don't have to do all the haulin' and shovelin'."

She had a point. He didn't exactly have a lot of experience with kids, but laying on the Thorndike charm was something he had a good twenty-four years of practice doing. He'd learned to play the gracious host at the knees of the masters, his parents, after all. And even if the whole reason he'd thrown a grenade into his life was so he didn't have to hide behind that mask anymore, this was for a good cause. Besides, it meant one less day of beating his head against the brick wall of Russ's disapproval. After four fruitless days on that front, he could use a break.

"I'm in," he said with a smile, and Phyllis's sweet blue-gray eyes glowed, warming him from the inside as he tucked into his food with a slightly improved appetite.

As IT turned out, charming people out of their money was something Jordan actually excelled at. It didn't hurt that his love for the ranch and its animals was surprisingly genuine, which he discovered as he led chattering families around to the pens and helped

Phyllis with funny and heartwarming stories so the people felt more connected.

Ernie's biggest charge, Ralph the Camel, was a big hit. The little boys loved the grunts he made and how he spit when he was irritated. Jordan steered everyone around the caution ropes in front of Calliope the Ostrich's pen, but he took great pleasure in relating the highlight of his week to any and all who would listen— that being the time he got to see Calliope knock Russ on his ass in the dirt as Russ dodged her grumpiness's precision beak strikes. Jordan told it as a cautionary tale, but he made sure his voice was loud enough the man in question couldn't help but overhear as he stomped by with another group of volunteers hauling feed. The scowl Jordan received in return for his efforts, as the kids let out peals of giggles, made Jordan's day that much brighter.

He could see where wrangling other people's children might get old after a while, particularly toward the end of the day when the kids started getting tired and cranky. But mostly, the little wide-eyed smiling faces following his every word were a balm to his tattered ego, and almost everyone was friendly and kind.

The only weird part of the day was when one of the dads eyeballed him. As a rule, Jordan had his fair share of good-looking guys eye-fucking him. In fact, he'd spent hours at the gym and in front of the mirror every week to make sure of it. So under normal circumstances, he would have preened under the attention. But there was something creepy about a guy with his wife and two little girls on a family outing, cruising him.

Call me a prude, but that's just wrong.

He shuddered as he lifted the tray of lemonade pitchers off the kitchen counter to carry outside, hoping the guy would have already left. He was just about to descend the stairs and head to several families hovering around a couple of picnic tables strewn with cups and plates of cookies, when he spotted the creepy guy again. Only this time, the guy was squaring off with Russ in the shade of the barn, a good distance from everyone else and mostly hidden from view by a tractor and a horse trailer.

His curiosity piqued, Jordan took a couple of steps to the side to get a better look. Russ's arms flailed as he exchanged what looked like heated words with the guy, but they were too far away for Jordan to even try to guess what they were saying. As Russ threw up his hands, turned his back on the guy, and stomped away, the screen door banged behind Jordan, making him jump.

Caught spying, Jordan blushed and straightened as he nodded over toward the barn. "What's that about?" he asked.

Phyllis followed his gesture and grimaced. She eyed Jordan speculatively for a moment before shrugging. "Ancient history. Todd's Russ's ex…. Never liked him, m'self. He's married now, with two adorable little girls, but he can't seem to help himself coming out here to stir up trouble every once in a great while. Luckily, Russ usually makes himself scarce when he knows Todd's about. Easier for everybody concerned."

Jordan blinked. He stared after Russ's retreating back for a couple of heartbeats before turning back to Phyllis. "His ex?"

Phyllis raised her eyebrows at his gobsmacked expression. "Yep. You don't got a problem with that, do you?"

"Uh… no." He shook his head, mostly to clear it. "No, not at all."

She grinned. "I didn't think you would."

At his puzzled look, she grinned wider. "Come on. Let's hand this out before the ice melts."

In a daze, he followed her down the steps and set the tray on the picnic table. He poured and handed out paper cups of lemonade while Phyllis did her part to thank everyone for coming.

He's gay? Russ is gay?

He was having a hard time wrapping his head around that fact, especially since it meant another blow to his ego. He wasn't so vain as to think every man on the planet would be hot for him, but he hadn't even gotten a hint of interest from Russ, not once in all the time they'd spent together. Jordan wasn't a troll, for God's sakes. A willing dick was a willing dick when you're horny, wasn't it? It wasn't as if the ranch held so many better options, and Russ hadn't been anywhere but to the local grocery store and one little home inspection in the time Jordan had been there.

I mean, what the hell?

Russ and Todd never rematerialized, that Jordan saw. But soon enough all the weekenders were packed into their vehicles and kicking up dust on their way off the ranch, including Todd's wife and kids, so he had to have come back at some point.

"You did good today," Phyllis said, tapping her paper cup full of lemonade to his in a toast.

Momentarily forgetting about his obsession with Russ, Jordan beamed at Phyllis. It was ridiculous how happy that tiny bit of praise made him, like a steak to a starving man.

Classic "middle child of an emotionally distant father" syndrome—always such a sucker for approval.

He shook his head. Knowing the whys and where-fores didn't make the feelings go away, though. He'd been in therapy from his midteens onward, so he knew all the right words and all the labels to put on things, but he'd lied to his therapist almost as much as he had to his parents. Judging by the reaction he'd gotten from telling the truth, he'd been smart to lie as long as he did.

"Thanks, Phyllis. You were right. It was fun."

"Call me Phyl."

She stood, grabbed the tray, and headed for the house while Jordan was still gaping after her with a stupid grin on his face and a hopeful little twinge in his chest.

"I'm going to get supper started. Why don't you go check in with Russ and see if there's anything still needs doing," she called over her shoulder before stepping through the screen door and letting it bang behind her.

Russ is gay... or at least bi? Holy shit.

CHAPTER NINE

WEDNESDAY MORNING, Russ woke to the screeching of his alarm clock and nearly sent the thing flying across the room. With a groan, he flopped onto his back and stared up at the shadowed ceiling. Although he still set it every night, he always woke way before the damned contraption had a chance to go off—always. Except over the last several days, he'd been lucky to get even a couple of hours of uninterrupted sleep before it was time to start the day all over again, and he knew exactly who to blame.

Jordan bloody Thorndike needed to "find himself" or his goddamned "inner peace"—or whatever the hell had brought him to the ranch—and move on, because Russ couldn't take another few days of being eyed like a stallion at auction. The doe eyes one minute, the sleepy eyes the next, the standing just a little too close, the accidental brushes against Russ's body, all of it was going to drive him out of his ever-lovin' mind.

"Goddamn you, Todd. Why couldn't you have just stayed away, lived your life, and let me live mine?"

His ex's most recent visit to the ranch had to be the reason for Jordan's sudden change in attitude from phony Pollyanna to cautious Casanova on the hunt. Nothing else had changed from the previous week. Russ sure as hell hadn't been any nicer to the brat. Somehow Jordan had figured out Russ and Todd had history, and he'd spent every day since Saturday examining Russ like a peach he thought might just be ripe enough to be plucked.

It got under Russ's skin something fierce, made him feel itchy all over. He hadn't had a decent night's sleep since.

With a growl, he rolled out of bed and glared in the general direction of Jordan's room. He was done pussyfooting around. He'd put a stop to it—whatever "it" was—sooner rather than later. Phyl wouldn't be happy, but this was Russ's home, not Jordan's, no matter how rich his parents were. If the kid didn't like being put in his place, he could damn well haul his pretty ass somewhere else to contact his inner child, because Russ had work to do.

Determined, he stomped to the bathroom, hosed off in the shower, and tugged on his work clothes for the day. He skipped breakfast, only grabbed a quick cup of coffee and a piece of buttered toast before heading for the horse barn as the first pink of a new dawn breached the horizon. He barely shared two words with Phyl, beyond the pleasantries, afraid she'd poke holes in the belly full of fire he'd worked up before he could unleash it all on the brat.

As he'd expected, Phyl stuck him with Jordan from dawn 'til dusk yet again. It didn't help matters any that the brat was actually pretty damned amazing with the horses. Under different circumstances, Russ might've considered training Jordan himself, just like Sean had done for him. But the brat wouldn't be around long enough to make that worth the effort, and Russ wouldn't be able to take that kind of one-on-one time and not do something he'd regret at some point.

"What's next, Boss?"

Russ scowled. Casting a reluctant glance over his shoulder, he found Jordan looking far too damned pretty for spending the last few hours ankle-deep in muck on a hot July day. Even sweaty and rumpled, he looked good enough to eat.

Russ had reached the end of his rope.

"You've been here more'n a week," he growled. "You oughtta know what needs doin' by now. You got eyes, look at the board. I ain't your nursemaid, and I ain't your daddy. Figure it out or get the hell out of my barn."

Jordan blinked at him for a couple of heartbeats, his blue eyes wide with surprise and maybe even a little hurt. Just as quickly, though, those pretty eyes narrowed and that smooth jaw tightened. Russ squared off with the brat, eager for a dustup to release the tension he'd been building for days. He wouldn't do any real damage to the pretty boy, but if Jordan threw a punch, he'd get a punch back.

Except that wasn't what happened. Instead of throwing a punch or stomping away in a huff, like the spoiled brat he was, Jordan's angry frown evaporated into thin air. His eyelids drooped, and his perfectly formed lips curved into a smile that spelled "trouble" in flashing neon letters, sending Russ's heart pounding.

Caught off guard, Russ stood there frozen as Jordan slunk a few steps closer, leaned in close, and murmured, "Oh, I know you're not my daddy. If you were, all the things I want you to do to me would be illegal and so very, very wrong... unless we're talking about a different kind of daddy."

With that, the cocky little shit spun on his heel and sauntered away, his tight ass wiggling in the pair of Russ's faded and far-too-thin old jeans that Phyl had given him.

"Well, shit," Russ swore to the empty barn when he was able to get his tongue back.

It seemed the brat had decided Russ was ripe enough to be plucked after all. Now what the hell was Russ going to do about it?

A horse down the line of stalls whickered, shaking him out of his stupor and reminding him he had work to do. After reaching down and adjusting himself with a grimace, Russ threw one last scowl in the direction Jordan had gone and went to find his farrier kit.

FOR THE rest of the day, Jordan avoided close contact with him, but that didn't stop the brat from throwing saucy winks and licking his lips every time he caught Russ's eye in the yard or passed him on the way to some of the other animal pens. Jon and Ernie weren't far off, and Phyl popped in from time to time, so Russ wasn't able to get some of his own back until just before quitting time.

Jon and Ernie weren't staying for supper that night. Ernie had his daughter's violin recital and Jon's in-laws were coming up that weekend, so his wife wanted him home to get the house in shape. That left Russ and Jordan alone outside to finish up for the night while Phyl cooked supper. Russ had shaken off his earlier discombobulation and had worked up another full head of steam by then. He strode into the barn with purpose. The brat's little comeback earlier had surprised him, and if he were honest with himself, it had gotten his dick's attention to the point where it took over for a few seconds. But that continued over-the-top flirting all afternoon had just pissed him off. He didn't like games.

"Hey," he called to Jordan's back as he came down the aisle.

Jordan was washing out some buckets, but he set them down at Russ's approach and turned to face him. A flirty smile played across the brat's lips as he leaned against the barn wall invitingly. He made a pretty picture. There was no denying that. But Russ was done with the bullshit.

"You and me, we need to have ourselves a little chat," he said, stopping a good eight feet away and folding his arms across his chest.

"Sure. What about?" Jordan asked, with a look that said butter wouldn't melt in his mouth.

"I think I need to set you straight on a couple of things, and I want you to listen real close, because I ain't gonna repeat myself."

"Okay." The brat stepped away from the wall, wet his lips, and sauntered a little closer. "I'm all ears."

"Good, then listen up. Phyl might be scared to step on your little pedicured toes, 'cause of how much your parents contribute to our little operation, but I'm not. She might feel pressured to be nice to you, but I don't give a good goddamn how much money your folks have. You want to stay here? Then you pull your weight like everyone else and don't make trouble. Otherwise I'll personally kick you out on your ass without sheddin' a tear. Ya got me?"

Jordan's mask slipped, showing a hint of something pained before his expression closed. Russ had worked long enough at the rescue to recognize a wounded creature when he saw one, even with only the tiniest glimpse. But he wasn't going to let that stop him. Jordan was a full-grown man, raised with more privilege than some people could even dream of, not a defenseless animal, and he needed to be reminded that he couldn't have anything or anyone he wanted with the snap of his fingers.

"Now I'm not sure what you think you know about me, boy," he continued relentlessly, "but just so we're clear, I ain't buyin' whatever it is you're sellin'. Got it? So you can keep your sashayin' little ass out of my way. And you can stuff your winks and your smiles where the sun don't shine while you're at it, because I got no use for a spoiled little rich kid slumming it down here with the rest of us just so you can *feel better about yourself*, no matter how pretty you think you are.... Been there. Done that. Bought the T-shirt. Never goin' back.... Now you stay out of my way, or you hop back in that expensive little toy that probably cost more than Ernie or Jon's house and find somewhere else to ease your conscience or seek out your inner child... or whatever the hell it is you're doin'."

Russ took a perverse pleasure in spinning on his heel and striding out of the barn, mimicking Jordan's dramatic exit from earlier, even if a slight twinge of guilt cast a pall over his satisfaction as Jordan's stunned expression burned itself into his memory.

"It had to be done," he murmured to himself as he climbed the stairs to his room to get washed up for supper. "He's probably just never had anyone actually say no to him before."

As he put on a fresh shirt and readied to go down for supper, he heard the screen door bang and the thud of boots move up the stairs and down the hall. He waited, but he didn't hear a door slam. He stepped out and cast a glance in the direction of Jordan's room. The door was slightly ajar, but only a weak light shone through the small opening. Russ rolled his shoulders and cracked his neck to ease some of the tightness there as he descended the stairs and went to see if Phyl needed any help.

Jordan said almost nothing at the supper table, and he never once met Russ's gaze. He talked to Phyl a bit. His magazine-cover smile was firmly back in place as he pushed his food around his plate and barely ate more than a bird—as usual—but Phyl must have seen through it anyway.

"Are you feelin' all right, darlin'?" she asked.

"I guess I'm just a little tired," Jordan replied, his phony smile dimming a bit. "I think I'll go to bed early tonight, if you don't mind."

"Of course not, hon. You go on. We'll take care of things down here."

"Thanks."

Jordan took his plate and glass to the sink before heading out of the kitchen. Phyl watched him go, a concerned frown knitting her brows, but a second before Jordan disappeared, she stood up and called after him. "Hey, hon, wait up a second. I need to talk to you about something, and it probably shouldn't wait."

From the hall, Russ heard her say, "Let's go outside and sit for a spell," before the screen door creaked open and banged shut.

Russ was actually relieved. He wouldn't have to play dumb with Phyl. He could do the dishes in peace and head on up to bed for what he hoped would be a full night's sleep at last, without being plagued by Jordan's puppy-dog eyes or Phyl's all-too-perceptive gaze boring into him. He'd get it from her eventually, if Jordan tattled, but she was unlikely to charge after him tonight with Jordan just down the hall, so he could go to bed free and easy if he was quick about cleaning up.

CHAPTER TEN

STILL RATTLED from the smackdown he'd received in the barn, Jordan wasn't sure he could handle any more serious conversations that night, but he didn't want to be rude, so he let Phyllis lead him to the rockers on the front porch and sat in the one she offered him.

"I can see you're tired, so I won't keep you long. I promise," Phyllis said gently.

"Okay. Thanks."

She pursed her lips and studied him for a few seconds before her weathered face twisted in a grimace. "I guess it's best if I just come right out and say it. No good ever came from dithering." She drew in a breath and blew it out. "I talked to your mama today."

Jordan felt the blood drain from his face. His stomach roiled as the meal he'd just eaten threatened to come back up. Swallowing bitter bile, he asked, "You did?"

Phyllis's expression softened. "Yeah. I got an email from her yesterday that was kinda confusing. She said she had to cancel the visit she planned for later this summer because she and her son weren't going to be able to make it. I thought it kind of odd that she didn't mention your being here or ask after you at all, so I gave her a call this afternoon."

"What did she say?"

"Now you know your mama's never been one for, uh, *sharing*, per se—at least not with people outside the family, that I can tell—but even she couldn't hide that she was upset."

"You told her I was here?"

"I did. I didn't know it was a secret, and she seemed awful worried about you."

He smiled bitterly. "She could have fooled me."

Phyllis frowned reprovingly. "Now darlin', no matter what, she's still your mama. Of course she cares."

"She hasn't tried to call or text me even once, except to get my brother and sister to harass me to go back home and apologize to all of them. All they want is for me to pretend it never happened, and I can't do that."

Phyllis's lined and tanned face fell, and she placed a warm, calloused hand over Jordan's on the armrest of the rocker. "I'm sorry. I had to read between the lines a bit, because she wouldn't say it outright, but I think I know what we're talking about here, and I'm so very sorry it turned out like that. Some folk are just taught to believe certain things their whole lives, and they're afraid to change their minds... like if they did, it would change everything and nothing would make sense anymore. But that don't make it right to hurt someone you care about."

Jordan had to turn away from her for a few seconds to get control. His eyes stung and his throat felt tight, and the last thing he wanted was to break down where anyone could see him. "Thanks, Phyllis, *Phyl*. Did she say anything else, after she found out where I was?"

Her eyes filled with regret. "Sorry, hon. She thanked me for telling her, but that was about it."

Jordan swallowed and nodded.

She squeezed his hand again and said, "I don't know much about the 'coming out' or anything, since Sean and I only had the one girl and she's happily married to a man in Tucson, with two grown kids of her own, but I do know family, and I got two good ears if you want to talk about it... anytime."

After a long drawn-out breath, he closed his eyes and nodded again. He was going to thank her one more time and make some sort of excuse to leave, but his stomach chose that moment for a full-on revolt. Too much was happening all at once, and the tidal wave threatened to drown him in feelings he didn't know how to deal with.

He clapped a hand over his mouth, leaped from the chair, and sprinted for the stairs as Phyllis called after him. He barely made it to the bathroom by his room before throwing up what he'd had at dinner. Over and over his body convulsed until he was left with only dry heaves. Tears spilled down his cheeks unchecked before he was able to beat back the floodwaters and put his walls back up.

If he had some sort of plan, any plan, he might be able to face what was beyond those walls, but he wasn't ready yet. He couldn't handle this now, especially after what happened with Russ. If he'd been even a little emotionally stable, he might've been able to brush off the slap across the face Russ gave him, but he was as brittle as glass, and he knew it. He had no defense mechanisms left.

"You're weak. You always have been," his father's voice said inside his head. *"Such a disappointment."*

Sitting down on the cool black-and-white tile floor, he wedged himself between the old bumblebee-yellow tub with frosted glass shower doors and the toilet, and shivered. After snagging a hand towel from the rod, he wiped his mouth, closed his eyes, and let his head thump back against the dimpled glass doors.

It had been almost two weeks since he'd taken a sledgehammer to his perfectly ordered life, and the pain hadn't lessened any. Wasn't it supposed to get better over time?

Suppress. Lock it away. Be proud. Be strong. Don't let the world see you hurt…. These were the only tools he'd ever been given by his family, so much so that he'd never been completely honest with anyone, not even his therapist. He wished he had now, because those tools weren't working. His walls were failing, crack by crack.

RUSS HAD just finished filling the dishwasher when he heard someone run up the stairs and a door slam overhead. He moved to the doorway of the kitchen in time to see Phyl come in from the porch calling Jordan's name. She looked really shook up.

"What's he done now?" Russ asked, ready to take him apart for putting that expression on her face.

She leveled a glare at him that set him back a step or two, placed her hands on her hips, and all but yelled, "Russell Patrick Niles, you need to stop ragging on that boy like he's done anything but show kindness, decency, and a generous spirit since the day he got here. Ya hear me? Now I need you to pull your head out of your ass for one minute, show the compassion and decency

I know you're capable of, and go up and check on that boy, make sure he's all right."

Taken aback, Russ just blinked at her. "Me?"

"Yes, you! Do you see me talking to anybody else?" she spat, narrowing her eyes.

With a grimace, he took the dishtowel off his shoulder and wiped his hands on it, stalling. He cleared his throat and stared down at his boots as he said, "I don't think that's a good idea. Me and him, we had a little exchange of words earlier. I don't think he's gonna have much interest in talkin' to me about anything, especially if he's upset about something."

"What did you do?"

A quick glance up showed she was spittin' mad, and Russ shrugged as the hairs on his neck prickled at the glare she was still giving him. "I just needed to set him straight about a couple of things, is all."

"Well, whatever it was, if you need to apologize, then you're gonna march right up there and apologize. Then you're going to dig deep for that sympathetic and caring heart I know you have, and you're gonna listen if that boy's willing to pour his heart out to you, you got me?"

"Phyyylll…." The only thing that stopped it from being a whine was that his voice had dropped an octave since he was a teenager. He lifted his chin, cleared his throat, and straightened his shoulders. "Why me?" he asked in a slightly more grown-up tone.

"Because, of the two of us, you're the only one here who might have a clue as to what he's going through."

Frowning, Russ threw the rag over his shoulder again and folded his arms. "What's that supposed to mean? What could I possibly have in common with a twentysomething spoiled trust-fund baby from the East Coast?"

That seemed to draw her up short, and Russ thought he'd dodged that particular bullet when she cast a glance up the stairs and sighed. That was, until she turned her soft, pleading blue-gray eyes back on him and said, "It's not really my secret to tell, but I'm pretty sure we're all he's got right now. He's been carrying this around ever since he got here, and none of us even had a clue. He's obviously upset enough to literally make himself sick, and I'm afraid if he keeps bottling everything up, he's gonna burst at some point."

"What are you talking about?"

With another sigh and a slight grimace, she said, "He came out to his folks, all right?" After a brief pause to let that sink in, she continued, "And, needless to say, it didn't go so well. From what I can tell, his momma's in complete denial, and I obviously can't know for sure, but his daddy was never what I would call the soft and understanding type. He's from that Jerry Falwell fire-and-brimstone country up there—not that we don't have more than our fair share of that here too, but you know what I mean."

Russ closed his eyes and slumped against the doorjamb. "Shit."

In the silence that followed his exclamation, they heard a toilet flush upstairs. When Russ opened his eyes, he found Phyl glaring at him again. "If you won't do it for him, then do it for me. I want you to check on him, make sure he's okay. If he won't talk to you 'cause of whatever happened between you, fine, but you're going to make an effort, you got me?"

With a resigned sigh, he moved to the stairs and handed her the dishtowel on his way past. "I'll do what I can, but I can't promise anything."

Her lips twisted. "I suppose that'll have to do. Just be kind. I know you know how to do that. If you have to pretend he's a horse, then do it."

Outside the bathroom door, Russ took a deep breath and let it out in a long sigh. He tapped on the door but received no response.

"Jordan, it's Russ. Can I come in?"

"Go away."

Dragging a palm over his whiskers, he blew out a breath and tried again.

"Now, Phyl won't let me do that, not until I've checked on you. Can I come in?"

"Whatever," came the somewhat petulant response.

Jordan sat curled up on the tile floor, crammed between the toilet and the tub. His face was pale, and beads of sweat dotted his forehead and upper lip. His blue eyes were red and wary, like a wounded animal, as he watched Russ step through the door. His fake smiles and flirty winks were nowhere to be seen, leaving only exhaustion and vulnerability in their wake.

Instead of coming the rest of the way into the room, Russ slid to the floor and propped himself against the jamb.

"She told you, didn't she?" Jordan asked, his voice raw with emotion.

"Yeah. Don't be mad. She was worried about you, and she thought I could help."

Jordan snorted, and Russ shared a wry smile with him as he nodded. "Yeah. I told her I probably wasn't your favorite person at the moment, but she thought I might be able to understand a little of what you're going through."

"And do you?"

"What?"

Jordan sat forward a little and pinned him with intense blue eyes. "Do you understand? Did you fuck up your entire life by coming out, like me, or were your parents actually decent about it?"

With a sigh, Russ pulled a knee to his chest and rested an arm on top of it. He worried the corner of his lip as he contemplated how to answer that.

"Sorry," Jordan rushed to say. "Of course you don't have to tell me, if you don't want to. It's personal. I get it. I know you don't really want to talk to me. I—"

Russ held up a hand to stop the flood of words. Jordan sounded so wounded right now, if he kept going, Russ would be over there pulling Jordan into his arms before he could stop himself.

Damned bleeding heart.

"It's not that I don't want to, Jordan. I'm just not sure how to say it. My situation was a little different from yours. I'm not sure that I ever actually *came out* to anyone."

Jordan frowned at him in confusion, and Russ sighed. "Look, my daddy wasn't exactly the kind of man I looked up to… like, *ever*. By the time I understood who I was, and that I wasn't going to be taking Mary Jo to the prom—or anywhere else, for that matter—my daddy wasn't in the picture much, and I didn't give a rat's ass for his approval of anything I did. I never bothered to tell him, because I didn't care enough to let him know me." He paused for a second and grimaced. "My mama was a different story, but not that different. She remarried a couple of times after my dad and had a few more kids, and since I was the oldest by several years—and a reminder of her early mistakes in life—I kinda got shoved by the wayside. I still got fed and had a roof over my head until I was eighteen, but I was more like a built-in babysitter than part of the family. She had a lot on her plate besides me, so when I could, I left. We exchange a Christmas card every year, but that's about it. I never really bothered to have the whole talk with her either. I think she knows, since I never mention a wife or girlfriend and neither does she, but we don't talk about it."

"I'm sorry," Jordan whispered.

"Don't be," he replied with a shrug. "I'm not."

Jordan searched his face as if he didn't quite believe that, but then he dropped his gaze to the tiled floor and shrugged too. "I've seen all those commercials, you know, the 'it gets better' ones, and I guess I just wanted to hear that from someone real, to know if it's true. That's why I asked."

Russ winced and dragged a hand down his stubbled jaw. "Look. I'm probably the last guy anyone should come to for a pep talk. Words—and people, for that matter—have never been my strong suit. I'm much better with animals. But I can tell you from experience that if you can't get the love and acceptance you need at home, you can find it elsewhere... as long as you're willing to go looking and withstand a few knocks along the way. I mean, look at Phyl. You've barely been here a couple of weeks, and she's already turning mother hen on you. That should tell you something."

The wariness was back in Jordan's eyes. "You said Phyl was only being nice to me because of my parents' money. She doesn't really like me."

Russ winced again. "I did?"

Jordan lifted an eyebrow and gave him a wry, watery smile. "Yeah, you did. And you know her a lot better than I do."

With a grimace, Russ waved that away. "Well, obviously I was wrong, wasn't I? She's down there right now wringing her hands about you. And she tore me a new one before I came up here. She wouldn't do that unless she cared."

Jordan sighed and rested his chin on his knees. "You can tell her I'm okay."

"I'm not gonna lie to her."

He held Jordan's stare as Jordan frowned at him in confusion.

"I don't get you at all," Jordan murmured after a long silence.

Russ groaned as he climbed to his feet and tried to rub some feeling back into his ass after sitting on a cold tile floor at the end of a long workday. "Listen," he said, clearing his throat, "I'm sorry if I've been too hard on you since you been here. I didn't know what you were dealing with, otherwise I might've laid off a bit." Jordan's expression had turned unreadable, which made Russ shift uncomfortably under his steady regard. "I'll go tell Phyl you're not going to pitch off the deep end tonight, but she's right, you're going to have to face what's happened with your life eventually. The B STAR's about healing, but only if you're willing to put the work in. It's not a place for running away… but we're here if you want to do that work."

"Okay. Thanks," Jordan croaked.

Russ stepped into the hall and closed the door behind him. He couldn't watch Jordan fall apart without doing something stupid. Besides, he didn't figure Jordan really wanted someone watching him right now anyway. At least not if that someone was Russ.

Straightening his shoulders, he took another deep breath and prepared to face Phyl again. Hopefully, he'd done enough to get him off her shit list.

CHAPTER ELEVEN

JORDAN SPENT the next few days in a fog. He and Russ had apparently formed some sort of truce. Russ stopped being quite so much of a dick, and Jordan stopped his campaign to get in Russ's pants. The problem was, all that tension with Russ had been a good distraction, even if it did little for his fragile ego. He still seemed to make Russ uncomfortable, though, probably because Russ appeared to be about as good at dealing with his own emotions as anyone in Jordan's family. Added to that, Phyllis had really taken to the mother hen role Russ had talked about—one she played with far more gushing tenderness than Jordan's reserved mother would have ever shown. So Jordan felt like a ping pong ball, bouncing between the unyielding blank granite wall he was used to and a mountain of marshmallow.

Russ was right, of course. Jordan couldn't avoid dealing with things forever, but was it so wrong to want

just a little more time? If Phyllis asked him how he was
doing again, he might just have a meltdown, right there,
out in the open, and that was next door to an unpardon-
able offense in the Thorndike family.

Kinda like being gay, apparently.

The only time he felt any peace at all was at night,
after supper, when everyone else was either gone or in
bed, and he could sit with Marina at the back of the
barn. Of all the horses on the ranch, she drew him the
strongest, probably because she was in the worst shape.

"We make a pair, don't we, girl?" he murmured as
he held out a bit of apple for her.

The last few nights, he'd spent hours just sitting
and talking nonsense to her. He'd even taken to sing-
ing snatches of whatever songs he could remember,
though he'd felt a little silly. It seemed to work, though,
because she'd finally rewarded him by coming close
enough to her stall door to let him rub her neck and
shoulder a couple of times.

"I'm probably still just using you as another excuse to avoid what I should be doing, but you don't
mind. And at least I'm doing something good while I'm
procrastinating."

He held the slice of apple out, but she made no
move to come closer to the door.

"Come on, girl. It's all right. You know me."

She shifted restlessly and swished her tail in
agitation.

"What's the matter, girl? Want to be left alone
tonight?"

She hadn't been this nervous with him since the
first time he saw her. She paced the confines of the stall
and let out a cross between a squeal and a grunt. The
other horses farther up the aisle poked their heads out

of their stalls and made nervous inquisitive noises of their own.

Concerned that she was acting a little strangely, he walked quickly back up the aisle and turned on the overhead lights. Blinking in the sudden glare, he trotted back to her stall.

"Nothing to worry about. Just want to get a better look at you."

He wasn't sure if the words were for him or her, but as he noticed her sweaty sides and the slight tremble in her legs, his anxiety grew.

"I'm going to go get Russ now. It's probably nothing, but I'd rather piss him off and be wrong than…."

Deciding he really didn't want to finish that sentence, he trotted back up the aisle and broke into a jog the rest of the way to the house.

"Russ?" He knocked lightly on the man's bedroom door. "Russ?"

"Yeah?" came the grumpy reply.

"Hey, it's probably nothing, but—"

Russ opened the door, fully dressed with his boots already on. Behind him, Jordan spotted a laptop open on the bed with what looked like a live feed from the barn on the screen in black-and-white.

"I saw the lights in the barn come on," he replied gruffly at Jordan's raised eyebrows. "What's wrong?"

"I don't know. It's Marina. She's sweating and upset. She wouldn't take the treat I offered, and she *loves* apples."

Russ pushed past him and headed down the stairs while Jordan followed close on his heels.

"Shit!" Russ exclaimed after peering into the stall.

"What?"

"See that discharge?" he asked, pointing toward her hindquarters. A disgusting-looking fluid ran down her back legs, partially obscured by her tail as she shifted and paced nervously. "It's either infection or labor, neither of which is good, since she's nowhere near time. Her udder is filling too, dammit."

Jordan's stomach twisted, and a ball of fear formed in his chest. "What do we do?"

"Stay here and try to keep her calm. I'll go call Dr. Watney."

Left alone again, Jordan moved closer and tried to coax her to him again. "It's okay, Marina. We're going to take good care of you."

He kept up a steady stream of gentle gibberish, and it seemed to help. She stopped pacing and moved to get some water from the bucket not far from where Jordan stood. By the time Russ came back, she'd even let him pat her neck once. She moved away when Russ stepped close, but not as far as before.

"Dr. Watney's on her way. Her house is about thirty minutes from here, so we have a little time to get her haltered and calmed enough to let the vet close."

"She doesn't really like much handling," Jordan said skeptically.

"I know," Russ said gently, without the harshness the obvious remark deserved.

Russ worked with her every day. He knew Marina better than anyone. Jordan just wasn't thinking very clearly at the moment.

When Russ brought the halter, it took both of them nearly the entire thirty minutes to coax her into it and get her settled. A car pulled up outside just as Jordan had gotten Marina to nibble on a bit of apple in his palm, and Russ walked out to meet the vet.

Dr. Watney was a short, slight woman with tightly braided black hair and smooth coffee-colored skin that made it hard to judge her age.

"Tish, this is Jordan, a new recruit. Marina's taken a real shine to him, so hopefully together we can keep her calm enough for you to do your job. Jordan, this is Dr. Latisha Watney, our savior on numerous occasions."

"I'd shake hands, but my hands are a little full right now."

Jordan held the halter lead loosely while he gently stroked Marina's neck with his other hand.

"That's okay, Jordan," Dr. Watney replied with a smile. "You just keep doing what you're doing. I've checked Marina out a couple of times since she's been here, and you guys seem to have worked a miracle yet again. She's much calmer than the last time, and I'm glad to see the weight she's put on."

Marina jerked her head slightly and snorted when the other two entered the stall, but Jordan kept murmuring to her until she settled a bit. She still seemed tense, and he was about to mention it, when Dr. Watney said, "I think it's safe to get Dallas. So far, she doesn't sound like it's any kind of respiratory infection."

Jordan threw a confused look at Russ.

"Having another good-tempered and well-trained horse nearby can sometimes calm the skittish," Russ explained as he exited the stall. "She seemed to like Dallas when we did this before."

Russ put Dallas in the stall next to Marina's so the mare could see and touch muzzles with the old gelding. It seemed to help, as a little more tension left her body. Jordan was prepared for Russ to take over and kick him out of the stall, but Russ merely settled outside, leaving Jordan and Dr. Watney with Marina.

While the vet worked her way slowly to the mare's hind end, Jordan tried not to think about anything other than comforting Marina. He became so focused on connecting with her and keeping her calm and happy, he didn't even notice when Dr. Watney finished her examination and stepped out of the stall.

It wasn't until he felt a broad hand on his shoulder that Jordan lifted his head and blinked away the fog. Russ studied Jordan's face with deep brown eyes, but his expression was unreadable.

"It's okay, Jordan. She's done with the examination." Russ's voice was softer and gentler than Jordan had ever heard it, which kind spooked him more than if Russ had snapped at him.

"Does she know what's wrong?"

"It's an infection," Russ replied somberly. "She's not sure what kind yet. She's taking samples back to her office tonight for the tests. Once she knows, she'll be back with medicine."

"That's a good thing, right?" Jordan asked hopefully. Except Russ looked anything but relieved.

Shaking his head, Russ said, "The infection has probably spread to the placenta. That's why we're seeing swelling in her udder. Signs like that usually mean the mare will abort the foal before it reaches full term."

Jordan's stomach twisted, and the fear he'd managed to banish while calming Marina returned as he stepped away from her and into the aisle with the others. "Isn't there something we can do?"

"We wait," Russ replied. "She's too thin to be pregnant anyway. It's probably better for her if she loses it now. Then she can concentrate on healing herself first without the added strain."

Jordan understood the logic. It just didn't make him feel much better. Marina was sick and might lose her baby. That was all his heart cared about.

Dr. Watney returned, drying her hands after washing them in the sink at the front of the barn. "I'll take the samples in now, and I'll call as soon as I have results on whether it's fungal or bacterial and we can decide on treatment. I recommend keeping a close eye on her. I have a bad feeling it won't be long before we know if the foal was affected. If she starts labor, give me a call and I'll come back. She just hasn't had enough time to get healthy for this yet, so she may need some help."

"I'll watch her," Jordan offered before Russ could say anything.

Russ flashed him one of his small smiles, which up until that point had seemed to be reserved for everyone else on the ranch *but* Jordan, before turning back to the vet. "I'll walk you out."

Over his shoulder, Russ said, "I'll bring you some coffee and your tablet, if you want it."

Jordan nodded, and they disappeared through the doors.

Once they were gone, he moved to Marina's stall door again and said, "It's just you and me tonight, girl. I'm going to keep an eye on you, and we're going to do everything we can for you."

Fifteen minutes later, Russ returned with a thermos full of coffee, a basket with some of Phyllis's muffins, a bowl of sugar, and a carton of half-and-half. He had a blanket draped over one shoulder and Jordan's tablet tucked under his arm.

"I'd stay out here too," Russ said apologetically, "but someone's got to see to everyone else tomorrow. Plus, tomorrow's Friday, so the weekenders will be here before we know it. I think we got another Girl Scout troop coming our way on Saturday."

"It's okay. It doesn't take two people to watch her. I'll let you know if anything changes."

"Yeah, all right." Russ turned to go but hesitated. "Eat those muffins. Don't want you keeling over on us too."

Jordan forced a smile and nodded. The last thing he wanted right now was to think about food. "Good night."

CHAPTER TWELVE

RUSS COULD tell the minute he stepped into the barn that Jordan needed to go to bed. Even from thirty feet away, he could see Jordan's sallow complexion and puffy purple-ringed eyes.

"How's she doing?" he asked as soon as he was close enough that he didn't have to shout.

Jordan shrugged. "About the same... suffering."

He looked ten times worse up close. His eyes were red with exhaustion, his normally perfect hair lank and sticking out at odd angles.

"Okay. Well, we can take it from here. Jon and Ernie will be here soon, along with a couple of Friday volunteers, and Phyl's going to come down as soon as she's finished in the kitchen. I filled her in this morning."

A glance at the basket he'd lugged out last night showed only one muffin had been picked at, less than half of it gone, and he frowned.

Stifling his exasperation, he said, "Get yourself on up to the house. Have some breakfast, and get some sleep."

With a slight bob of his head, Jordan collected the basket and the rest of his things and shuffled toward the house. Hopefully Phyl would take one look at him and go into hyper mother hen mode… stuff some food into him before tucking him in.

"How are we this morning, little lady?" he murmured to Marina as he stepped up to the stall. She stood in the far corner. Her muscles quivered every once in a while, a shiver running down her body, and her head hung low. Russ clicked his tongue and shook his head.

"Hang in there, sweetie. You ain't never been mothered like ol' Phyl's gonna mother you. You just wait."

Less than two hours later, Russ was returning Missy to the pasture after running her through her paces when he spotted a familiar blond-highlighted head pushing a wheelbarrow through the yard.

"What the hell?"

He set Missy free and closed the gate before charging after Jordan.

"What are you doing out here?" he barked as soon as he was close enough. "You should be in bed."

Jordan turned dull eyes in his direction and shrugged. "Couldn't sleep."

"I don't care if you sleep or not, but you need to lie down before you fall down," he growled.

"I can't," Jordan argued. "All I see is her, Marina, suffering, when I close my eyes. I need a distraction, so I might as well work."

Russ forced a breath out his nose and gritted his teeth. What he wanted to say was Jordan was being a damned fool, but Jordan was still all kinds of raw on several fronts, and he'd promised Phyl and Jordan he'd be *nicer* from now on. After another longer, slower inhale and exhale, Russ said, "Look, I get it. But you're working on no sleep and, knowing you, probably less than half the calories you should."

Jordan frowned, but Russ held up a placating hand. "Put that wheelbarrow away and come back here. You can get some of our less placid beauties prettied up for our guests tomorrow. Give as many of the horses that are ready for adoption a bath as you can, but start with the least friendly and work your way up, so whoever's left are the sweetest tempered to hand over to the volunteers tomorrow. Is that enough of a distraction?"

It was a testament to how tired Jordan had to be that he didn't even pull a face. Horse bathing wasn't exactly the most skilled of their labors, but cleaning a fractious mountain of muscle, bone, teeth, and hooves wasn't exactly child's play either. He'd need to keep his mind on what he was doing or he'd regret it.

Russ spent the whole day checking in on both Marina and Jordan, in addition to all his other charges. Phyl wanted to spend all day with Marina, but someone had to field phone calls and deal with all the minutia of running a charity, so the others took turns watching her.

Tish called at three to say Marina had a bacterial infection and to start her on some of the antibiotics they already had for a couple of the other sick horses, and she'd be by with the rest after work. But as it happened, they needed her sooner than that.

Marina went into labor a little over an hour later. Jordan was right there with her and Phyl before Russ even got back from making the phone call to Tish.

The poor mare shivered and groaned with discomfort, her flanks dewy with sweat as Jordan leaned close and murmured to her. Marina let out a shuddering breath and moved closer to Jordan, seeking comfort in her distress, and Russ's throat got a little tight for a second before he swallowed the constriction down.

"Tish is on her way."

"Will she be able to save the foal?" Jordan asked, still running a soothing hand over Marina's neck and shoulder.

Russ grimaced, but Phyl was the one who answered gently, "From what the sheriff's office got from the previous owners, she's not even three hundred days, Jordan. There's nothing we can do for the foal."

Jordan's jaw tightened, and he turned back to Marina without saying anything more.

The next few hours were a solemn affair. No one really said much beyond Tish's orders. Jordan stayed at Marina's head, soothing her, while they waited for enough of the foal to breech the canal so they could get a rope around it and pull it the rest of the way out. They all agreed Marina was still too weak from malnourishment and all the complications that came with it to be left to do it on her own, despite the mare's obvious distress at having so many people crowding into her space.

Jordan worked a minor miracle there. He kept her calm and cooperative while they removed the poor little thing from the stall, and Tish made sure Marina was cleaned up and treated for the infection, inside and out. Thankfully, as far as they could tell, the foal hadn't had time to turn septic, but they'd still have to keep a close eye on Marina until the infection passed.

After he and Phyl saw Tish out to her car and waved her on her way, Russ returned to the barn to find Jordan still standing at Marina's head.

"Come on, Jordan. We should let her get some rest. One of the volunteers, Michelle, I think, has offered to stay until about eight or nine tonight so we can get some food in us and a little sleep ourselves." When Jordan didn't even twitch, Russ stepped closer. "Jordan?"

He called again, but it wasn't until he put a hand on his shoulder that Jordan started out of whatever trance-like state he'd been in.

"What?"

Glazed blue eyes stared up at him. "Food. Bed. Rest, for all of us. It's been a long day."

With one last pat to Marina's neck, Jordan allowed Russ to drag him from the barn.

"Do you think she'll mourn her baby?" Jordan slurred as he shuffled along beside Russ.

"I don't think so," Russ said kindly. "She didn't really get a chance to see it, let alone bond with it. But we'll take good care of her, and hopefully, when she's feeling better, her spirits will pick up too."

"Good."

Russ had no warning. One second Jordan was walking beside him. The next he dropped to the dirt like a box of rocks.

"Shit!"

Russ crouched next to him and rolled him over. Bleary blue eyes blinked up at him.

"When was the last time you ate or drank anything?" he growled.

Jordan's eyebrows drew together, but he just stared as if he wasn't quite getting what Russ was saying.

"Goddammit. Jon! Ernie! You guys still in the house?" he shouted.

Ernie came trotting from the yard to his left.

"Help me get this fool up the stairs," Russ grated.

As he and Ernie got their arms under Jordan's and helped him to his feet, Jon came out onto the porch.

"Jon, will you grab some Gatorade for this idiot?"

He deposited Jordan on one of the rockers on the front porch. Thankfully by then, Jordan was a bit more alert, so Russ didn't have to worry about it being more than just a little exhaustion and dehydration at work.

"Drink," Russ ordered as he shoved the plastic bottle Jon brought into Jordan's hand.

Luckily, Jordan wasn't fool enough to do anything beyond what he was told. He chugged about a third of it before trying to hand it back, but Russ folded his arms and glared. "All of it," he growled.

Jordan sighed, but he put the bottle back to his lips. Satisfied the idiot was going to cooperate, Russ thanked Jon and Ernie and shooed them on their way. The dimwit didn't need an audience.

While Jordan was drinking, Phyl came out and hovered for a bit, but once she was satisfied Jordan was feeling better, she went back inside to find food for everyone else. They were all feeling low and tired, and Russ assured her he could handle one fool of a man.

Once he'd drained the dregs from the bottle, Jordan grimaced and waved the plastic at Russ with a scowl. But that was fine by Russ. Cantankerous he could handle just fine.

"Good," he said, "Now do you need help going upstairs to your bed, or can you manage it on your own?"

Jordan rolled his eyes. His stubborn jaw, now shadowed with dirty blond stubble and whatever grime he'd run into that afternoon, twitched like he was itching to argue, but Russ just scowled right back at him.

"There's enough sugar in that Gatorade to tide you over while you rest, so where you're going isn't up for debate. The only thing you get to decide is how you get there."

Jordan defiantly held his gaze for a few more seconds before slumping back in the chair and throwing up his hands. "Fine. I'll go take a nap if it's so damned important to you." He brushed Russ's offered hand to the side and stood. "I don't need to be carried. I can get there on my own."

Making a grand gesture of it, Russ held the screen door for the little shit, and then he waited at the bottom of the stairs until Jordan had disappeared from sight.

"Someone needs to get that kid a Snickers bar. He's a real diva when he's hungry." Russ chuckled to himself as he made his way to the kitchen to fill his own belly and help Phyl find some food for the volunteer that was staying.

Maybe he should order and set up another security camera, actually *in* one of the stalls, so they could keep an eye on their more worrisome charges from the comfort of the house. Except the cameras didn't show everything, and sometimes nothing beat a real person watching, listening, and even smelling for problems.

After running a tray out to Michelle in the barn, Russ went upstairs to check on Jordan. Sleeping Beauty was passed out cold on his bed. He'd taken the time to hose off in the shower before collapsing in a disordered heap on the mattress, because his hair was still wet, and as far as Russ could tell, he was naked under the sheet he'd draped over his lap.

Russ lingered in the doorway longer than he should have. Jordan Thorndike of the Virginia Thorndikes was, without a doubt, a beautiful man—perfectly put together, from his artfully highlighted dark blond hair to his elegant, pedicured feet.

He's a hard worker, smart, funny, and with a good heart too... at least when it comes to the horses, a traitorous voice inside Russ's head whispered.

Yeah, and he's a vain, spoiled rich kid who's been pampered every day of his life and has no idea what the real world is like, he argued back. *He's also got more issues than Reader's Digest.*

Closing his eyes, Russ forced himself to turn around and leave. The image of Jordan naked and splayed out on rumpled sheets was burned into his brain, but the most he ever intended to do about it was pull it out for spanking material from time to time... or possibly every day until Jordan left for greener pastures.

CHAPTER THIRTEEN

THE ROOM was dark when Jordan woke. His phone on the nightstand said one thirty when he tapped the button. With a groan, he dragged himself upright. His head pounded, telling him he was probably still dehydrated, so after taking a quick leak, he downed a glass of water from the bathroom sink.

As he replayed the events of that afternoon, he cringed. He'd been really stupid not to stop and drink something in the Texas heat. He'd been so worried about Marina, he knew he wouldn't be hungry, but he should have forced himself to drink. Crumpling to the dirt in front of Russ and everyone else was 100 percent mortifying. He was going to have real trouble facing any of them in the morning.

A quick glance in the mirror made him wince. His eyes were bloodshot and underscored with deep purple rings. His cheeks looked sunken and sallow.

"And you wondered why Russ didn't jump all over this," he grumbled to himself. "You should be lucky he didn't run away screaming."

Except he hadn't looked this bad when he was flirting with Russ. He'd spent forever in front of the mirror to make sure of that, and Russ still hadn't wanted him.

The rejection stung, no matter how many times he tried to convince himself that Russ was just an asshole who had a hang-up about rich people—that it was nothing personal. It felt personal. It felt all kinds of personal.

Not good enough.

That was what it always boiled down to. He wasn't deluded about his looks, his abilities, or his intelligence. He had a decent amount of all of that… just never enough, it seemed, not for anyone in his life.

Closing his eyes, he dragged his hands down his face and shuffled out of the bathroom. If he kept looking in the mirror, the rest of the night might turn into a downward spiral of those kinds of thoughts and he'd be useless in the morning. It was Saturday. The weekenders would be coming, and both Phyllis and Russ had warned him of an impending Girl Scout troop they'd need his help with.

He shivered. After the emotional upheavals of that week, he wasn't sure he had it in him to be "on" all day tomorrow. Maybe he should just tell Phyllis he wasn't feeling well and stay in bed. He'd fainted, after all. She'd hardly begrudge him a bit of time off. It wasn't like he was getting paid for his time.

An image of Russ's disapproving scowl flashed in his mind and refused to be banished. Jordan couldn't do it. Russ would probably make some crack about the trust-fund baby needing a *personal* day or something. He'd already shown enough weakness for one week.

He'd spend the entire day fighting with himself and battling that tidal wave with no distractions if he didn't go to work, so looking at it that way, he really had no choice.

Dragging his weary body over to the dresser, he grabbed a fresh set of borrowed work clothes and pulled them on. As he buttoned and zipped the jeans, a small smile fought its way to the surface. At least he'd managed to get in Russ's pants... in a manner of speaking.

At Marina's stall, Jordan saw that the mare seemed to be resting comfortably for the night. He checked her over as best he could with a flashlight, but couldn't detect any problems with his admittedly limited experience. Not wanting to disturb her, he moved back up the aisle and rubbed the neck of any curious head that poked out.

The short trek out to the barn reminded him of how tired he really was, so after snagging some leftover chicken and rice and beans from the kitchen and downing another glass of water, he returned to his room. Thankfully, sleep came quickly again, and he didn't wake up until he heard his door creak just before dawn.

Blinking blearily at the paneled white wood in the semidarkness, he was confused for a second, since it remained closed, but eventually he just shrugged and rolled out of bed to get ready for the day.

After his shower, he spent several long minutes in front of the mirror again, inspecting himself. He still didn't exactly look his best, but after a shave and using the last of a very fancy bottle of face cream he probably couldn't afford to replace, he doubted he'd scare the kiddies.

He didn't feel up to putting on the charm today. He really didn't. He felt useless and weak and just a little broken, but the show must go on. He was still a Thorndike, after all, even if his father didn't want him to be. Thorndikes weren't quitters, whatever else they might be.

Breakfast was as bad as he'd thought it would be. Everyone hovered over him, making sure he ate until he felt like he was going to throw up. He kept his smile firmly in place and thanked them politely for all their concern. With effort, he managed to wipe the worry from their faces and get them all laughing and kidding around again. Russ didn't count. He never stopped frowning, so Jordan couldn't quite make out whether that was concern or disapproval, and he didn't want to know the answer anyway.

As promised, he waded into the fray of excited, horse-crazy little girls right alongside Phyllis. He charmed and flattered. He was funny and upbeat. His mask didn't even slip when Russ's ex, Todd, showed up as one of the troop's chaperones for the day and eyed him like a Christmas present come early.

Despite being creeped out again that the guy was cruising when his daughters were barely ten feet away currycombing a sweet little donkey named Jasmine, Jordan had to admit to a certain amount of morbid curiosity as he studied the man out of the corner of his eye. At about five foot ten, with artfully layered short light-brown hair, Todd wasn't a bad-looking guy, but he wasn't underwear-ad material either. Judging by the general age of his kids, and that Russ didn't seem the type to go on the down-low with a married man, their relationship had probably ended close to a decade ago. Maybe Todd had let himself go a little in the interim, and he'd been a real stunner ten years ago.

As he was now, Todd might've been fine for a hookup, but Phyllis had made it sound like he and Russ were in an actual relationship. Jordan just didn't get it. What did Todd have that he didn't?

Maybe the guy had a monster cock hiding in those jeans?

And why the hell couldn't Jordan just let it go?

Russ was super hot, but he wasn't the only dick on the planet. Jordan didn't know how long he'd even be on the ranch, so who gave a shit if one stupid, hot asshole of a cowboy rejected him anyway?

God, he was so fucked-up right now.

BY TWO that afternoon, Jordan's mask was wearing very thin. The girls in the troop were starting to get a little tired and whiny, and the stress of the last few days was catching up to him. After the troop finished lunch and while they were busy with some craft project they intended to sell to raise money for the ranch, Jordan made a quick run up to his room and dug out his bottle of bourbon in desperation. He wasn't going to get drunk. In fact, he'd barely had any of it since coming to the ranch, but today, just this once, he needed something to soften the edges and loosen his limbs. The girls' shrill little giggles and whines were like ice picks in his skull, and the last thing he wanted was to lose his temper with any of them, for Phyllis's sake, if nothing else. He needed the world to be a little hazy around the edges.

After a couple of quick swigs from the bottle, he put it back in the closet, brushed his teeth, grabbed a water bottle, and headed right back out. Some of the girls were decorating old, worn horseshoes, while others made leather and bead bracelets. Jordan helped where he could, but crafting wasn't exactly his strong suit. Eventually, Phyllis took pity on him and sent him off to the barn.

"We'll be done here soon. Go check on Marina and then see if Russ needs you for anything. I'm sure you'd much rather be doing that anyway."

Jordan's smile of relief was the first real one he'd had all day. He gave a startled Phyllis a quick squeeze before heading for the barn at a jog. The bourbon had been just enough to loosen him up a little, and after being set free from babysitting duty, he practically danced his way down to see Marina. Despite the sadness of what happened with her foal, the mare seemed better even after less than a day, and Jordan had to admit it had been the best thing for her.

He lingered in the barn rather than going in search of Russ. He was still a bit on the warm and fuzzy side and wasn't sure seeking out that particular man was the best idea. He'd already embarrassed himself more than enough for one lifetime where Russ was concerned.

The barn was empty of humans, despite all the activity on the ranch. Most of the horses had been let out in the pasture or were moved to a pen or paddock to get a little sunshine and fresh air or get worked on by a volunteer. Deciding he'd put in more than enough work for one day, he stepped into the empty stall where they stacked extra straw and slumped onto a couple of bales to shut his eyes for a few minutes. He'd help clean up when everyone was gone, but a quick nap wasn't too much to ask, was it?

"There you are."

Jordan had just dozed off when the unfamiliar voice woke him. Blinking awake, he found Russ's creepy ex, Todd, propped against the opening to the stall.

Clearing his throat, Jordan sat up and brushed his hair out of his face. "I'm sorry. Did you need something?"

A lazy smile played across Todd's face. "I could use a sip of that water, if you don't mind."

He sauntered into the stall and plucked Jordan's water bottle from the bale where Jordan had propped it. Standing close enough that his denim-clad knee brushed Jordan's, Todd wrapped his lips around the bottle, tilted his head back, and took a long pull. His Adam's apple bobbed, and a little water escaped to trickle down his chin to his neck as Jordan watched with mild curiosity and a sliver of interest.

The devil and angel on each of Jordan's shoulders had a little debate as Todd stopped drinking and offered the bottle to Jordan with hot eyes, and Jordan drank what was left.

On the one hand, Todd was obviously a jerk. Being married with two kids wasn't stopping him from cruising the local animal rescue for some tail on the side. On the other hand, Jordan was lonely and in need of a little boost to his ego, so what harm would a little flirting do?

"Damn," Todd husked. "You're the hottest thing I've seen round here in a long time."

Jordan couldn't help himself. He preened under the compliment. He hadn't been to a bar or hooked up with anyone from Grindr in weeks, even before his talk with his parents. And, weak as it might be, he needed *someone* to tell him he was desirable, even if it came from a bit of a sleaze.

He grinned and stretched, enjoying the feel of Todd's eyes on him. "Glad you think so."

"After spotting you the last time I was here, I definitely wanted a closer look."

Jordan wet his lips and cocked his head. "I thought you were a little preoccupied with someone else the last time you were here."

Todd had been angling his body closer but paused. "No. If you mean Russ, he just gets his panties in a bunch sometimes and thinks he has a right to interfere in other people's business. Believe me, baby, you're the only one I'm looking at."

The devil was still winning the argument in his head, so Jordan stood up and propped himself against the stack of bales, spreading his boots wide enough that Todd could step in close.

"You think I'm worth looking at?"

Todd's hazel eyes took a lazy journey down and back up Jordan's body. "You know you are," he said huskily.

It wasn't until Todd stepped close enough to press his erection to Jordan's thigh that reason began to return.

What the hell was he doing?

Yes, he was lonely. Yes, he was weak and needy and hurting and horny. But since when was he enough of any of those things to mess around with a guy he didn't even like, less than a hundred yards away from the man's little girls?

Just, ew.

Deciding the game had gone far enough, Jordan moved to extricate himself from the situation, but before he could manage to get a word out, Todd fisted Jordan's package through his jeans... and then all hell broke loose.

"What the fuck are you doing?" Russ shouted from the door to the stall.

"Oh shit."

Chapter Fourteen

Russ was so mad, he didn't even stop to think. He grabbed Todd by the shoulder, yanked him out of the stall, and shoved him into the dirt.

"Russ—"

Turning on Jordan, he glared and spat, "Shut up. I'll deal with you in a minute."

He swung back around, and Todd crab-walked backward a bit before scrambling to his feet. Todd put his hands out in front of him to ward off Russ's advance and continued to back up.

"Calm down, Russ," Todd said, regaining some of his composure. "This isn't any of your business."

"The hell—" he started to shout, but cast a quick glance at the open barn doors and lowered his voice. "The hell it ain't," he hissed. "This is *my* ranch, *my* home. I told you I didn't want you here causing trouble. I told you not to come back. This ain't a goddamned pickup spot. This is an animal rescue, and your kids are barely fifty yards away. What the hell were you thinking?"

Hands still raised in a placating gesture, Todd replied, "All right. All right. You're absolutely right. I didn't come here to cruise. I swear. I had to come because the troop needed another chaperone, and Molly had a migraine this morning and couldn't make it. Your friend over there was just flirting with me all day, and I got a little carried away."

"What?" Jordan gasped behind him, but Russ ignored him.

"Get out, Todd," Russ sighed tiredly. "If you want to cheat on your wife and risk screwing up the best thing you're ever gonna get, that's your business. But this ranch is mine, and you're not gonna do it here. You got me?"

Todd rolled his eyes. He opened his mouth to retort, but paused and glanced back and forth between Russ and Jordan. A slow smirk spread across his face. "Oh, I got it," he said. He turned to leave but stopped and grinned over his shoulder. "If that's how it is, Russ, you really need to keep a tighter leash on your boy there, or you're not going to have him for long. I know how you are about faithfulness and fidelity and all that." He laughed. "But I have to tell you, you're betting on the wrong horse with that one."

Russ rolled his shoulders and spat in the dirt in the direction of Todd's receding back. The asshole had done him a favor by dumping him all those years ago to take the straight-and-narrow path with Molly. He proved it every time he showed up. Russ felt sorry for the kids, but he hoped Todd was a better father than a husband.

"What the fuck is that supposed to mean?" Jordan shouted belligerently behind him, and Russ's anger spiked again.

He rounded on Jordan and crowded him back into the stall. "Keep your goddamned voice down," he growled. He kept going until Jordan was backed up against a wall and got right in his face. "Bad enough you were fucking around with one of the dads where anyone could walk by, you don't have to swear loud enough for the kiddies to overhear and let everyone know what you were doing."

Jordan had opened his mouth, probably to argue, but clamped it shut again and winced. Russ's smile was not pleasant. "Good. You can stop being self-centered for one damned minute, enough to think about those kids. Maybe there's some hope for you after all."

"Hey!"

"What?" Russ shot back. "Am I wrong? Were you not just in here with Todd's hand down your pants two seconds ago, while his daughters were making bracelets not fifty yards away?"

"His hand wasn't down my pants," Jordan argued petulantly, but he wouldn't meet Russ's eye.

"Fine. But he was still grabbing your dick, and who knows how far you two would have gone if I hadn't come in."

"It wouldn't have gone any further."

"Bullshit." Struggling to get a hold of himself, Russ took a couple steps back, rolled his shoulders, and worked his jaw. After blowing out a cooling breath, he said, "Listen. What you do on your own time, that's your business. But pull another stunt like this, and I don't care what emotional trauma you're going through or who your goddamned parents are, I'll personally kick your ass off this ranch. You hear me?"

He spun around without waiting for a reply. He was too hot right now to listen to excuses or promises.

And if Jordan decided to try to win him over with any of that fake-ass charm, Russ might really lose it and do or say something he'd regret later.

Instead of even trying to get back to work, Russ figured he'd better take a long walk until he cooled off. The crowd at the ranch was already thinning out, people heading home to get dinner ready and let tired families decompress from a hot, busy day. He could help finish cleaning up when everyone was gone, and that way he wouldn't have to try to make polite conversation with strangers, which was painful on a good day.

At the first big rise overlooking the ranch, he plopped his ass down in the shade of his favorite live oak, crossed his arms and ankles, tipped his straw hat forward, and closed his eyes. A slight breeze stirred the hot, dusty air, rustling the grasses and wildflowers. Insects buzzed and clicked nearby, but most of the noise and bustle from the ranch had thankfully faded… at least until the crunch of boots on the dirt track cut in on his peaceful interlude.

When the footsteps grew close, Russ sighed and opened his eyes to find Jordan standing over him. Jordan didn't look guilty anymore. He looked good and mad. And Russ's heart rate kicked up a notch.

"Our conversation wasn't finished," Jordan fired.

Russ shrugged. "It was as far as I'm concerned. Grow up or get out. I don't think I can be any clearer."

"Fuck you, Russ. You didn't even stay to hear me out. You just assumed you knew everything you needed to, judged me, and walked off, as usual."

"Are you trying to tell me I didn't see you and Todd groping each other in the barn while the kiddies did their craft projects right outside?"

Jordan groaned. "Yes, okay? I know. I fucked up," he said, flinging his arms wide. "I'm sorry. If you haven't noticed, I'm not exactly at my best right now, and I was starved for a little attention, so sue me. I had a *major* momentary lapse in judgment, but that's all it was, *momentary*. I swear I was going to put a stop to it. I'm not a complete asshole, despite what you seem to think. Todd grabbed me like a second before I was about to tell him to back off, and you stepped in all wrath-of-God, fire-and-brimstone before I could get a word out."

Russ snorted, climbed to his feet, and dusted off the seat of his jeans before lifting his gaze to meet Jordan's. "I left the barn because I didn't particularly care what your excuses were, and I still don't. If you're looking for a shoulder to cry on in your emotional distress, try Phyl. I'm all out of fucks to give."

He turned to head back to the barn, but Jordan grabbed his arm and spun him around. "What the hell is your problem?"

Getting up in Jordan's pretty face again, Russ growled, "My problem is guys like you thinking you can do anything you want, and because of who you are, no one will dare call you on it. My problem is poor little rich kids who think the whole damned world revolves around them and *their* problems. Oh, boo hoo, my mommy and daddy don't love me enough. They only gave me a fifty-thousand-dollar red convertible for Christmas instead of the private jet I wanted. They want to pay hundreds of thousands of dollars to send me to college to get a degree that would open doors pretty much anywhere for me, but that's not what I really want for my life. Why can't they understand?"

Jordan dropped Russ's arm and stepped back like Russ had slapped him. Guilt doused some of the fire in

Russ's belly. He hadn't wanted to lash out like that, but Jordan wouldn't let him be long enough to cool down.

Jordan regarded him with wounded eyes for a few breaths before he croaked, "That's really what you think?"

Anger crept back into Jordan's face by slow degrees as Russ tried to think of something to say that wouldn't make things worse, but Jordan recovered quicker.

"Fuck you, Russ. You know what? You made up your mind about me the first day I got here, based on one bit of information about me that I have no control over. Nothing I do, no matter how nice I am or how hard I work, is ever going to be good enough, is it? Nothing could possibly change your mind, with your head crammed so firmly up your ass."

Jordan advanced on him until they were nose to nose again. "I'm sorry, Russ. Is that what you want to hear?" he spat. "I'm sorry I was born with a silver spoon in my mouth. I'm sorry my parents were rich and gave me everything they thought I could possibly want. I've had privileges other people only dream of, so *obviously*, I have no right to ever be sad, or lonely, or to complain about anything. No one and nothing could possibly ever hurt me, and I sure as hell should never be so human as to make a mistake, because my parents have *money*, lots and lots of money." He stepped back and hugged himself. "Who cares that I had no control over who I was born to? Who cares that none of that money is actually mine? Who cares that they set standards for me I couldn't possibly achieve, and every penny of that oh-so-important money was taken away the second I failed... and all of their supposed love and support right along with it? Who cares that I was so afraid of losing all of that—not the money, but the rest—that I spent nearly my entire life pretending to be someone I'm not? Obviously, no one should care, because the spoiled little rich kid doesn't deserve it."

Jordan's voice caught, and he blinked rapidly. All his masks were gone, leaving only naked pain behind. Russ had done that. He'd taken someone wounded and hurt him some more. This wasn't who he was. He wasn't supposed to be the bad guy, but right now he sure as hell felt like it.

Before Jordan could catch his second wind, Russ fisted a hand in Jordan's borrowed T-shirt and dragged him into a hug. Jordan jerked in his arms and made a startled noise, but didn't pull away. His chest heaved against Russ's as Russ tightened his arms.

"I'm sorry," Russ murmured against his temple, putting as much feeling into it as he could.

Jordan was still breathing heavily when Russ cautiously leaned back to get a peek at his face. Wounded and wary blue eyes searched Russ's and held his gaze.

"I'm sorry," Russ whispered again.

Giving in to the impulse—anything to wipe that hurt look off Jordan's face—Russ cupped Jordan's jaw and tentatively pressed his lips to the corner of Jordan's mouth. Jordan jerked in his arms a second time, but didn't pull away. Instead he turned into the kiss and sealed their lips together, opening for Russ's tongue and giving just as good as he got. Jordan moaned into the kiss, and Russ gorged himself on the lips he'd craved since the first second he'd laid eyes on Jordan. His blood heated, and his cock stirred as Jordan's lean, hard body molded to his.

When Russ finally broke the kiss so they could breathe, he squinted at Jordan and braced himself, half expecting a fist in his face. He deserved it. But Jordan just stared at him as he panted for breath. Russ was the one to finally break the stand-off, as the pain and confusion slowly returned to Jordan's gaze. He wrapped a hand around the back of Jordan's neck and pulled him to his chest once more, and even more heartbreaking than the look on Jordan's face was the way he sighed and shivered in Russ's arms. Clutching him closer, Russ pressed his lips to Jordan's temple.

The silence stretched as Russ held him. Eventually, Jordan relaxed completely in Russ's arms. He turned his face away and rested his cheek on Russ's shoulder, the gesture so trusting it tore at Russ's heart.

With a sigh of his own, Russ repeated, "I'm sorry."

After letting out a shuddering breath, Jordan nodded against his shoulder.

Resting his chin on the top of Jordan's head, Russ's lips slowly split into a wry grin. "You know, you're the second person this week to tell me to get my head out of my ass." Jordan huffed out a weak chuckle, and Russ smiled. "I guess maybe I should take that as a sign."

"Maybe you should," Jordan replied without pulling away, and Russ closed his eyes.

After a while, with Jordan making no move to break their embrace and Russ in no hurry for it to end either, despite the heat of the Texas sun beating down on them, Russ began to move his hands in soothing circles along Jordan's back and shoulders. Jordan's hands slid down along his flanks to grip Russ's belt at his hips.

"Russ?"

"Hmm?"

"What are we doing?"

Russ sighed. Despite all of his best efforts at being logical and all his growls to the contrary, he couldn't deny it anymore. He was well and truly hooked, and he supposed he had no more reason to lie about it.

"Anything you'll let me," he murmured.

Jordan lifted his head and searched Russ's face, his perfectly shaped eyebrows drawing together above his too damned pretty blue eyes. "I really don't understand you at all. A couple of minutes ago you were treating me like something you scraped off your boots. Now you're holding me like you don't want to let me go and offering me what? Whatever I want?"

With another sigh, Russ dragged the backs of his fingers down Jordan's cheek and smiled when Jordan didn't pull away. "You told me to get my head out of my ass, so that's what I'm doing. You're right. I've been an asshole. I've been judging you based on someone I knew a long time ago. It wasn't fair and it wasn't right."

"I'm me, not anybody else."

"I know," Russ agreed. "I'm sorry."

"So now what?"

Russ's lips quirked as he eyed Jordan hopefully. "Now I hope you forgive me and let me show you just how sorry I really am."

He trailed his fingers down Jordan's back again, and Jordan drew in a quick breath. "Just like that. Now you want me?"

He crooked a smile and shook his head. "Baby, I've wanted you since the second you stepped out of that shiny red sports car of yours. I just didn't want to admit it."

"Yeah?" Jordan grinned. But his grin quickly faded. "You're a hard man to figure out."

"Not really. I'm pretty simple, once you get to know me…. Do you want to get to know me?"

Jordan licked his pink and slightly swollen lips and nodded. "Yeah, I do. I'm just having a little trouble keeping up here," he said with a chuckle. "I'm not used to switching gears quite this fast."

"Take your time." Russ pursed his lips. "Only, maybe not too much time." He chuckled, pressing his hips forward so Jordan could feel the evidence of his desire.

Jordan's already flushed cheeks grew a little ruddier as heat sparked in his eyes. "Okay, let's go."

"You sure?" Russ teased. "I don't want to rush you now."

"Move it, cowboy. You have some apologizing to do," Jordan shot back with a grin.

CHAPTER FIFTEEN

APPARENTLY RUSS didn't need to be told twice. He grabbed Jordan by the wrist and set off toward the ranch. Jordan was perfectly fine with that plan. Thinking and logic were overrated anyway.

"You know I'm not actually a cowboy," Russ huffed conversationally as they trotted down the hill.

"What?"

"I don't raise or work with cattle beyond the few bovines we have at the rescue."

"Uh, okay."

Russ had gotten him all worked up and now he wanted conversation? Was he kidding? Thinking time was done. Otherwise Jordan might realize how crazy this was and put a stop to it, or at least put on the brakes for a second while he processed... and his dick was so not interested in that plan.

Russ just grinned over his shoulder and shook his head.

Phyllis and a couple of people at the table looked up as Russ charged into the yard—including Todd, who was helping his little girls pack up for the day—but Russ didn't slow down. He let go of Jordan's wrist—seemingly his only concession to the onlookers—but he marched up the stairs and into the house without a backward glance, and Jordan followed on his heels.

Before Jordan knew it, he was in Russ's bedroom. As soon as the door closed, Russ spun around, tossed his hat into a chair, and pressed Jordan back against it. Russ's mouth came down on his, wet and demanding and so fucking hot. That hard body and talented mouth scrambled his brains even more, and he gladly surrendered to the demands of his dick.

With a couple of quick yanks, Jordan's T-shirt hit the floor, followed by Russ's. Jordan had been fantasizing about Russ's chest from the first day, and he wasn't disappointed. A smattering of dark brown hair covered hard pecs, thickening around his brown nipples and trailing downward across his belly. But before Jordan could get a taste, Russ stepped away and pulled him toward the bed.

"Mind helping me with my boots?" Russ asked with a cocky grin.

"It would be my pleasure."

Jordan yanked off Russ's boots and socks, then dove for his turquoise-studded belt buckle. After hurriedly fumbling the button fly open, a quick yank revealed Russ went commando, and Jordan groaned. He pressed his face to Russ's trimmed bush and rubbed his cheek along Russ's rapidly hardening dick, breathing him in as his own cock throbbed in his jeans. As hard as Jordan was right now, he could probably come just from sucking Russ off. He wouldn't even need to touch his dick.

Russ cupped the back of Jordan's head and pulled him up, taking Jordan's mouth in another hot kiss.

"Now you," he growled. "I've been waiting far too long to see you completely naked."

Jordan tried to kick off his hiking boots without undoing the laces, but he'd tied them too tight. Russ chuckled at Jordan's growl of frustration, grabbed his arm, and shoved him onto the bed.

"I got it," Russ said as he shimmied the rest of the way out of his own jeans, kicked them to the side, and dropped to his knees between Jordan's thighs.

While Russ worked the knots loose and yanked at his boots, Jordan unbuckled his belt and undid the button and zipper on his borrowed jeans. Jordan's cock throbbed at the look on Russ's face when he saw Jordan's tight red boxer briefs.

"Nice," Russ growled.

"Yeah?"

"Hell yeah."

Russ draped himself over Jordan, pressing him into the mattress and grinding their cocks together as Jordan kicked the rest of the way out of his jeans and underwear and spread his legs. Skin to skin at last, Jordan moaned eagerly into Russ's kiss and mapped every inch of Russ's work-hardened body he could reach. Russ's muscles were lean and wiry, not gym-pumped for show, but that didn't make him any less hot. In fact, the scents of hay and horse and sweat combined with Russ's musk were driving Jordan crazy with need. Up until that moment he'd never quite realized he had such a thing for a hard-working, physical man... or maybe it was just Russ who drove him wild.

Jordan shoved a hand between their bodies, wrapped both their cocks in his fist, and pumped feverishly, desperate to come, but before Jordan could work up a good rhythm, Russ clamped a hand over his fist and forced him to stop. Russ grabbed both Jordan's wrists and pinned them to the mattress by his head.

"Hold on there a second," Russ murmured, smiling down at him.

"What?" Jordan breathed in frustrated need. "You want something else? You want to maybe fuck me into this mattress?" Despite being restrained, Jordan lifted up and bit Russ's chin, giving it a soothing suck and lick as he released it.

Russ shuddered and groaned, but didn't release Jordan's wrists. "Yeah, baby, I want all that and more, but there's no rush. I wanna touch and taste every inch of you. I wanna hear every pant and moan you make. I wanna find every little spot on this hot body that makes you wild. You gonna let me do that before we rush to the finish line?"

Jordan's cock throbbed with every gruff dirty word out of Russ's mouth, but Jordan wasn't sure if his dick was cheering Russ on or protesting the delay.

"Jesus, Russ, anything. Just touch me," he panted.

Russ's grin could've been described as evil, but since he slid down Jordan's chest, kissing and licking a trail in the general direction of Jordan's dick, he supposed he couldn't complain.

The first hot, wet swipe of Russ's tongue over Jordan's cock was pure torture, but Russ didn't make him wait long. He took Jordan's dick deep after only a few seconds of teasing, and Jordan moaned his approval loudly. It was a good thing the ranch house had central air and all the windows were closed, or those little kiddies outside might've gotten a little more of a nature lesson than they bargained for.

Jordan threaded his fingers into Russ's thick brown hair and spread his legs wide to give Russ plenty of room to work. Russ was a man of many talents, and cocksucking was definitely not the least of them. He played around down there for what felt like hours, ferreting out every little bundle of nerves that made Jordan jump and swear and whine. He brought Jordan to the edge several times, until Jordan thought he really would go crazy if he had to wait even a second longer.

"Jesus, Russ, I need to come... *please*!"

Russ lifted his head, rasped his stubbled chin along Jordan's sensitive inner thigh, and grinned. "Okay, baby. How do you want it?"

"You scrambled my brains, and *now* you want me to make a decision? Are you kidding me?"

With a chuckle, Russ climbed up Jordan's body, draped himself over him, and kissed him slow and sweet. "How about an either-or, then?" he asked placatingly. "Do you want to come in my mouth or come while riding my cock?"

"That one! The second. Fuck me."

Jordan hooked his heels under Russ's ass and thrust against Russ's belly, distracting Russ as he stretched to yank open the top drawer of his nightstand.

"Hurry up, or I just might finish without you," Jordan teased.

"You better not," Russ growled.

Tube of lube and condoms in hand, Russ sat back on his heels. He slid the condom on and slicked it up while Jordan licked his lips and thrust his hips impatiently. When Russ breeched Jordan's ass with two wet fingers, Jordan threw his head back and bore down.

"Slow down, darlin', let me get you ready or you'll regret it."

"I was ready half an hour ago," Jordan complained.

"Not for this you ain't." Russ wrapped a fist around his admittedly impressive erection, and Jordan rolled his eyes and chuckled.

"Okay, okay. Just hurry up."

Jordan was used to quick and dirty, but it had been a while. Forcing a little blood back into his brain, he concentrated on relaxing his overheated body and enjoying Russ's talented fingers inside him without whining too much in frustration.

"You ready for me?" Russ growled after bringing Jordan a little too close to the edge yet one more time with his fingers.

"Yes! Fuck me."

Lifting Jordan's thighs over his arms, Russ pressed slowly inside until he bottomed out. Jordan gasped and groaned, so unbelievably full, and Russ stilled. He placed tender kisses to Jordan's temple, his cheek, and then his lips.

"Okay, darlin'?" Russ panted.

"Yeah," Jordan breathed. "Move. Do it."

Russ started slow, fucking Jordan deep with each careful thrust, but as soon as Jordan pushed back and dug his heels under Russ's ass, Russ got the hint and rode him hard. Jordan had to brace a hand on the headboard, which in turn banged against the wall, but he sure as hell wasn't going to tell him to stop. Precum dribbled from his cock in a steady flow as Russ pounded his ass, and Jordan moaned, "Yes. Fuck. Harder. God."

Eventually he just couldn't take it anymore and he fisted his dick, pumping hard until he shot all over his stomach and chest with one last cry before collapsing back to the mattress. Russ hammered a few ragged thrusts home and shouted his release soon after.

With a chuckle, Russ pulled out, got rid of the condom, and dropped to the mattress next to Jordan.

"Damn, darlin'. Just damn!" Russ panted.

Jordan grinned as he tried to catch his breath. Russ had fucked him boneless. He wasn't sure he could make it back to his room, even if he tried, so he hoped that wasn't what Russ wanted. But he didn't want to take his welcome for granted either.

Before Jordan could work himself around to asking, Russ snagged his T-shirt off the floor and gave it to Jordan to clean up. Then he slid an arm under Jordan's back and urged him to drape himself over Russ's chest.

The ceiling fan above them spun and rattled as it cooled their sweating bodies, and Jordan decided that was a good enough answer for him. Closing his eyes, he let the weight of a long day and postorgasmic warm fuzzies drag him under. If Russ wanted him to move at some point, he could wake him up.

CLOSE TO dinnertime according to the somewhat battered clock on Russ's nightstand, Jordan once again lay partially draped over Russ's chest, with his chin propped on the backs of his hands, watching Russ sleep. They'd made love two more times since the first, and Jordan's body was still humming and tingling from head to toe. He probably looked like an idiot, staring all gooey-eyed, but he didn't care. One-night stands and hurried hookups in bathrooms, alleys, and bathhouses had nothing on a few hours of Russ's undivided attention in his creaky old bed. Russ was incredibly intense once he'd made up his mind about something, and Jordan still hadn't quite caught up.

Unfortunately, the bang of the screen door downstairs ended any further uninterrupted study. Russ cracked open sleepy brown eyes, and a small, sexy smile curved his hard lips.

"What?" Russ asked.

Caught staring, Jordan flushed, smiled sheepishly, and shook his head. "Nothing."

Russ did a full-body stretch before folding an arm behind his head and resting his other hand on Jordan's flank. As he'd done pretty much all afternoon, Russ started exploring and petting Jordan's skin like he couldn't help himself, and Jordan wanted to purr. He'd had no idea Russ was such a sensualist, and now that he knew, he had this ridiculous urge to do a little happy dance around the room.

"You were looking at me awful intently for it being nothin'," Russ said with a chuckle.

"Sorry."

"Don't apologize. I didn't say it was a bad thing. But obviously somethin's on your mind."

Jordan worried his lower lip and squinted at him. "I just…. You're going to have to bear with me for a bit. Like I said before, I got a little whiplash here. This is going to take some getting used to."

"Which part?"

"You being nice to me. I mean, like, *really* nice to me. Like so nice I'm kind of melted over here."

"Are you saying you want me to stop?" Russ asked, raising his dark eyebrows and stilling the fingertips he'd been trailing down Jordan's spine.

"Hell no, I don't want you to stop. I'm just going to need a bit to wrap my head around everything that's happened over the last few days… hell, the last few weeks. Nothing is what I'd thought it was, I guess. I don't know."

He frowned helplessly. He wasn't explaining himself very well. Russ's small smile faded, and he dropped both hands to Jordan's sides and urged him up. Russ rolled onto his side, and when they were face-to-face, he kissed Jordan, plucking at Jordan's lips until he stopped worrying and sank into it. When they broke apart, Jordan laid his head on the pillow next to Russ's and held his concerned gaze.

"Boy, when you make up your mind about something, you really make up your mind," Jordan teased breathlessly.

Russ's face sobered, and he nodded. "Maybe we should start there, because that's probably something you should know about me up-front before this goes any further."

A spike of unease made his stomach clench. "What's that?"

"You haven't known me long enough to see for yourself, but for better or worse, I'm an all or nothin' kinda guy. I'm either all in or all out. I don't have an in-between. I've been that way my whole life." He let that sink in for a few seconds before continuing. "It's not something I'm necessarily proud of per se, but at this stage in my life, I don't think it's gonna change. So, if that's not something you want—not something you can promise back—you should probably let me know now."

Jordan's eyes widened and his eyebrows climbed toward his hairline as he pulled away a little. "Uh, I'm not really sure what that means. I mean, I'm kind of in flux right now. I have no idea what I want to do with my life or where I'm going. I'm here to figure that out.

So if you need me to make, like, long-term promises, I don't think I can do that."

Russ chuckled. "Baby, I'm not blind. Despite all evidence to the contrary, I do realize you've got a lot to work through right now—even if I haven't exactly been all that understanding about it. You don't know where you'll be next week, let alone next year. I get it. I'm not asking for that."

"What are you asking for, then?"

"I'm asking you to say you're all in, for right now. I don't play games. I don't mess around. Casual doesn't interest me. If you're gonna be with me, you're gonna be with *me*. Just you and me, in a real relationship, no tiptoeing around the edges of one. Obviously we're going to see each other every day, so there won't be any of that 'will he call?' bullshit, but I don't want to dick around with all that 'does he like me?' 'does he want to spend time with me?' BS, 'cause the answer's yes. And, if you got somethin' on your mind, you say it. You want something, you ask for it, and I'll do the same… for as long as it lasts."

After sucking in a deep breath, he searched Russ's face. "Exclusive?"

"Yup."

"Like real boyfriends, not just dating?"

"'Boyfriends' sounds a little high school for my taste, but yeah, that's what I mean."

"Sleeping next to each other? Hand-holding? PDAs? Cuddling? Long walks on the beach?"

Russ snorted. "We ain't got a beach. But we can take a long walk holding hands anywhere you want. So, what do you say?"

"Jesus, you move fast."

Russ grimaced and nodded. "I know. It's not always a good thing."

"I didn't say it was a bad thing either," Jordan argued. More noises from downstairs distracted him, and he sighed. "Guess we should get up before someone comes looking for us, huh?"

"Only if you want to. We've probably already missed cleanup, so there's not much point. Phyl saw us come up here together. If she needs us, she can always holler up the stairs."

"We should probably check on Marina, though, shouldn't we?" Jordan continued, realizing with a small stab of guilt that he hadn't thought about her for hours.

Russ rolled away from him, dug by the side of the bed, and returned with his laptop. He popped it open and pulled up a video feed from the barn, but this time, Marina's stall was front and center.

"Chances are Phyl already had someone in to see her or checked on her herself, but I moved the camera this afternoon so I could look in on her at night."

The mare looked fine. She was chewing placidly on her feed, her tail swishing at flies, showing no obvious signs of distress.

Jordan smiled up at Russ. "You thought of everything, huh? Got it all planned out?"

Giving Jordan a wry smile, Russ shook his head. "I don't think I've had anything go to plan since you got here."

"You could've fooled me."

Russ's smile widened into a grin. "Well, that's the trick, ain't it? A man's got his pride to look after."

Jordan shared his grin for a few seconds before he sobered again. "Is that all it was, pride? Because I got the feeling you really just didn't like me."

With a sigh, Russ propped himself on an elbow and held Jordan's gaze. "I'm sorry about that. Like I said, you were right. Despite evidence to the contrary, I judged you based on things you had no control over, and you called me on it. The real you is pretty damned irresistible, as far as I can tell, and I was afraid to let you get too close—pure and simple."

For several seconds, Jordan just blinked. "Wow. You really do just put it all out there, don't you?"

A deep chuckle rumbled in Russ's chest as his face split into a wry grin. "I meant what I said. Once I'm in, I'm in. I don't play stupid games. With the people I choose to care about, I'm honest to a fault. I put everything out there…. Maybe you can understand now why I'm extra careful about who I let in. Why I'm a bit prickly on the outside."

"So you don't get hurt," Jordan reasoned. "Because you've been hurt before."

With a nod and a small smile, Russ started running his fingers over Jordan's scalp, down his throat, and over his collarbones, and Jordan shivered. His eyes drooped and he leaned into the touches, but he struggled not to lose his train of thought. This conversation was important.

"Did Todd hurt you?"

Russ's fingers stilled for a second before resuming their drugging caresses. "Naw, he—well, yeah, I guess he did. The way he's acting now makes me feel like he did me a favor, dumping me for a 'normal' life with Molly Shelton, all those years ago. But at the time, I'd be lying if I said it hadn't hurt."

"You were pretty angry with him in the barn," Jordan countered.

"I was annoyed with him, and disappointed, but he wasn't the one I was hot over."

Shifting uncomfortably under Russ's wry smile, Jordan cleared his throat and pressed on. "He wasn't the one who made you hate rich people either," he guessed. At Russ's raised eyebrows, Jordan shrugged. "He does pretty well, whatever his or his wife's jobs are, but I didn't get the feeling he came from money."

"You can tell that just from looking at him, huh?"

Jordan rolled his eyes. "I know. I know. I'm contradicting everything I said earlier about stereotypes, but sometimes you can just tell. It wasn't him, was it?"

"Nope. It wasn't him. That was Theo. I was younger than you are now…. We both were. I worked on his daddy's ranch one summer." Russ waved his hand dismissively before returning it to Jordan's skin. "He was bright and shiny, and I was too young and stupid to look beneath the surface until it was too late. He dumped me like a bad penny as soon as the newest bit of rough caught his eye."

"I'm sorry."

Russ smiled and kissed him tenderly. "Wasn't your fault. He was my first love, is all. And I know you're not the same as him."

Jordan grimaced. "I'm not exactly the most stable person to bet on right now either," he reluctantly admitted. "You said you didn't want to play games, and we should be honest, so to be fair, I should probably point out to you that I'm all kinds of messed-up right now… if you haven't already guessed."

With a soft smile, Russ kissed his temple. "I know you got a lot to work out. I'll help if I can, and you let me know if I'm making things worse. Be honest with me. That's all I ask. I won't put pressure on you for any promises you can't make. This is new, and we'll see where it goes. All I'm asking is that you be all in with me, right here, right now. That's it, okay?"

Jordan nodded. He was getting choked up again, like the emotional basket case he was. Being an adult and giving Russ some equally kind assurances in return was apparently beyond him.

"Come on," Russ said, rolling out of bed. "Let's go down and see if there's anything to eat. I'm starving, and you have to be too."

Food was the last thing on Jordan's mind, but Russ had already donned his jeans, so Jordan reluctantly stood and went in search of his own discarded clothes.

CHAPTER SIXTEEN

BEFORE DAWN, Russ crept out of his room and down the stairs so he didn't wake Jordan. They'd gone to bed early after Russ made sure Jordan ate as much as an active grown man should, but they hadn't slept all of that time. Some of it had been fun, but Jordan tossing with bad dreams for part of the night hadn't.

At least getting Jordan to eat hadn't been as difficult as Russ had feared, so maybe, whatever Jordan's issue with food was, it had more to do with the stress he was under than anything long-term. Russ had probably been worried over nothing. After all, Jordan's body certainly didn't seem to be suffering from any signs of deprivation, beyond that one fainting spell. Jordan was magazine-cover gorgeous from head to toe.

Phyl wasn't in the kitchen, but the coffeepot was full and hot. He poured himself a cup and shuffled out to his spot on the front porch. With a groan, he settled into Sean's rocker and propped his boots on the railing.

His leg muscles and pretty much everything else protested the stretch, but he needed to loosen up a bit. He wasn't as young as he once was, and he hadn't had an honest-to-God lover—someone he could take his time with and do the job right—in almost three years. Apparently there were a few muscles that working on the ranch and the occasional online date from Dallas just didn't exercise.

At the sound of the screen door creaking open, he quickly hid his grin behind his mug.

"Don't bother trying to hide it," Phyl said as she sat down in her rocker. "I've seen that look before, and I know full well what it means."

"Why, Phyl darlin', I have no earthly idea what you mean."

She rolled her blue-gray eyes and smiled. "Don't bother trying to work the charm either. It ain't your forte."

With a chuckle, he sipped at his coffee and dropped the innocent act. "You know I've been trying to tell you that for years. You're the one who keeps trying to make me practice so I can charm the donors like you do."

"I take it our boy is still asleep?" she asked, changing the subject.

"He was when I left," Russ answered, seeing no point in tiptoeing around.

"I have to tell you, I was a bit surprised, given how you've been acting toward him since he got here. I guess I can assume you've ironed out your differences?"

Russ couldn't stop his smile. "You could say that."

She was quiet for a while, but Russ could tell she was working her way up to something, so he sat and sipped his coffee and waited.

"I know this ain't really my business," she began hesitantly. "You're a grown man, and so is he. But are you sure this is a good idea? That young man has a lot on his plate right now. I don't think he even knows if he's coming or going, if you catch my meaning."

Russ choked on his coffee at the unintended pun. Wiping his mouth on the back of his hand, he cleared his throat. "I know he's got problems. I can tell you're worried about him. But believe it or not, we've talked about it. I'm not going to hurt him, Phyl."

"It ain't him I'm worried about."

At Russ's confused frown, Phyl rolled her eyes. "Well, of course I'm a little worried about him. He seems a sweet young man, and he's obviously hurting."

"I distinctly remember you telling me to pull my head out of my ass and be nice to him… and reminding me on several occasions how important his parents' contributions are to this ranch."

"Yeah, and I meant it, but there's a difference between being kind to a person in need and fallin' for one," she huffed. "You forget Sean and I were right here when Isaiah left. I don't want to see you hurtin' like that again. You gotta know your happiness means more to me than any donation, *always*. And you gotta know by now that *I* know you're not as tough as you let on. That boy upstairs is gonna leave eventually. This place isn't where he belongs."

"I know," Russ sighed. "Don't worry, I know. Isaiah was a surprise. Although looking back, he shouldn't have been. He had too many dreams for this little part of the world, even if his family was all here. Jordan won't be. When he figures out what he needs to figure out, I'll be ready for him to move on."

Russ had to smile at the unadulterated skepticism in the look she threw him. "I'm not saying I'll be happy about it," he qualified, "but my eyes are open going in this time. This thing is only temporary. And honestly, I think we might just do each other some good in the meantime, so…." He shrugged.

With a sigh of her own, she pushed herself out of the rocker. "I'll take your word for it. I'm gonna make breakfast."

Jordan shuffled into the kitchen about half an hour later, looking almost as shiny as he had that first week, but even more beautiful in Russ's old faded jeans and T-shirt.

"My clothes look good on you," Russ murmured huskily as he sauntered over and gave him a quick kiss.

Jordan's eyes widened and he cast a nervous glance at Phyl, and Russ chuckled.

"I promised PDAs, didn't I?"

Jordan's return smile was tentative but sweet. Russ couldn't wait to get him alone in the barn later.

"You two quit cooing like doves and eat," Phyl ordered, placing a giant platter of toast, sausage, and bacon on the table. "It's Sunday, in case you forgot. You got a little time, but after church lets out, we'll be up to our eyeballs in regulars and newbies all fired up and just bursting to do 'God's good works.' Best fuel up now, while you got the chance."

Jordan eyed the platter skeptically, but Russ managed to get him to take a decent portion, plus the eggs Phyl fried, by threatening to feed Jordan one bite at a time from his fingertips, right there in front of Phyl.

As promised, the crowd of volunteers and visitors flooded in right after Sunday brunch. As a rule, Russ actually enjoyed meeting with prospective adopters, discussing pros and cons, determining if the family would be the right fit for an animal. Seeing his hard work bear fruit as a once neglected or abused animal found its forever home never got old. It was just all the others that severely tested his patience. By the end of every weekend, he was done dealing with the general public and well on his way to needing a quiet sit and a few beers. This Sunday was no exception. Even though parts of him were still happily humming from all that had happened with Jordan, his patience was wearing perilously thin under the heat of the late afternoon sun.

"We need them.... *All* of them, every nickel and dime, every bit of exposure on social media, every child that sees the right way to treat an animal," he repeated under his breath like a mantra as a pair of seemingly unattended screaming and giggling little boys ran by him, spooking the donkeys in their pen.

The regular volunteers, Phyl, and now Jordan, were pretty good at wrangling the unruly, but they couldn't be everywhere at once. These days, with parents paying more attention to their cell phones than their kids, everyone had to be vigilant.

The shrieking, unattended boys streaked by again, and Russ's irritation reached the end of its tether. With a growl, he started after them to herd them back to whoever they belonged to, but he wasn't fast enough to stop them from ducking under the caution ropes around Calliope's pen, apparently paying no attention to the Stay back! She bites! signs posted on her fence. A jolt of real fear made his temper spike, and he charged after them. The last thing the ranch needed was a lawsuit or their insurance to skyrocket.

Stepping in between the boys and Calliope, Russ shouted, "Out! Get out! Can't you read?"

The boys looked at him in stunned silence for two seconds before screaming and running away from him. He had to duck a swipe from Calliope's beak, but she still caught a bit of flesh on his shoulder. Swearing under his breath, he glared at the bird, who he knew was laughing at him. Rubbing the spot, he stomped after the boys to give them and their parents a talking-to, but Jordan's hand on his shoulder, rubbing the sore spot, pulled him up short only a couple of steps beyond the ropes.

"The day's almost over. Just a couple of hours and they'll all be gone," Jordan murmured. He stepped a little closer and lowered his voice so only Russ could hear, his warm breath ghosting over Russ's sensitive ear. "And only a couple of hours more before I'm under you in your bed… or over you, or in you, whatever you want."

Startled out of his temper, Russ blinked at him as a slow grin spread over Jordan's face. Jordan moved to saunter away, but Russ gripped his upper arm to stop him. Turning so his back was toward the rest of the yard, he murmured under his breath, "I prefer to be over you so I can keep an eye on you. You're beautiful all the time, but you're stunning when you come."

Russ was the one to saunter this time, but his tone was a lot more reasonable as he confronted the two boys and their parents and gave them a mini lecture on the dangers even "domesticated" animals could pose to the unwary.

When he caught Jordan smiling warmly at him from over by the goat pen, Russ couldn't help but puff up a little. He found himself leading the family back to Calliope's pen and launching into a speech about all the things he'd learned about ostriches since she'd come to the ranch.

"Is she up for adoption too?" one of the little boys asked as Russ wound down.

Russ had seen the little boy's eyes light up when he'd likened Calliope to a modern-day dinosaur. The horrified look on the boy's parents' faces got chuckles out of the small crowd that had assembled while he talked, and Russ laughed too. "Sorry, she's probably going to stay here with us. She was someone's adored pet for a very long time, until that person couldn't take care of her anymore. We don't think it would be right to send her to a farm now, and not many people would want her at her age. But don't worry, we're going to take good care of her, right here, and you can come visit. Just don't get too close. I speak from experience when I say she can be pretty cranky."

Russ headed for the barn immediately after the crowd dispersed, his brief spate of sociability all but petered out. Families were already moving toward their cars. It wouldn't be long before he had his blessed silence back.

"That was quite a little lecture you gave out there. I was impressed," Jordan said, coming up behind him.

Russ didn't bother with a verbal response. He grabbed Jordan's arm and dragged him into an empty stall, out of sight. He swallowed Jordan's surprised gasp in the hot kiss he'd been dying to plant on him since breakfast. When Russ finally let him go, Jordan swept their immediate vicinity with a nervous glance.

"What happened to the guy from yesterday who was incensed about inappropriate behavior in front of the kiddies?" Jordan huffed.

"None of those kiddies are mine, and all we're doing here is kissing."

Jordan licked his lips and eyed Russ hotly. "You're going to make it very difficult to walk out of here without displaying something very inappropriate in front of those kiddies," he said, grimacing and adjusting himself in his jeans.

"I'd offer to help you out, but that probably would only make things worse," Russ replied with a grin.

After shooting Russ a mock glare, Jordan smoothed a hand down his neatly tucked T-shirt and blew out a breath. "If you've got a room with a locked door around here I haven't seen, then maybe I'd take you up on that, but since you don't, and I still need to help Phyl, I'm going to need you to keep your hands and lips to yourself while I make myself presentable again."

Russ would have apologized, but he really wasn't sorry. He'd need a little cooling-off time himself before he was decent for company, but he had selfishly relieved some of the tension from the day, and Jordan didn't appear to be too upset over it.

"After dinner—or maybe before, if we can sneak away—I'll make it up to you," he promised.

With a pained groan, Jordan closed his eyes and *thunked* his head on the wood post closest to him. "Russ," he whined. "Now that's all I'm going to be able to think about, and I have families I still need to schmooze."

Taking pity on him, Russ stepped out of the stall and headed outside.

"I'll go check on Missy and some of the others. We had a couple of families fill out adoption applications today, so I'll need to make sure the horses they're interested in are as ready as I can get them. Why don't you spend a couple minutes with Marina and cool down?" he said on his way.

CHAPTER SEVENTEEN

CONCENTRATING ON charming strangers and spreading the word about the ranch and all the good it did was a challenge when all Jordan wanted was to climb back into Russ's bed and spend the rest of his life there. Even the wreckage he'd left behind in Virginia didn't seem so overwhelming while his body and heart were humming with happy hormones. The floodwaters of the tidal wave had receded for the moment, and he sure as hell wasn't going to look that gift horse in the mouth.

Was that responsible adulting?

No.

Was he going to do it anyway?

Hells, yeah.

"Jordan, is that it?" Phyllis called as the last SUV headed up the gravel drive toward the road.

"I think so."

She blew out a breath and shook her head. "Another Sunday over and done with. I think we did well today."

"Me too."

She put a hand on her lower back, stretched, and groaned. "Will you check all the gates one more time for me, make sure no one forgot to lock up? I'll go in and get supper ready."

She moved slowly toward the house and leaned heavily on the railing as she climbed the steps.

"Hey, Phyl," Jordan called.

"Yeah?"

"Why don't you just take it easy? We've all had a long day. Russ and I can scrounge something for dinner. You don't have to cook for us."

Even from his short time on the ranch, Jordan expected her to argue, but she smiled tiredly and nodded instead. "Thanks, hon. I could use a little lie-down, I won't lie."

"Do you want us to bring you something later?"

"That's sweet, thank you, but I'll grab something on my way. There's plenty of leftovers tucked away in the fridge." She paused for a second as a grin split her face. "I think I'll spend the rest of the night in my room, so you two enjoy your evenin', all right?"

Jordan wasn't exactly sure if she was talking about what he thought she was talking about, but he felt himself flush anyway. After clearing his throat, he said, "Good night, Phyllis."

"Good niiiigghht," she sang back to him as she opened the screen door and disappeared into the house.

After inspecting all the pens and making sure everyone had been fed, watered, and settled for the night, he jogged back to the house and up the stairs to the second floor, taking them two at a time. In the bath-room, he ripped off his sweat-stained, dirty clothes and hopped into the shower for a thorough scrub. If to-night was anything like last night, he needed to make sure every inch of him was clean and ready. His cock throbbed, filling as his mind replayed all that Russ had done, but he resisted the urge to take care of it. If he'd learned anything last night, it was the power of delayed gratification. His one-night stands had been all about the rush to get off—still fun in their own way, but ulti-mately unsatisfying. Apparently, deep down, he was a romantic… or a sensualist, at the very least.

"Who knew?"

His reflection in the bathroom mirror didn't answer back.

"Shit," he swore as he turned this way and that in front of it, frowning.

His muscle definition was slipping. The ranch worked him hard, so he hadn't put on any weight, but the six-pack abs and high and tight ass apparently only came from the gym. He'd need to find one soon. Now that he had someone who wanted to be familiar with every inch of him, he couldn't afford to let himself go.

Except thoughts of the gym stirred the floodwaters of everything he was trying to avoid. He couldn't really afford a gym membership now. How far would he have to go to find one? He couldn't get an extended mem-bership because he didn't know how long he'd even be here. And even if he went, he'd have to pay for gas. And what about insurance? There was no way he could afford to continue insurance on the convertible.

Closing his eyes, he gave himself a shake, shoving those thoughts down as far as they would go. He wasn't ready yet, and somewhere downstairs, a super-hot, horny cowboy was just waiting to rock his night.

After quickly blow-drying his hair and sculpting it with product, he changed into a pair of designer khakis and a polo shirt. Hopefully, he'd be naked for the only working he was going to do tonight, so he could wear his own clothes in the meantime.

The screen door banging closed downstairs was his cue to hurry up and get down there. After one last quick look in the mirror to make sure he hadn't missed anything, he hurried down the hall and the stairs to meet Russ by the front door.

"Hey there," Jordan said as he sauntered down the last couple of steps.

Russ's eyes sparked as they raked Jordan from head to toe. "Well, don't you look shiny."

Jordan stepped in close, but Russ moved back. "I'm all over dirt. I just got back from a ride. Wouldn't want to muss you up, with you looking so nice and all." He glanced over Jordan's shoulder, and a slight *V* formed between his eyebrows. "Where's Phyl?"

Jordan's grin widened. "She was tired, so I told her we could fend for ourselves. She said she was going to spend the night in her room."

"Oh yeah?" Russ's lips curved into a crooked smile. He left his hands in his pockets, but he leaned forward and pressed a kiss to Jordan's neck, just beneath his ear. "I suppose we could find something to do with ourselves," he murmured between light nibbles, nuzzling, and warm sweeps of his tongue over Jordan's surprisingly sensitive flesh. "I can think of something I'd like you to feed me right now."

The hairs on Jordan's arms and the back of his neck stood up, and he shivered. It was still going to take some getting used to, but this instant-boyfriend thing definitely had its perks. Russ didn't waffle or hesitate. He acted like they'd been dating for months, not hours—or at least what Jordan imagined that would be like. If Jordan hadn't held them in his own hands and felt for himself how soft they were, he would've sworn Russ had balls of steel, and that confidence was so fucking sexy.

Without any more warning than that, Russ leaned back, hooked a finger over Jordan's belt, and dragged him into the living room. He shoved Jordan against the wall, dropped to his knees, and opened Jordan's belt, button, and zipper. Jordan's brain had no chance to catch up before Russ sucked Jordan's cock to the back of his throat in one quick, hot slide.

"Jesus, Russ!"

Russ hummed, and Jordan's knees wobbled. Drawing off with a wet pop, Russ winked up at him and said, "Keep an ear out for Phyl, just in case."

Before Jordan could form a reply, Russ sucked him back into that fantastic, heavenly mouth, and Jordan was gone. Phyllis could have come out of her room with a marching band and he wouldn't have heard her, nor would he have cared. No way was he going to tell Russ to stop.

He spread his legs as wide as his bunched pants would let him and tilted his hips forward. He thrust tentatively at first, until Russ moved his hand from the base of Jordan's cock to Jordan's hip and gripped him tightly, urging him on. With a stifled groan, Jordan fucked Russ's mouth, keeping his eyes wide open, afraid to miss one second of his cock sliding in and out of that gorgeous, talented mouth.

"I'm going to come," he warned breathlessly.

Russ sucked harder and dug his fingers into Jordan's hip, egging him on. Jordan's balls drew up tight. He gripped Russ's thick brown hair, curled inward, and unloaded into his mouth, biting his lip to stifle his cry. The muscles in Russ's throat worked, milking every drop out of him. Then Russ pulled off and placed a gentle kiss on Jordan's cockhead and another on his inner thigh before grinning up at him.

"I'm a man of my word," Russ panted.

"Come up here," Jordan ordered lazily.

Jordan pulled him in for a kiss, but Russ didn't let him meld their bodies together. "I wouldn't want to get you dirty."

With a chuckle, Jordan rolled his eyes. "You just sucked my dick not thirty feet from Phyllis's bedroom door. I think I might already be just a *little* dirty."

As Jordan blinked up at him in postorgasmic lassitude, Russ dragged the backs of his fingers down Jordan's cheek. "I'm going to go get washed up. Why don't you see if you can scrounge us somethin' to eat? I'm gonna need my strength to keep up with you."

"Okay," Jordan replied, but he was the one feeling like he needed to catch up. "Hey," Jordan called when Russ reached the bottom of the staircase.

"Yeah?"

"What about you? I feel like a little reciprocation is in order."

"No need," Russ said with a grin. "I busted when you did." He held up both hands and wiggled his fingers. "I'm a multitasker, and like I said, you're fuckin' gorgeous when you come."

Jordan watched Russ's ass all the way up the stairs, but he waited to let out a completely besotted sigh until Russ was out of earshot.

In the kitchen while Russ showered, Jordan stood in front of the refrigerator at a loss. Neatly stacked plastic containers held the remnants from previous meals, plus the rest of the shelves and drawers were packed full of ingredients, if Jordan only knew how to cook. After having a housekeeper and cook to rely on his whole life, he didn't have a clue what to do in a kitchen. At school, he'd always just eaten out. No insult to Phyllis's cooking—in fact, the food was quite tasty—but everything in Texas was so damned *heavy*. Even the salads had cheese and bread in them, and he hadn't seen a leaf of kale or a scoop of quinoa in weeks.

He'd have gone to the grocery store for himself except that required not only money—of which he had a limited supply at the moment—but some sort of knowledge of what to do with the food once he got it. Just the thought of that made his stomach and chest tighten with a sense of dread. Plus, he didn't want to insult Phyl by bringing in his own food, and he was pretty sure that was what would happen if he tried. He was Southern enough to know at least some of the rules of being a good guest.

He was still staring into the refrigerator and worrying his lip when Russ strode into the kitchen. He was wearing a pair of boxers and T-shirt so worn, Jordan could almost see through them, and his dark hair was still damp and curling against his forehead.

"Find something?"

With a grimace, Jordan shrugged. "I wasn't sure what you'd want."

After a slight hesitation in which a hint of a frown came and went on Russ's face, he smiled and clapped his hands together as he joined Jordan in front of the refrigerator. "I'll eat pretty much anything. We can have more of the chicken we had yesterday, or I could whip us up a few sandwiches. What're you in the mood for?"

Sex.

With Russ looking and smelling good enough to eat, it was pretty much all Jordan could come up with, but he figured Russ wouldn't go for that just yet. He had some weird fetish about making sure Jordan ate. Maybe he had an Italian grandmother somewhere back home, though he hadn't made it sound like he had anything quite so loving and traditional in his family tree.

"Whatever you feel like is fine. I had a big lunch."

Russ pulled out far too many containers and heaped two plates with way too much food before popping each in the microwave. While they ate at one end of the enormous scarred rustic wood table, they traded anecdotes from the day and soft, tender touches. Russ didn't even seem to be aware he was doing it, but Jordan felt every caress of Russ's rough fingers or brush of his thigh beneath the table. Coming from a family that barely managed hugs on birthdays, Christmas, and after long absences, this sort of intimacy didn't come naturally. Jordan had to make a conscious choice to reciprocate, but he loved and craved every single touch he received.

"I'm almost done," Russ said, wiping his mouth on a napkin. "You need to get busy and finish so we can take this conversation upstairs."

"I'm done," Jordan replied eagerly, grabbing his plate to take it to the sink.

"Hold on there," Russ said, gripping Jordan's arm. "You haven't even eaten half of what's on the plate."

Jordan was about to laugh and blow it off, but that slight frown came and went on Russ's face again, and Jordan plopped his butt back on the bench. After studying Russ's face for a few seconds, he said, "You seem awfully concerned with my eating habits. Is there something I should know?"

"I just want to make sure you're getting enough calories is all. Ranch work burns a lot more than you're probably used to. Don't want you fainting on us again."

Jordan rolled his eyes. "That was dehydration. I just didn't drink enough, and I was exhausted from not enough sleep. I'm not a complete wuss. I've never fainted before in my life."

His concerned frown didn't ease as much as Jordan would have liked, but Russ said, "I know you're not a wuss. I never said you were. But I do know for a scientific fact that you're burning more calories than you're taking in, and that's going to leave its mark on you eventually."

Now it was Jordan's turn to frown as he smoothed his shirt over his belly and shifted self-consciously. "I like to watch what I eat. Everyone where I'm from does the same thing. It's not a crime to want to look good."

"I didn't say it was. Don't go reading anything into what I'm sayin' here." Russ grabbed the hand Jordan had been fidgeting with. "Look at me," he said.

Jordan met his gaze, and Russ smiled softly. "I've been doing this for a long time, so maybe just trust me that I know what the work takes from a man. Every inch of you is fucking gorgeous, inside and out, just as you are. I can't believe my luck that you want to spend time with a gristly old man like me."

Jordan snorted out a laugh and rolled his eyes. "You're neither old nor gristly, whatever that even means, and you know it."

"Yeah?" Russ grinned. "You like what you see?"

"You know I do."

"Then maybe I know a little bit of what I'm talking about?"

Jordan narrowed his eyes and huffed. "Fine. See? I'm eating." He shoved a few more forkfuls of food into his mouth and forced them down. "Happy?"

"Ecstatic," Russ agreed. "Now you eat just a little more while I clean up. Then we can go upstairs, give Marina a quick check on my laptop, and see where the rest of the night takes us. How does that sound?"

"A little like blackmail. You're going to make me fat with the promise of sex."

Russ laughed on his way to the sink. "I'm sure we can find some way of working off a few of those calories. And if you're really worried about it, we can think up a *rigorous* exercise program we can perform together, whenever and wherever you like."

Jordan's cock jerked in his slacks even as he groaned at the cheesy pun and threw his napkin in Russ's general direction.

It wasn't a bad thought, though. Instead of a gym, maybe he'd just google the best sexual positions to work his abs and his glutes. Squats could be hot, depending on what he was squatting over.

He took another few mouthfuls and pushed away from the table. He was not going to be some kid showing he'd cleaned his plate so he could have dessert. He might be feeling a bit pathetic and helpless everywhere else in his life right now, but he was an adult, and he'd eat when he was hungry, not because someone told him he should.

He scraped what was left in the trash and set his plate in Russ's outstretched hand. Russ didn't say anything as he rinsed it off and added it to the rest of the dishes in the dishwasher, so Jordan couldn't help but hover anxiously at his elbow. Despite his pretentions of maturity and independence, Jordan hated not meeting peoples' expectations of him, even if those expectations were wrong or unfair. It was one of the few things he *had* talked with his therapist about, at length—not that it had done much good, as his life up until a few weeks ago clearly demonstrated. The look of disappointment on his parents' faces still haunted his nightmares, no matter how hard he tried to avoid thinking about it during the day.

Pulling his shoulders back and narrowing his eyes, Jordan decided if Russ wanted to judge him over something as stupid as how much he ate, he would let Russ have it like he had on Saturday. But apparently their disagreement was all in his head, because, after wiping his hands on a dishtowel, Russ turned to him, wrapped an arm around Jordan's waist, and tugged him close. With a lazy smile, Russ pressed their bodies together from bellies to knees and said, "You ready to go to bed?"

"It's only a little after six."

Russ licked his lips, and his smile widened. "I think we can find some way to pass the time. Don't you?"

"Maybe," Jordan said with an answering grin.

This time Jordan led the way, all too aware of Russ following close behind him. The night before had been a bit of a blur. Jordan hadn't really had time to think before he'd found himself in Russ's bed. Now all he wanted was for his brain to shut up and let him enjoy his very first "second date" with a guy.

Luckily, Russ appeared to be a master at making Jordan's brain shut down. The man had supernatural skills in that department. Jordan didn't even get a chance to work up more than a hint of performance anxiety before Russ was there with his magic hands and whispered compliments in his slow Texas drawl that made Jordan want to melt at the same time it made him hard as a rock.

Damn, but Russ knew all of his buttons already. How was that even possible?

Jordan hated feeling this needy, but gobbled up every caress and every word like he was starving anyway. Still, he liked to think he gave as good as he got too.

Naked, straddling Russ, his knees pressed into the mattress, Jordan lowered himself onto Russ's cock with a long, low groan. He'd never taken his time like this before, never had the opportunity to put on a show. But Russ had said he liked to watch, and Jordan was more than happy to oblige. Daylight still streamed through Russ's bedroom windows as Jordan rocked his hips experimentally and arched his back. He could feel Russ's hot gaze on him like a physical touch. The man's eyes were almost black with passion as he looked at Jordan as if he were the only thing in the world.

"You can keep an eye on me this way too," Jordan gasped out as he fucked himself on Russ's fat cock.

"Oh hell yeah, I can," Russ moaned.

The thick muscles in his neck corded, and the veins popped beneath his darkly tanned skin as Russ threw his head back, gripped Jordan's hips hard, and thrust upward, meeting Jordan's downward slide.

As Jordan picked up speed, Russ wrapped his fist around Jordan's cock and pumped.

"Shit," Jordan gasped. "I'm not going to last long."

Russ grinned and propped himself on his free arm. "Go ahead. Do it. We got all night, remember?"

Russ's grip on Jordan's cock tightened, and Jordan saw stars. He shot between them as his rhythm faltered. He only had the chance to gasp a few breaths before

Russ pulled out and flipped him onto his back. Kneeling between Jordan's thighs, Russ pulled off the condom and pumped his dick until he cried out and shot all over Jordan's spent cock and belly.

"You're pretty gorgeous when you come too," Jordan panted, blinking up at him.

Russ gave a lopsided grin before flopping to the mattress next to him. "Glad you think so," he said between breaths. He rolled onto his side and kissed Jordan tenderly. "Not bad for an old man, eh?"

Jordan rolled his eyes. "You're not old."

"I'm past forty. In some circles that's close to being put out to pasture."

"Well, lucky for you, I haven't spent much time in these circles you speak of, so I haven't developed stupid prejudices like that," he said primly.

Russ propped himself on an elbow and worried a corner of his lower lip. "Out of curiosity, how much time have you spent?"

Jordan quirked an eyebrow. "Are you asking me about my sexual exploits?"

Russ grimaced. "No. I can tell you've had experience. But you said you just came out, so I wondered…."

When it became obvious Russ wasn't going to finish that statement, Jordan shrugged. "I've been to the clubs up near Dartmouth and a few other places, but I was completely in the closet, so it wasn't like I could really make gay friends or do much actual socializing in 'the community.' There's a reason it's going to take me a while to get used to the whole boyfriend thing, since I've never actually had one before."

Russ pursed his lips. "Am I going too fast for you? Pushing too hard too soon? It's okay. You can tell me…. You wouldn't be the first to say it."

With a helpless shrug, Jordan shook his head. "To be honest, I wouldn't know if you were going too fast. But I don't want you to slow down. You make me feel good and wanted... and happy. I need this. I want it. I've never felt like this before. I don't want you to change a thing."

Russ's smile made Jordan feel about ten feet tall. Trailing gentle fingertips over Jordan's chest and through his hair, Russ said, "I'm glad. I like seeing you happy. I'm giving you the reins on this one, though, because you've got a bit more to deal with than I do right now. Use 'em if you need to, okay? Promise?"

"Yeah, okay. I promise."

CHAPTER EIGHTEEN

JORDAN STRETCHED and groaned as the piercing light of dawn blazed through Russ's windows. Russ needed some blackout curtains ASAP... or at least some blinds.

He was alone, but that wasn't a surprise. At some point, he was going to convince Russ to sleep in so they could wake up together, but he hadn't felt comfortable broaching the subject yet. He was already pretty sure Russ thought him needy as fuck. Jordan didn't want to give him even more proof of that.

Still, even alone, he woke up giddy every day from the realization that Russ wanted him for his boyfriend. He hadn't slept a single night in his own bed in more than a week, and Russ didn't appear to be in any hurry to kick him out. In fact, those affectionate touches and tender words that Jordan craved like crack just kept coming and coming.

It was surreal.

As Jordan rolled out of bed and rubbed the sleep from his eyes, he heard Jon and Ernesto pull up outside, their tires crunching loudly in the gravel. He needed to get downstairs soon or he'd catch all kinds of shit for being the last to the table. At first he'd taken the teasing personally, but Russ had finally explained that it meant the others were warming up to him, treating him like part of the family. He wasn't quite comfortable giving it back yet, but he had an older brother. He knew how to trash talk and give as good as he got, so Ernie and Jon were in for it when he finally got over that hurdle and relaxed.

As for reactions to him and Russ being a couple, Ernesto had been a little weird that first Monday morning when they'd sat together at the breakfast table and Russ had been his usual wonderfully unashamed, affectionate self, but Ernie was the only one. Phyllis had even taken him aside after breakfast to make sure he was okay, and she'd been the one he'd worried about most.

"Don't you worry about Ernie," she'd said.

"What do you mean?"

"I mean that happy smile that's been plastered on your face since Saturday has suddenly vanished, and I'm trying to tell you it doesn't need to."

"Am I that obvious?"

She'd smiled. "I'd tell ya to stay away from the poker tables, except I know you were hiding a lot more than you showed when you first got here. And you must've done a fair job of hiding your feelings at home, if your parents didn't catch on before you broke it to 'em."

"I finally told them because I was tired of all the hiding," he admitted.

With a nod, she'd patted him on the shoulder. "And you shouldn't have to. Least not among friends. But I saw you pulling away from Russ a bit, so I figured I'd poke my nose in and tell you that you don't have to. We may be a bit more rural than you're used to, but that don't mean we're all as closed-minded as your folks. Jon's pretty oblivious to affairs of the heart, but he's never had a problem with Russ." She paused and grimaced. "Ernie was a slightly different story. The man's Catholic, born and raised, so he and Russ had a bit of a problem to start. I think it even came to blows at some point. I wasn't there or I'd have taken a switch to both their hides and had Sean dunk 'em in a horse trough to cool off. But whatever happened, they came to some sort of understanding between 'em, and when Isaiah came into the picture, well—"

"Who's Isaiah?"

She'd blinked at him for a second before waving her hands in the air. "Oh, he's just a boy Russ dated a while back. The point is, Ernie's made some sort of peace between his faith and his friends, so you don't have to hold back or make yourself uncomfortable on his account. Okay? You got enough on your mind without havin' to add to your worries."

"Okay," he'd agreed absently.

"Good. Now you go on and get to work. I have a kitchen to clean up, adoption paperwork to review, and donations from the weekend to take to the bank."

She'd shooed him out the door and left him standing on the porch, wondering just how many boyfriends Russ had had. For being out in the middle of nowhere, Russ certainly seemed to be popular.

Even more than a week later, Jordan was still too chicken to ask. The answer would probably give him an anxiety attack anyway, since he was pretty sure he'd fallen head over heels already, stupid as that was in his current life situation.

"You're so fucked-up right now it isn't even funny," he said to his reflection in the bathroom mirror before turning his back on it and hurrying down to breakfast.

AFTER LUNCH, and a furtive heavy petting session with Russ in the tack room, Jordan led Marina out into one of the pens to sun herself and get some fresh air while he mucked out her stall. Another week on antibiotics and a high-calorie diet had her looking better than ever, and Russ assured him her gentling was going so well they'd be getting her training started before he knew it. Of course, that meant she'd be that much closer to being adopted and leaving the ranch, which would probably break his heart a little, but maybe she'd be adopted somewhere close by and he could visit.

He froze halfway up the main aisle of the barn, still holding the handles of the wheelbarrow. What was he thinking? He might not even be at the B STAR in a few months' time. He might not even be in Texas, so what did it matter where Marina ended up?

Shaking himself out of his daze, he finished pushing the wheelbarrow to the compost heap and dumped it. Thoughts of leaving the ranch left his stomach almost as twisted up as that ever-lurking emotional tidal wave from Virginia. It might be the coward's way out, but he still wasn't ready to deal with either. There were worse sins than a little procrastination, right? He wasn't hurting anyone by putting off dealing with his shit just a little while longer.

The crunch of tires on the gravel drive outside the barn was a welcome distraction, bringing him back to the here and now. Trucks and cars came and went all the time, delivering supplies, prospective adopters, or curious visitors. Russ, Jon, and Ernie tended to hide from the latter, so that left Jordan to greet, if Phyl was busy. Poking his head around the side of the barn, he saw a white convertible pull in and park next to his red one. As the dust settled and a windblown mane of high-lighted blonde hair came into focus, Jordan's stomach flipped.

"Gemma," he croaked.

His sister —in bling-encrusted brown Dolce and Gabbana sunglasses, tight white short shorts, and a pink tank top with "Extra AF" printed in silver glitter on the front—stepped out of the car. She didn't see him at first, because she was busy talking to someone on her cell, but when she spotted him, she threw up her hands and squealed.

"Lacey, I gotta go. Hit me up later, 'kay?" she said into the phone before throwing her hands wide again and scampering toward Jordan in her white leather sandals.

Off-balance, all he could do was smile weakly at her as she gripped his upper arms and pulled him in for the two-cheek air kiss. He should have been overjoyed at having someone from his family so obviously happy to see him, but her presence on the ranch was jarring.

"Gemma, this is a surprise. I wasn't expecting you," he said lamely.

She shoved her sunglasses on top of her head and rolled her expertly made-up blue eyes. "That's because you're stupid… which seems to be running in the family these days."

He was saved from trying to come up with a response to that when Phyllis came down the stairs from the house. A quick glance around showed Russ moving toward them from the horse pasture fence and Jon and Ernie watching from the other animal pens.

"Uh, Phyllis, you remember my sister, Gemma," he stuttered out as Phyl joined them.

Phyl had been wearing her usual open, welcoming smile, but it widened even further as she took Gemma in. "My word, look at you! You've grown so much I woulda hardly recognized ya. How are you, darlin'?"

"Phyllis!" Gemma squealed. She danced over to Phyllis and threw her arms around the woman, giving her a real kiss on the cheek before withdrawing. "It has been forever since I've been here, but you look exactly as I remember you."

Jordan felt Russ come up behind him. Russ didn't touch him, but he hovered close, like he wanted to. As off-center as Jordan was at that moment, he didn't know if he should be grateful or resentful of Russ's restraint.

God, he was so fucked-up, and not at all prepared to deal with his little sister. She didn't belong there with her polish and bling.

At a pointed look from Phyl, Jordan was jarred out of his self-absorption and minor internal freak-out. "Oh, uh, Gemma, this is Russ, Phyllis's right-hand man. Russ, this is my sister, Gemma," he stuttered out.

"Nice to meet you," Russ said, giving her a nod. His voice was like warm honey over Jordan's raw nerves, and Jordan felt himself leaning toward him before he snapped himself out of it.

Gemma eyed Russ speculatively and tossed her windblown blonde hair over her shoulder. She extended a limp pink-nailed hand and threw him a flirty smile. "And you."

As Russ took the hand and gave it a gentle squeeze, Jordan frowned. Jealousy wasn't an emotion he'd experienced often, but at least it helped snap him out of the mental tailspin he'd been in.

Before he could tell Gemma to keep her eyes and hands to herself, Phyl said, "You've had a long drive, darlin'. Why don't you come on up to the house, and I'll get you something to drink and a place to freshen up, if you like? You and Jordan here probably have some catching up to do."

And just like that, Jordan's stomach churned, he tensed back up again, and he forgot all about his jealousy. His sister wasn't there for a friendly visit. She wasn't even there to steal his boyfriend. She was there to talk about family and everything else Jordan had been doing his best to avoid. He threw a panicked look at Russ, but Russ just gave him a reassuring half smile back.

"You visit with your family. I'll take over in the barn," Russ said.

Jordan swallowed and nodded. "Thanks," he murmured, not really meaning it.

He followed Phyl and Gemma up the stairs as his stomach tried to claw its way past his spine.

Chickenshit.

Man up a little. It's just your baby sister, for Christ's sake.

There went his father's voice again, but he found himself stiffening his spine despite how much he resented it.

In the kitchen, Phyllis bustled to the cabinets and then the refrigerator. "Would you like some lemonade, sweetie?"

"That'd be great, thanks."

Gemma threw Jordan a smile that said how quaint she found all of this as she scanned the country-style kitchen, and Jordan winced. He'd had a similar reaction his first few days on the ranch. It seemed like a lifetime ago now, but in just a few weeks, the ranch had come to feel like a second home—or his only home, for that matter.

"There you go," Phyllis said as she handed over two tall glasses, already damp with condensation. "Are you hungry, Gemma? Can I get ya somethin'?"

"Oh, no thank you, Phyllis. I had lunch at the airport while I waited for them to bring me the car I wanted."

"All right," Phyllis replied without batting a lash. "Then I think you two probably have some catching up to do, so I'll leave you to it. Jordan here knows where everything is by now, if you do need anything, and I hope you stay for dinner so I can hear all about what you've been up to."

In true Thorndike family style, Gemma's answering smile was radiant. It lit up her whole face and made the recipient feel like they'd been given a gift.

Holy hell, is that what it looks like from the other side? He'd never really paid attention before.

"Thank you so much, Phyllis," Gemma gushed, and Jordan felt a little sick.

Do people hear and see the noblesse oblige, but they're just too polite to say anything? No wonder Russ acted like a dick toward me. He probably thought I was a giant douche from the second I walked in.

As soon as Phyllis stepped out of the kitchen, Gemma's smile fell away and she narrowed her eyes at Jordan. "I'm mad at you," she said, poking a manicured pink fingernail at his chest.

"Okay."

"Okay? That's all you have to say?" she huffed, placing her free hand on her hip. "No one tells me *anything*, except Mom and Dad aren't talking to you anymore and they kicked you out. You don't answer my texts except to say 'ask Mom and Dad.' Mom calls me crying. I come home from my girls' trip to West Palm Beach so she can tell me you've decided you're gay now, and she just found out you're staying at the charity ranch we used to go to as kids. And all you have to say is *okay*?"

With a sigh, he rubbed his temples, trying to ease his burgeoning headache. He wasn't ready for this. Why couldn't he have had a few more weeks? At least it was Gemma and not Will Jr. barreling down on him—or, God forbid, his parents. He might've totally lost it then.

Offering her the seat opposite him, he collapsed on the bench at the kitchen table and set his drink down. "What do you want me to say? I came out. They *flipped* out. And I didn't exactly have anywhere else to go, with Father canceling my credit cards and emptying the joint bank accounts. I'm sorry you felt left out, Gemma, but if you haven't noticed, I'm kind of going through some shit right now. I just had my entire life implode, so forgive me for not being sensitive to your feelings."

Crossing her arms across her sparkly chest, she pouted. "Well, I might have been able to help, if you'd given me a chance."

"And what exactly would you have done?"

"I don't know, but nobody gave me a chance to find out, did they? I'm just as much a member of this family as you and Will, you know, even if everybody conveniently forgets that."

Jordan opened his mouth to return fire, but closed it again and took a calming breath. He wasn't a child.

He really shouldn't act like one if he wanted people to believe that. He was arguing over something stupid, because he was pretty sure he didn't want to hear whatever else she'd come to tell him.

A horse neighed out in the pasture, and Jordan glanced longingly out the window. All he wanted was to go back out there with Russ and leave all this painful family shit behind, but he couldn't exactly look down his nose at his sister's immaturity while refusing to be an adult himself.

"I'm sorry, okay? If it makes you feel any better, I didn't return Will Jr.'s texts either."

She rolled her eyes. "No, it doesn't. Of course you didn't text him back. He's an asshole. But I'm not."

Barking out a laugh, Jordan shook his head. "Who are you and what have you done with my annoying little sister who used to follow me around threatening me with hellfire and tattling over every swear word?"

"I just finished my first year at Brown, in case you forgot. I'm not a little kid anymore, no matter what everyone in this family seems to think," she huffed, narrowing her eyes at him again.

Holding up his hands in surrender, he said, "Okay. You're right. My little sister grew up while I wasn't paying attention."

"Damn right I did," she said, tossing her hair.

They shared a smile, but Jordan's faded as he took a steadying breath. "Okay, grown-up Gemma, what do you suggest?"

Her confident grin fell away. She blinked at him and bit her lip. "I don't know," she admitted miserably. Frowning in confusion, she said, "So you're really gay now? You're not just saying it to get back at Mom and Dad for something?"

He nodded, watching her face carefully. "Yeah." Forcing a chuckle, he said, "I've actually been gay for a long time. It's not a new thing. I just didn't have the balls to tell anyone until now."

"You never acted gay," she argued, worrying her lip some more.

Apparently her horizons hadn't been widened too much with her first year of college. She fiddled with the gold-and-diamond sorority pendant glittering on its fourteen-carat chain around her neck, reminding him that a person could be as sheltered or open as they chose to be, no matter how far from home they wandered.

With a sigh, he took her hand in his and squeezed. "There's no such thing as acting gay, you know? Unless you mean having gay sex, then I suppose that's *acting* gay. But you're right. I dated a lot of women and did all the things a proper son is supposed to. I pretended to be someone I wasn't because I was afraid of disappointing everyone. Given Father and Mother's reaction, I was right to be worried, wasn't I?"

"Do they know?" she asked, crooking a thumb toward the door to indicate the rest of the ranch.

"Yeah. They figured it out when Phyllis called Mom."

She withdrew her hand from his, tapped her pink nails against her glass of lemonade, and frowned. "Everybody at home is so upset. Daddy stays in his study and growls. He and Mom are fighting all the time. Will Jr. and Sherryl and the kids came over while I was there, but nobody really talked, and Will and Daddy disappeared into his study after dinner. Everything was awkward and uncomfortable, and everyone's bitchy."

With a wince, Jordan leaned back in his chair. "I guess that's all my fault, huh?"

"Well, no… I mean, yes, but I guess you can't help it, right? I just want everything back the way it was."

"Everything? Even you being treated like the baby?"

She threw him a sour look. "Of course not that."

"Because you've changed and you want everyone to respect that, right?"

"Yes."

He waited two beats, and she huffed and rolled her eyes again. "I get what you're saying. I'm not an idiot. But this is different. I'm not asking them to change their faith, their whole belief system. You can't expect them to be okay with this overnight."

"I'm not. I wasn't."

"Well, you ran away to the middle of nowhere. You didn't even give them a chance."

"I didn't run away, Gemma. Father threw me out, and Mom just sat back and let it happen."

His voice cracked, and he clamped his mouth shut before any more of the hurt could come pouring out. He absolutely refused to start crying in front of his little sister.

Not appearing to notice, she waved a dismissive hand. "He didn't mean it."

"Since when has Father ever said anything he didn't mean? He cut me off, Gemma. He canceled my credit cards. The only things I have left are my car and what I took with me from the house. That's it. And neither one of them has messaged or called me since that day. Mom even knows where I am, and she didn't ask to speak to me or anything."

"No. She sent me instead," she countered.

Blinking in surprise, he asked hopefully, "She sent you? Really?"

She grimaced. "Well... not exactly. I mean, I kept pushing for answers, and she told me where you were.... But I know she's worried about you, and obviously if she agreed with Daddy, they wouldn't be fighting so much, right? They never fight, not like this."

"Like what?"

"Well, they aren't getting into screaming matches or anything—at least not where any of us can hear—but they're totally not talking to each other. And when they have to, it's barely civil."

Wow, you go, Mom. Way to stick up for me, he thought acidly.

The thought was unfair. He didn't know what was going on between his parents, but since he hadn't heard from either of them, it didn't make much difference.

"That's something, I guess," he replied, less than enthusiastically.

"God, Jordan, emo much?"

With a glare, he pushed away from the table and paced the room. "What do you want me to say? Father threw me out and cut me off. I'm sorry if that's making me a little moody. With no other information forthcoming, I have to plan the rest of my life based on what I have right now. I don't have any other choice."

"I could give you some money," Gemma offered hopefully. "I just got my allowance. I could give you some to tide you over until...."

She left it hanging there, and Jordan sighed. "Until what? Until Father changes his entire personality and core belief system?"

"So, what, you're just going to walk away from us?" she asked, staring up at him with the glistening puppy-dog eyes of the little sister he remembered.

With a groan, he threw up his hands. "It's not like I want this, Gemma. I just can't be the son they want me to. I'm never going to marry a woman and make grandkids. I never actually *wanted* to be a lawyer. I can't pretend to be someone I'm not for the rest of my life. I can't do it. So if they can't accept the person I am, I don't know what to tell you."

She continued to gaze at him with hurt shining in her blue eyes, and he sighed and slumped onto the bench next to her. "I'm always going to be your big brother, if you let me. But the rest really isn't up to me, is it? I love Mom. I'll always love all of you... even Father. As for the rest, I have no clue. I don't exactly know what I'm doing here, if you haven't figured that out yet."

She gave him a watery smile and nodded.

Unable to take any more family talk without crying like a baby himself, Jordan said, "Hey. Did you pack any pants or decent shoes?"

"What?"

"Let's go riding together... just like old times."

"Yeah?"

"Yeah. Come on. I'm sure Russ can find us a couple of mounts, and Phyl should have some clothes if you need them."

Her lips curved as she smoothed a hand over her hair. "Russ?"

He rolled his eyes. "Yes, Russ, who's gay too, by the way... and mine."

While she gaped at him, Jordan stood on somewhat shaky legs and grinned. "Come on."

CHAPTER NINETEEN

AFTER COMING back from their ride, Jordan's sister confessed to being tired from her trip, so Jordan showed her upstairs for a nap, while the rest of the ranch inhabitants hovered curiously outside. When Jordan came back down, he sported that fake smile Russ hated and waved everyone's concern away before heading to the barn to get back to work.

Phyl stood at the base of the porch steps, frowning after him, so Russ rested a hand on her shoulder and squeezed. "I'll talk to him."

"Good."

In the barn, he found Jordan in the tack room furiously cleaning tack that wasn't actually dirty.

"You did everything else," Jordan complained without glancing up from his task.

Crossing his arms and ankles, Russ leaned against the doorframe. "There's always plenty of work needs doing, if you want to go see Ernie or Jon…. Calliope's water bucket needs cleaning."

Jordan finally looked up and gagged theatrically. "No way. I'm not that desperate for something to do. Besides, I did it last week. It's not my turn again until after Ernie." He set the gear aside and stood. "But I can go see if they need help with anything else."

When Jordan moved to pass him, Russ put a hand on his chest. "It's almost quittin' time anyway, and I think maybe you have something a little more important on your mind than cleaning up goat and donkey shit."

Jordan closed his eyes and hung his head. "Don't. I can't right now, Russ."

Sliding his hand up and around Jordan's neck, Russ pulled him in until their foreheads rested together. "You're wound tighter than a spring," he murmured into the close air between them. "If you don't release some of it soon, you're gonna snap. Would you rather do it out here with me or in there in front of your little sister and everybody?"

Jordan's jaw worked, and his nostrils flared. "I don't want to do it anywhere," he grated.

"That ain't an option," Russ whispered, not unsympathetically.

With a huff of breath, Jordan tried to pull away, but Russ didn't let him. "I don't want to do this in front of you."

"Why?"

"I don't want you to think less of me."

"I won't."

This time Russ let him pull away when Jordan drew back and eyed him skeptically. "You weren't exactly impressed with me from day one," he pointed out.

Russ grimaced. "I thought we'd been over that and put it to bed already. I said I was sorry for prejudging.

I told you I wanted you the whole time. What more do you need me to say?"

Wrapping his arms protectively around himself, Jordan took another step back. "There's a difference between wanting to fuck someone and being impressed by them."

"Picking a fight with me ain't gonna make the rest of this stuff with your family go away, you know," Russ countered, taking a step forward. "I told you from the start, words weren't my strong suit, but if you want me to lay it all out there again—even though I thought I'd given you plenty of demonstrations to convince you this past week or so—I will." He advanced until Jordan's back hit the wall. Crowding Jordan against it and placing his palms flat on the wood to either side of Jordan's head, Russ said, "You're kind. You're smart. You're generous and sensitive. You're beautiful... and stronger than you think you are. Even with everything you're going through, I can see the fight in you. But nobody's strong all the time. Nobody can make it all the way through life without some help."

"Not even you?" Jordan's lips wobbled into a wry smile, and Russ grinned.

"Especially not me. One of these days you'll see what a softy I am underneath, and it'll all be over. You won't look at me the same ever again. Now quit being an ass and talk to me."

Jordan grimaced and let his head thump back against the wall. "I'm sorry I'm such a wreck. I'm sure you didn't need another lost soul to rescue."

With a roll of his eyes, Russ slipped a hand behind Jordan's neck and tugged him into a kiss.

"Ain't your fault life kicked your legs out from under you. It's what you do about it now that matters.

You're gonna land on your feet, though. I'm sure of that."

"Wish I could be so sure," he whispered.

Jordan's breath hitched, and he buried his face in Russ's shoulder. Wrapping him up tight, Russ just held on as Jordan shook and fought not to cry.

"I'm the only one here, baby. Let it out."

"It won't do any good," Jordan sniffled.

"It might. Have you tried?"

With a snort, Jordan pulled back and shook his head. "God, I must look like shit right now."

He smoothed his hair back and tugged at his clothes until Russ captured his hands. "You look like you're hurtin', which is the truth. Now what happened with your sister? Did things go all right? She seemed pretty happy to see you, at least."

With an exhausted sigh, Jordan moved around him and slumped on the bench just inside the tack room door.

"I think so? I mean, she didn't tell me I was going to hell or call me a pervert or anything, so that's a plus," he said as Russ joined him on the bench. "But she didn't tell me anything I didn't know already, except my parents are fighting a lot… which might mean my mom isn't ready to just write me off quite as easily as my father did."

"That's something, right? One parent's better than none."

Jordan grimaced. "Sorry. I guess this sounds like a lot of whining over nothing to you, after everything with your family."

With a frown, Russ gripped the back of Jordan's neck and gave him a shake. "Don't be stupid. Just because my family problems are different from yours doesn't mean you don't have a right to be hurt. If I remember correctly, you let me have it over that exact thing that night on the trail, and you were right. I told you that."

After taking a deep breath and blowing it out, Jordan nodded. "Yeah. Sorry."

"You say sorry one more time and I'm gonna have to kiss you 'til you stop," Russ growled.

Jordan blinked at him for a couple of beats before his lips curved. "Sorry?"

Russ took great pride in being a man of his word, but he cut things off before they ended up naked in front of the open tack room door.

"Okay. Enough distractions now," he chastised breathlessly. "You gonna be okay? Really?"

"Better now." Jordan smiled. "I feel stupid enough for freaking out over a visit from my little sister. She flew all the way out to see me. She even offered to help if she could. But I was just settling in here, you know? Just trying to get my head on straight, and she comes and stirs all this stuff up again. I still have no idea what I'm going to do with the rest of my life, but at least I knew what I was doing right now." He groaned and rolled his shoulders as he tipped his head back and gazed at the ceiling. "I feel like I need to get all my ducks in a row before I can have the energy to deal with that other stuff. It's like from my old Psych 101 textbooks from my freshman year—what was that guy's name, Maslove? Maslow? The hierarchy of needs thing?"

Pursing his lips, Russ shrugged helplessly. "Sorry, you lost me. Name sounds familiar, but I didn't go to college, and psychology textbooks aren't really my first choice for a good read."

Waving his hands, Jordan continued, "Well, whatever it's called. It's like a pyramid with the basic needs like air, water, shelter, food, and that kind of stuff on the bottom. You need to have all that and other things like safety and financial security before you can deal with anything else. So that was kind of my plan, I guess. Maybe… I don't know. I'm sounding really stupid right now. Please just stop me. Jesus, one visit from my little sister and I'm a mess. I don't know why you want to put up with me."

Jordan moved to get up, but Russ grabbed his hand and tugged him back down. "Easy there. Take a breath and give me a second, okay? I think I get what you're trying to say. You're focusing on the things you can control and putting aside the stuff you can't."

"Is that what I'm doing?" Jordan said with a self-deprecating smile.

Russ chuckled. "Yes. It's a good thing. It's smart. But your sister being here could be a good thing too. You *can* control your relationship with her… or at least you can do your best to keep the lines of communication open, stay connected with her. You love her. She loves you. Nothing bad about that. Deal with her as she is, not what she represents."

"Except she makes me think of everything else I've lost. She wants something from me that I can't give her. She wants her family back the way it was."

"But she also doesn't want to lose her brother, right? You can give her that."

Jordan propped his elbows on his knees and dropped his head into his hands. "I wasn't ready to deal with this yet," he grumbled.

Threading his fingers through Jordan's hair, Russ gave his scalp a gentle rub. "I get that."

Turning his head so one blue eye peeped past his fingers at Russ, Jordan let out a muffled chuckle and said, "You know, for a guy who claims to be bad with words, you're doing a really good job right now."

"Fair warnin', I'm probably shooting my wad right here."

Jordan dropped his hands to hang loosely between his knees and grinned at him. "Not yet you aren't."

Rolling his eyes, Russ pushed to his feet and headed for the door. "Come on. That's enough jawin' for now. Let's go see what shit job Ernie or Jon can find to keep you occupied until Phyl rings the bell for supper."

When Jordan caught up with him, the little bastard slid a hand into one of Russ's back pockets and squeezed. "I could just ride the fence and watch while you work with one of the horses," he breathed in Russ's ear. "Think of it as furthering my training… absorbing your genius."

"Careful or I'll make you clean up that load of horseshit you're layin' down," he replied, stepping away and giving Jordan a playful shove in the direction of the donkey pasture. "Now go find Jon before neither one of us is fit to sit at the table with company."

Jordan's throaty chuckle followed him as Russ adjusted himself in his jeans and went to find his own distraction.

CHAPTER TWENTY

GEMMA STAYED another full day before driving out Thursday morning to catch her flight home. Though Jordan felt guilty about it, he was relieved to see her go. He and Russ hadn't exactly been falling all over each other in front of everyone before. But Russ had cut way back on those little touches Jordan loved—obviously because they made Gemma uncomfortable—and Jordan missed them terribly.

He and Russ still had their nights together. He wasn't willing to go that far for his sister's comfort, but Jordan could admit he was needy enough to resent the loss of any of Russ's attention. One of these days, he promised his pride that he really would get a grip. He just wasn't there yet.

Despite having longer conversations than he and his little sister had had in years, Gemma had remained jarringly out of place in her expensive but completely impractical clothes and shoes, a painful reminder of the life he'd left behind. She and Jordan had the love of riding in common, and their childhood, of course, but that was about all. And while she'd laid on the Thorndike charm like a pro with the rest of the ranch, she'd remained an outsider—another reminder that Jordan himself was only passing through, that everything he had now was only temporary, even Russ.

He'd been quite happy living in a paradise of denial, and she'd pricked little holes in his bubble. The tidal wave was harder to push away. The need to make decisions about his life and get on with it prickled more insistently at the edges of his consciousness. And his excuses for not doing so sounded more and more pathetic.

For the first couple of days after she left, everyone continued to treat him like glass. But luckily, once the weekend hit in full force, Russ and Phyllis had their hands too full to tiptoe around him anymore. Russ was as crabby as ever by the end of the day, and Phyllis was too tired to mother him. Every time Russ barked out an order or growled under his breath, Jordan had to hide a smile. Things were getting back to normal, and Jordan couldn't have been happier about it, even if he felt a few twinges of guilt for grabbing on to the distraction like a lifeline.

BY TUESDAY morning, Jon and Ernie had taken their cues from Russ and went back to ribbing Jordan at the breakfast table. When Russ's hand slid almost absently onto Jordan's thigh under the table as he teased Phyllis about something, Jordan closed his eyes, let out a happy sigh, and sipped his coffee.

Normal. That was all he wanted.

Marina was doing better by the day. Missy and Daisy were being picked up by their new family by the end of the week. Three of the goats had found a new home with a family in Waco. Over the weekend, a rancher from Clifton had agreed to donate two hundred bales of extra harvested feed hay after Jordan had given the man's wife and kids the grand tour—and possibly talked them into taking a horse or pony in the bargain.

Life was pretty good.

Russ squeezed his thigh again, breaking him out of his daydream.

"Jordan, hon, you feelin' all right?" Phyllis asked as she cleared dishes from the table.

"I'm fine. My mind just wandered a little," he said, flushing in embarrassment.

Phyllis gave him a gentle smile as she collected his plate. "Well, at least your appetite's back. You didn't eat hardly anything when your sister was here. Of course, she barely ate more'n a mouse too. Must be a family thing."

That worried V appeared between Russ's eyebrows again, but Jordan took his hand under the table and squeezed it reassuringly. "Really, I'm fine. I was actually just thinking we had a pretty good weekend, all things considered."

Her smile widened. "Yeah, we did. You were great with that Barton woman from Clifton. I think you might have just made a new regular donor out of her. We're gonna need that extra feed, which is something I wanted to talk to you two about."

Russ and Jordan both stopped clearing the last of breakfast from the table. "What's that?" Russ asked.

"I got an email this morning from Bailey's Rescue outside of Muskogee. Seems they got a big case from a debunked 'rescue' in Arkansas they need help with, and they're reaching out to every good rescue they know, looking for help. This is a big one, dozens of neglected horses. They're hoping we can take three or four at the least, maybe more later. Russ, you and I can sit down and decide just how many we can afford, but I figured, while I had the two of you together, I'd see if you were willing to take a little overnight trip north."

"I think we just might be able to manage that. Don't you?" Russ said, his smile widening as he cocked an eyebrow at Jordan.

"It's an eight-hour trek each way, so if you'd rather I asked Jon to go with Russ…," Phyllis teased.

"No." Jordan flushed as her grin widened. "No. I'm happy to help any way I can."

"Good," she replied, nodding. "You go on ahead out to the barn while Russ and me look at some numbers and talk. Then I'll call around to find someone to come in for bit Wednesday and Thursday 'til you get back."

Russ joined him in the barn an hour later. "Phyl got Michelle and another regular to agree to stop by when they can," he began without preamble. "You sure you want to do this? It hasn't been that long since your road trip down here."

Jordan grinned up at him as he tapped a finger to his chin. "Hmmmm. Let me see. Almost two whole days, just the two of us, and a night alone in a hotel with you? I think I can make the sacrifice for the good of the horses."

Russ tugged him close and gave him a deep, slow kiss. "Told you you had a generous heart." He chuckled. "It's still gonna be sixteen hours in a truck, so it won't all be fun and games."

"I'll manage."

With a swat to Jordan's ass, Russ strode away. "Well then, get back to work so we have time to get the trailer ready and pack. We're leaving before first light," he threw over his shoulder.

"I love it when you're bossy," he called after him with a grin.

DESPITE BEING on the ranch for weeks now, Jordan still shuffled down the stairs like the undead come morning. Russ pretty much dragged him to the truck and shoved a travel mug into his hand. Russ would have to do all the driving, since Jordan had never hauled a trailer in his life, but that was probably the safest bet for all concerned.

"Damn morning people," Jordan grumbled into his mug as Phyllis waved them a cheery goodbye.

"Gotta be up with the animals," Russ replied with a smile. "Don't worry, baby. I know you're not used to it yet. I can keep quiet for a while if you want to go back to sleep."

"Wouldn't be much of a copilot if I left you all alone," Jordan mumbled around a yawn.

"This time of day I'm fine. Now when the sun goes down, that's a different story."

"You're more than fine when the sun goes down too. I speak from experience."

Russ threw him a grin and batted his eyelashes. "Why, thank you, kind sir."

Jordan nearly snorted his coffee. Teasing, playful Russ might just be worth rolling out of bed at the ass-crack of dawn.

When Jordan was finished coughing and wiping his mouth, Russ picked up his phone, unlocked it, and handed it over. "There's a few books on Audible on there, plus a couple I still have from the library on Overdrive, if you want to pick one for us to listen to." His grin turned a little sheepish. "I figured that might be better than us trying to find common ground with music."

"What? You don't want me to entertain you with my witty repartee for the next eight hours? I'm hurt."

"If you got something you want to talk about, you know I'll listen," Russ replied, his voice and his gaze entirely too serious.

"Nope. I'm good," Jordan rushed to reply.

They hadn't had another heart-to-heart since the one in the barn, and Jordan was perfectly happy with that for the time being. He was still cringing in embarrassment from the last time.

"Didn't think so," Russ murmured, shooting Jordan the side-eye and a wry grin.

Keeping his head down, Jordan scrolled through the titles on Russ's phone, surprised at the sheer size of his library. "I didn't know you read so much. I mean, I saw the ones on the bookshelf in your bedroom, but this is impressive."

Russ shrugged. "I discovered e-books and audio-books about the time I started at the B STAR, so I only lugged my favorite hard copies when I moved and donated the rest. You have lots of time to listen to a book when you're mucking stalls and doing the busy work, and I read a lot before bed, but most of it's digital."

"I've only seen you pick up a book a couple of times at night. I didn't even know you had an e-reader."

"That's because I had my hands full with something else."

Jordan returned his grin and rolled his eyes. "Sorry. I didn't realize I was keeping you away from your favorite hobby."

Russ reached across the bench seat and squeezed Jordan's thigh. "It was worth it."

Hiding a pleased shiver, Jordan scrolled until he found a John Grisham that sounded interesting. With all the reading he'd had to do for school, Jordan hadn't done much for pleasure, but maybe he'd follow Russ's lead from now on and look into some audiobooks, especially if the library had them for free.

Look at me, being all frugal and fiscally responsible.

By lunchtime, Jordan was convinced audiobooks were the best road-trip idea ever. His family had never been one for road trips. His father's bank had a private jet, so they mostly used that and commercial flights in first class to go where they wanted. After four hours in the truck, with another four to go, Jordan could understand why.

"My ass is numb," he whined.

"That's why we're stopping, that and I'm starving. Don't worry. I'll massage it tonight when we get to the hotel."

"Promise?"

"I'm a man of my word, ain't I?"

Outside the restaurant, Russ eyed Jordan's salad dubiously as they headed to one of the tables, but he didn't say anything, and far too soon they were climbing back into the truck.

Just before they took the last turn to the rescue, according to GPS, Russ asked Jordan to pause the book. "We'll be there soon, so I figured I should warn you now. We don't know what kind of shape these horses are going to be in. Some of them might not make it. This won't be as bad as visiting the actual place where the neglect happened. Bailey's a good man and runs a great rescue. But I thought I should give you a heads-up before we roll in. The sight of that many animals in

such bad shape breaks my heart every time, even after
ten years at the B STAR."

Russ eyed him soberly until Jordan nodded. After
drawing in a deep breath and letting it out, he said, "I
understand. Thanks for reminding me."

Bailey's had a cute painted wood sign at the en-
trance to the ranch, nestled among tall yellow and white
wildflowers. Halfway up the dirt drive, they had to stop
to wait for a mama goose and her goslings to cross.
A long-haired highland cow munched lazily in a field
to the right, eyeing them curiously through his russet
bangs as they pulled into the gravel circle by the house.

The ranch itself was considerably smaller than the
B STAR. When Jordan mentioned it, Russ said, "Bailey
does mainly horses. I think he might have a donkey or
two and a few other farm animals around, but the rescue is for horses."

"Hey there!" a balding man in overalls pulled tight
over an impressive belly and barrel chest descended the
stairs of the ranch house when they pulled in. Sunlight
gleamed off his dark brown scalp as he wiped a rag
over it. "You made good time. Russ, right?"

Russ smiled, tipped his tan felt Stetson—which he
reserved for "dressing up" when he was out in public
off the ranch—and shook the man's hand. "Yes, and
this is Jordan."

"Nice to meet you, Jordan, I'm Jedediah, but everyone just calls me Bailey. It's hotter'n hades out here.
You boys come inside, and Naomi'll help get us something cold to drink."

Naomi turned out to be Bailey's seventeen-year-old
daughter. She took time away from poring over papers
in a makeshift office that was probably meant to be a
dining room to say hi and help her dad serve iced tea.

The house was small, the furniture, wood floors, and rugs old and worn. Only a few weeks ago, Jordan might've internally turned up his nose at sitting on the ragged couch while they all exchanged small talk—just like his sister had. But now all he could think was how kind these people had to be to give every extra penny they had to something greater than themselves. His parents had always given a lot to charity, and his mother could be quite passionate about some of her causes, but they'd never actually sacrificed for it. They'd never felt the pinch of going without to help someone else. There was nobility in giving when you had little.

Russ got paid for his work, but he probably could have made more somewhere else, and he definitely put in more hours than a normal job would require. He did it for love, just like the Baileys must.

Jordan turned doe eyes and a sappy smile on Russ, and Russ frowned back. "Are you okay?" he mouthed when Bailey went to get refills for their drinks.

Jordan refrained from sighing and fluttering his eyelashes. "I'm fine."

"Ooookay."

Russ probably thought he was crazy, but Jordan didn't mind. He had a whole night in a hotel bed—without Phyllis within hearing distance—to convince Russ otherwise and show just how much he admired him.

After they'd talked for a while, Bailey showed them to the pasture where the newest rescues were being kept. Jordan's stomach twisted as he got a good look at the emaciated and ragged animals.

"We've got 'em all on a high-calorie diet and antibiotics for the sickest. We could only take about a dozen, even on a temporary basis. The rest have been scattered around at any rescue that had space. Phyllis said you could take four with you now?"

Russ nodded. "Yeah. We can fit four in the trailer. After we get 'em settled and figure out everything they're gonna need, we might be able to come back for a few more. It depends on how the adoptions go this week and the next."

"We're grateful for any help you can give," Bailey said with a smile. "Naomi's got paperwork on four pulled out and ready for you. We can get 'em separated tonight so it's easier to load 'em tomorrow morning."

"That would be a big help, thanks."

Between the three of them, they found the horses that corresponded to the numbered files and moved them to a pen. After checking them over, Russ decided they were gentle enough that he could trim their badly overgrown and thrush-infected hooves so they'd be a little more comfortable for the trip. Seriously, Jordan had never seen hooves grow that long in his life. Some of them even curled up like elf shoes. It was horrible, and they stank to high heaven once Russ started cutting into the infected areas.

By the time Russ finished a cursory clipping of the four they were taking, the sun was getting low and Jordan was way more tired than he should have been after sitting on his ass all day. But Russ still offered to work on some of the other horses while they had the light. Thankfully, Bailey shook his head. "I got a guy coming day after tomorrow. You drove a long way today, and you got a long way back tomorrow. Go get some rest, and we'll see you in the morning."

They unhooked the trailer from the pickup and left it in Bailey's yard. After hopping in the truck, they headed back toward the highway. Jordan insisted on driving this time, since Russ looked dead on his feet.

"I'm sorry, baby," Russ murmured as Jordan pulled out onto the main drag that led to the small town of Summit outside Muskogee.

"For what?"

With a yawn, Russ laid his head back against the seat. "I had big plans of taking you out to a nice dinner, like a real date, before we headed to the hotel, but I'm beat. I'd probably fall asleep on you before we got through the appetizer."

Jordan's smile was just a tad besotted as he cast Russ a sideways glance. "Yeah? You wanted to ask me on a date, huh?"

"Should've done it sooner, but pickings are kind of slim around the ranch, if you don't want chain food—not much for the refined palate, if you know what I mean. Thought maybe I'd find someplace near here that was quaint and homey, if not five-star cuisine."

"I don't care where we go, Russ, really. And don't worry about tonight. You were sawing and clipping and sanding for hours, even after an eight-hour drive up here. Of course you're tired. I'm tired, and I barely did anything today…. Let's just find a hotel, I'll drop you off to shower and relax, and I'll go looking for something to bring back for dinner."

Russ's smile was a tad sappy too. He was utterly adorable when he was sleepy, damned precious really, but Jordan would never say that out loud.

"My hero," Russ murmured sleepily.

CHAPTER TWENTY-ONE

JORDAN PICKED up carry-out from a Chili's, because it was the first sign he recognized. He wasn't in the mood to be adventurous with the local fare, although he would have done it if Russ had been up for that date. If he were honest, he hadn't even thought about them not having been on a real date yet, but obviously Russ had.

Jordan worried his lip as he cut off the engine and climbed out of the truck. The B STAR was his escape from reality—his island in the storm, detached from everything else—but was that fair to Russ? The ranch *was* Russ's life. Russ had said he understood, but was Jordan playing house while Russ had actually been serious?

"Jesus, Jordan, get a grip," he mumbled to himself. "It was supposed to be one date. The guy didn't ask you to marry him."

Grabbing the to-go bags, he slammed the truck door and headed for their room.

"Hey, baby," Russ called sleepily from the bed as Jordan came through the door.

"I bring sustenance," Jordan announced, arranging the foam containers on the tiny round table as Russ clicked on the lamp by the bed.

"My hero," Russ said again.

Surprisingly hungry for having done next to nothing all day, Jordan polished off anything Russ didn't, even though Jordan hadn't stinted on ordering food. He'd had a bit of a moment in the restaurant when he'd handed over his card—flashback from that first day after leaving home and his mortification at the gas station. But the sale went through, much to his relief.

The card was for his private bank account, and he'd hardly used it since coming to the ranch, so he shouldn't have worried, but this whole being aware of every penny he spent was going to take some getting used to. In his old life, a few thousand dollars was barely a month's spending money, with more to fall back on if he overspent. Now it was all he had until he figured out what to do with himself. The thought was just a bit terrifying.

How fucking helpless was that? He couldn't even order food without getting nervous. He'd never realized just how dependent on his parents he was until all the little things he had to think about now started adding up. Those things had always just been taken care of before, without his ever needing to know how. The real world was creeping closer, and he wouldn't be able to put it off forever.

After they finished eating, Russ helped him gather up the empty containers and tuck them back in the bags. When the table was clear and the bags set by the tiny trash can, Russ stepped in close and kissed him.

Russ's tongue tasted of garlic and barbecue sauce, and Jordan returned the kiss eagerly.

"Since I bought you dinner, does that mean you have to put out?" Jordan asked between kisses.

Russ grinned. "Have to? No. Want to? Always."

"Even though you're exhausted and have to get up early and do it all over again tomorrow?" Jordan asked, cocking an eyebrow.

"Darlin', I'd have to be dead to say no to you," he said, tugging at Jordan's belt. "Now, I may not last more than one round, but I promise I'll make that round count."

"We'd better get a move on, then," Jordan teased. He pushed Russ away and started working off his boots. When he tugged his shirt over his head, he found Russ just standing there, watching. "What are you doing?"

"Enjoying the show," Russ answered with a grin.

Jordan frowned even though he preened on the inside. "Stop watching and start getting naked. If I've only got a limited time before you pass out, every second counts."

Russ's lopsided grin widened. "Yes, sir."

Since all Russ had put back on after his shower was his T-shirt and a pair of boxers, he was gloriously naked a lot sooner than Jordan, and it was a sight Jordan never got tired of. Lean and tanned, every inch of him was hard from work. Brown nipples peeked out of a scattering of dark chest hair, begging to be tasted and touched.

Russ had looked at Jordan like he was crazy the one time he'd asked about a place where he might get waxed, but even Russ was vain enough to trim with an electric shaver every once in a while. Jordan knew this for a fact since he'd offered to help the last time—which had led to quite an enjoyable evening romp afterward.

"Now who's slowing down the process?" Russ asked with a grin.

"Just getting a good look myself… taking it all in."

"Well, come a little closer and I'll make sure you take it all in."

Jordan groaned at Russ's truly awful joke, but his cock waved eagerly as he closed the distance between them. "You're lucky you're pretty, because your jokes are terrible," Jordan teased as he wrapped his arms around Russ's slim waist and tugged their bodies together.

"Who's joking?" Russ shot back as he ground his cock against Jordan's.

Banter was wasting precious time, so Jordan sealed their mouths together rather than answer. Russ steered them toward the bed as Jordan kissed and fondled every inch of Russ he could reach. Russ was clean and fresh from his shower, making Jordan uncomfortably aware he hadn't had one since that morning. Luckily, he hadn't actually done much other than sit in the car and keep the horses still and calm while Russ had done most of the work. Plus, Russ actually seemed to like it when Jordan was a little mussed up and dirty, which was a bit of a change from the overly primped, producted, powdered, and manscaped men Jordan had hooked up with before.

With a growl, Russ gave Jordan a little shove onto the bed.

"Oof," Jordan said, when the mattress didn't give as much as he'd expected. With a grimace, he rolled up and rubbed a hand over his ass.

The springs squeaked when Russ knelt on the bed and crawled over him. Russ bent down, pushed Jordan's hand aside, and kissed one asscheek, then the other.

"Sorry, baby. Forgot the mattress was a bit on the Flintstones side. Let me kiss it and make it better."

Russ nudged and Jordan happily rolled over. Words weren't necessary after that, even if Jordan had been capable of anything beyond "fuck," "yeah," "God," or slurred gibberish. Russ's mouth and tongue were absolute magic, a fact Jordan had become well-acquainted with over the last few weeks—add in just that little hint of stubble burn on sensitive skin and Jordan was in heaven. Going to bed with an older, more experienced man definitely had its perks. Though Russ had had a long day and probably shouldn't be doing all the work, Jordan couldn't seem to get the words to that effect to come out of his mouth.

The best he could come up with was "God, Russ, just fuck me already, before I lose it and leave you hanging."

Not the most romantic or generous of utterances, but it did the trick. Jordan heard a rustle and then the tearing of condom and lube packets before Russ filled his needy hole in one long smooth glide.

Jordan reared up, placed one palm on the slab of wood mounted to the wall in lieu of a headboard, gripped Russ's hip with the other, and began to move. Obviously getting the hint that this wasn't going to be a slow, gentle fuck, Russ pulled out and slammed back in while Jordan thrust his ass back, meeting every stroke. Russ rode him hard, grunting and swearing as drops of his sweat dripped onto Jordan's back. Jordan hadn't been kidding that he was ready to lose it, so it wasn't long before his balls drew up, he arched his back, and yelled, shooting his load all over the sheets. Russ grunted behind him, slammed into him a few more times, and froze. Russ's grip on Jordan's hip was hard enough to leave marks, but Jordan only sighed happily as Russ pressed lazy kisses to his shoulders and the back of his neck between panted breaths.

With a groan, Russ pulled out and flopped onto the mattress. After removing and getting rid of the condom, Russ closed his eyes, but Jordan gave him a little shake.

"Not yet, sleepyhead. Come on. I'm not sleeping in the wet spot."

He dragged a half-conscious Russ over to the second bed in the room. He stripped off the shiny, hideous comforter and pilled polyester blanket underneath and tucked Russ between the sheets before crawling in after him.

THE CLOCK on the nightstand between the beds told him it was barely eleven when he woke from his little postsex nap. Russ was still out cold, but he was a quintessential morning person, so Jordan was used to that by now.

With a soft smile, he braced his fist against his temple, propped himself on an elbow, and gazed fondly at the sleeping man beside him. Obviously, he didn't know much about boyfriends and all that stuff, but Russ had to be one of the better ones. Russ could be surly and short-tempered, but it was only because he cared so much. Jordan had spent his entire life being taught how to hide his feelings behind coolness and detachment, so that kind of passion took some getting used to, but damned if it wasn't a beautiful thing to behold. His parents would consider Russ loud and common—low. But Jordan loved it. In fact, he couldn't imagine surviving the last few weeks without Russ.

He was in a crappy, damp, musty hotel room, permeated by the faint smell of old cigarettes. The air conditioner sounded like a jet airplane. The sheets were cheap and scratchy. He was surrounded by some of the worst pastel "hotel art" he'd ever seen. He was lying on a mattress that would probably separate a few disks in his spine by morning—and he wouldn't even go there about the bathroom... but he was happy as a clam.

I wouldn't mind spending the rest of my life, just like this.

He froze. His breath stilled in his chest, and his eyes went round.

Holy shit.

He *was* happy—like *really* happy—happier than he could remember being since he was a little kid. He might have been wandering around for weeks, afraid to make any kind of decision about the rest of his life, but *today*, today he'd done something good, something he could be proud of.

He didn't have a job, a home, or most of his family, but he had Russ... and Phyllis, and Jon and Ernesto—all really good people who cared about him—*right now*.

Struggling to breathe around the constriction in his throat as thoughts and feelings took shape inside him, he sat up and pulled his knees to his chest, staring blindly into the mostly darkened hotel room.

Maybe life didn't have to be some grand future plan with degrees, letters after his name, and a career his father could be proud of. Even after the crushing blow his father dealt, Jordan had still been so intimidated by "What To Do with His Life" that he'd run away from even the thought of it every chance he got. He'd still been playing by his father's rules in his head, looking at his future like his father expected—a career, an office in a big building, and a fancy condo or house in a trendy neighborhood to go to on evenings and weekends. But he'd had it right earlier, the ranch *was* life for Russ... and for Phyllis, Jon, and Ernesto, and a lot of other people. That was their home and their career, and Jordan didn't think any less of them for choosing it. In fact, he admired them for it. So why couldn't he live a life like that too? It might not be a six-figure salary with his name engraved on a brass plate, but it was a life, a good one, one he'd been happier in than anywhere else.

He took in a long breath and blew it out, trying to calm his racing heart.

Don't get too far ahead of yourself.

No one had actually asked him to stay on permanently at the ranch, not even Russ. Jordan had made it pretty clear that he was only there temporarily. But he could talk to Phyllis about that, couldn't he? He'd helped enough with the paperwork to know they couldn't support another paid full-timer, but he could work around that. He was pretty good at the schmoozing and fundraising stuff. He knew a lot of rich, influential families he could contact to find more donors, and he could always take a desk job in the meantime. Two years of law school should be enough to get a job as a legal assistant or clerk or something. Though he shuddered to think about climbing behind a desk again, he could deal with it in the short term if it meant he could stay.

Swallowing his nerves, he tried to think of practicalities—like Russ had said, the things he could control rather than the things he couldn't. Everything he'd been running from didn't seem so scary anymore when he felt like he was running toward something instead of away. The half-formed thoughts he'd been pushing to the side weren't quite so overwhelming when he looked at them in light of being able to stay with Russ and his newfound friends.

If they'll have me.

Thrusting his nerves aside, he concentrated on the basics. As soon as he could get away again after they got back, he'd take a trip to Dallas to sell his car. He couldn't afford the insurance on it anymore anyway. He'd get a cheap sedan of some sort to tide him over. He'd also pawn his Rolex and his jewelry. That, with the money left over from the car, should be enough to make a comfortable cushion until he found a paying job. He could always move the rest of the way into Russ's room if Phyllis needed the extra space when they did the whole B and B thing. It wasn't as if he spent much time in his own room anyway.

Russ had said this boyfriend thing would last until Jordan left. He might not have anticipated that being never, but things were going pretty well between them, weren't they?

And if Russ doesn't want you on a more permanent basis? If he's only willing to put up with your crazy neurotic drama because he knows it's not forever?

Jordan shook his head and stretched out beside his still-sleeping boyfriend.

Fuck off, he said to his father's voice.

He couldn't let it stop him. Russ and Phyllis and everyone else had been patiently waiting for him to make a plan. He couldn't disappoint them forever.

This was it. This was the plan. He'd been hiding from it for weeks, and now he had it. It might not be the best plan ever, and he'd sort of fallen into it. A lot depended on the kindness and generosity of others, but he was willing to work hard to repay that generosity. Working with horses was something he loved and something he was good at. Everyone said so. He could do this.

HIS ALREADY shaky confidence waned a bit as the hours passed on their trip back the next day. Jordan couldn't talk to Russ about it, not yet. He needed to see Phyl first. The ranch was hers, even if Russ was her right-hand man. Whether he stayed or not had to be up to her and had to be on his own merit.

He replayed what he was going to say to her, and to Russ afterward, so many times in his head, he barely heard a word of the audiobook he'd chosen.

"You okay?" Russ asked a couple of hours into their trip.

"Yeah. Just thinking."

"Anything I can help with?"

Jordan squeezed his thigh. "I'll let you know."

"Okay." Russ gave him a side-eye, but turned his attention back to the road and continued on in silence.

By the time they arrived at the ranch, Jordan was too tired to even think, let alone have his big talk with Phyl. They'd left a little later in the morning than the day before, plus, with loading the horses and stopping every so often to check on them, it took a lot longer to get home than the drive out. It was close to quitting time when they pulled in, but Jon and Ernie stayed on to help them unload and get the new horses situated in their stalls. They'd be kept completely separate from the others until Dr. Watney could take a look at them, and after that, the four might be allowed into one of the fenced corrals so they could start introducing them to the herd.

Jon and Ernie hung around for a bit to chat about Bailey's place and the trip, but it soon became obvious that neither Jordan nor Russ were up for much sparkling conversation, and the men headed home. As soon as Jordan and Russ's plates were clean, Phyl shooed them out of the kitchen.

"Go rest up. Read a book if you're not quite ready to go to sleep, though you look like you're pretty much dead on your feet."

"Thanks, Phyl," Russ murmured, flashing her a tired smile.

"It amazes me how exhausting sitting on my ass all day can be. I mean, I didn't even do anything, and I can't keep my eyes open," Jordan complained on the way up the stairs.

"It was all that thinkin' you were doin'. Can be hard on a fella if he's not used to it."

At the top of the stairs, Jordan stopped and stared. Russ's grin was broad as he playfully bumped his shoulder against Jordan's on his way past. Glaring, Jordan huffed and followed him into the bedroom.

"You're lucky I'm too tired to make you eat those words," Jordan said before flopping face-first onto their mattress. The sheets were still mussed from the day before, and they smelled like Russ and home. He groaned and snuggled deeper.

"No, you don't. Being tired is no excuse for wearing your boots to bed… which reminds me, we really should get you a decent pair of cowboy boots."

Jordan flopped onto his back and started untying his bootlaces. "Yeah? Think I'd look sexy in a pair like yours?"

Russ's grin was tired but full of warmth. "Baby, you'd look sexy in about anything, or nothing… and you know it."

After kicking off his boots, Jordan shimmied out of his jeans without sitting up. A quick tug and his T-shirt went to join his jeans and socks on the floor.

"There's a hamper in the corner, you know," Russ grumbled without much force behind it.

"I'll get it in the morning. I promise," Jordan said around a yawn.

"Good." Russ yawned too. "'Cause there's no maid service, and I sure as hell ain't picking up after you."

Russ flopped onto the mattress next to him, and Jordan snuggled close. Phyllis didn't exactly set the thermostat to a chilly seventy-two degrees in the Texas heat, like Jordan was used to back home, but he was willing to accept a little stickiness in exchange for skin-on-skin contact. Thankfully, Russ didn't seem to mind, and they usually drifted apart sometime in the night anyway.

Usually it took Jordan forever to fall asleep, while Russ just dropped off like flipping a switch. That night Jordan barely remembered closing his eyes before Russ jostled the bed, climbing out just before dawn like he always did.

CHAPTER TWENTY-TWO

AFTER BREAKFAST there was too much to do before Jordan could have his talk with Phyl; at least that was what he told himself. He wanted to check on Marina and some of their other problem children. Plus, they had four new horses in pretty rough shape to deal with now, and Russ needed his help giving each of them a thorough examination and taking notes on problems to discuss with Dr. Watney.

Eventually, though, the rush of activity slowed to normal, and Russ moved on to his training sessions, leaving Jordan to his regular barn upkeep duties. Despite an attack of nerves, Jordan squared his shoulders, put his wheelbarrow and shovel aside, and headed for the house with a determined stride before he completely chickened out.

What's the worst that could happen?

She could say no, and he'd lose his safety net.

But he wasn't a child. In some areas, he might be almost as helpless and ignorant as one, but he had options. He'd rather not just leap from the nest, but he could if it became necessary.

Internal pep talk done, he marched up to Phyllis's small office and knocked on the doorjamb before poking his head through the opening.

"Got a minute?" he asked when she lifted her head and smiled at him.

She pulled off her reading glasses and raised her eyebrows. "Sure, hon. What can I do for you?"

So this was what a job interview felt like. Not quite as bad as facing his father across the man's carved mahogany desk, but still a little unnerving.

With a nervous swallow, he sat in the small wood chair in front of her desk and launched into his proposal, hardly stopping for breath.

"You want to stay on here, full-time?" Phyllis asked.

"Yes."

Her brows knit. "Are you sure, hon? I mean, this isn't exactly where you're from, if you catch my meaning. And what about your folks and all that business back home? I know your mom's gotta be worried about you. Now might not be the best time for you to be making big decisions."

"If that's all you're worried about, don't be. You may not know my father well, but believe me, I do. He's made his decision. And even though I can hold out some future hope my mother or some earth-shattering event might change his mind somewhere down the road, I can't plan my life around that. He'll either come around or he won't, but that makes no difference to the fact that I need to take control of my own life. I need to find a new direction to go in because the old one was wrong. I'm happy here, Phyl. I'm proud of what the ranch does, and I'm proud of being able to contribute to that."

Her gaze turned soft as her tanned, weathered face crinkled into smile lines. "Thank you, sweetheart."

"Look. I've seen the books. I know you can't afford to bring me on as an employee right now, but like I said, I have ideas to help with the fundraising, and I'm willing to make improvements and updates to the blog and website, and find a job somewhere around here to pay the bills in the meantime. Hopefully I won't have to commute all the way to Dallas every day, but I'm willing to, if it means I can stay on here with all of you. I'll still put in all the hours I can at the ranch, to earn my keep. I promise."

She pursed her lips, but her eyes were smiling at him. "We'll need to talk to Russ before I give a final say," she warned.

"I know. I'd like to talk to him alone, first. I just wanted to discuss it with you before I broached the subject, since, in the end, it's your ranch, and I do think I can be useful here."

"You already are, hon." Her smile fell away as she studied his face. "You know, Russ isn't as tough as he likes to let on. Once he gives his heart to somethin', that's it. He's done. Whatever it is you two got going on really isn't my business. But as a friend, I'm gonna ask you to think real hard before you make any promises to him."

"I will. I have been."

"You've got a lot goin' on in the emotion department right now. I can't pretend to understand all you're feelin', but are you sure you don't want to take a bit more time to settle into your skin?"

Blowing out a long breath, Jordan shook his head and smiled ruefully. "My life's been on hold for as long as I can remember. I can't pretend to know what I'm going to want five years down the road, but at some point, I need to start living instead of just thinking about it. The last thing I want to do is hurt Russ. You have my word I'll do everything in my power to keep that from happening, okay?"

With a sigh, she nodded and gave him a small smile. She opened her mouth, but whatever she was going to stay was cut off by the sound of tires on the gravel drive. Frowning, she stood and peeked out the window.

"We're not expecting any deliveries today," she murmured. "Wonder who that could be."

She came around the desk and patted him on the arm as Jordan stood. "Come on. You go have that talk with Russ while I go see who that is, and we can all get together over lunch after. How's that sound?"

Blowing out a relieved breath, Jordan smiled. "It sounds great. Thanks, Phyllis."

"Phyl," she corrected.

"Phyl," he said with a smile.

If he were a hugger, he would have totally picked her up and swung her around, but he wasn't quite there yet... maybe in time.

Giddy with possibilities and butterflies in his stomach over the upcoming talk with Russ, Jordan almost plowed into Phyllis's back on the front porch when she stopped dead at the top of the stairs.

"Oh Lordy," Phyllis whispered.

Following her gaze, Jordan saw a young dark-skinned man in jeans and a green-and-white-striped short-sleeve polo striding across the gravel toward the paddock where Russ had been gentling Aubrey, a gray-and-white splotched palomino. As they watched, Russ hopped over the fence and jogged toward the man. The two collided in a hug, and Russ lifted the other man off the ground.

"Is that—" Jon asked from the bottom of the stairs.

"Yup," Ernie answered, coming up to join the three of them.

"Well, I'll be damned," Jon said with a laugh. "The one that got away came back for another go."

"Jon!" Phyllis hissed.

"What?"

All three of them turned to look at Jordan. Phyllis gave Jon a pointed look, and the man actually blushed.

"Oh."

With a sinking feeling in his stomach, Jordan cleared his throat and asked, "Who's that?"

He tried to make it sound like he was only mildly curious, but the look on Phyllis's face told him he failed miserably.

"That's Isaiah," she answered gently.

He and Phyllis moved to join Jon and Ernie at the bottom of the stairs as Russ and Isaiah ended their enthusiastic greeting and headed their way. Phyllis gave Jordan's arm a little squeeze before stepping forward to greet the newcomer.

"Hey there, stranger. Welcome back," she called.

Russ's cheeks were flushed beneath his tan, and his grin was wider than Jordan had ever seen it. He practically glowed.

Jordan studied the newcomer, his earlier joy fading with each second that ticked past. Close up, Isaiah was intimidatingly beautiful. He topped everyone there by a good couple of inches in height. His amber eyes were striking in contrast to the rich deep brown of his skin and black close-cropped hair. His well-muscled frame belonged on a magazine cover. Jordan smoothed a hand down his shirt until he realized how ridiculous the effort was, given he was dressed in one of Russ's faded work T-shirts. Without lifting a finger, Russ's ex made him feel scrawny, plain, and shabby, a sensation he was definitely not accustomed to anywhere other than his father's office.

He'd thought he was jealous when his little sister drooled over Russ. He'd been mistaken. This was what real jealousy felt like.

It hurt.

Russ had dropped his arm from the other man's shoulder when they drew close, but the image was still burned into Jordan's psyche. Swallowing down a sudden queasiness, he plastered on his patented Thorndike smile and joined the rest of them.

"Phyl!" Isaiah boomed as he swooped in and lifted the woman into a hug. "You look as stunning as ever."

"Oh, go on with you," she chuckled, but her cheeks reddened just the same.

"Jon… Ernie," Isaiah said to each man before shaking their hands in turn. "Glad to see you guys still holding down the fort. The ranch looks incredible. You've made a lot of improvements while I've been gone."

Isaiah's gaze landed curiously on Jordan. Phyllis opened her mouth, but thankfully—before Jordan could throw one hell of an internal tantrum—Russ stepped forward and draped an arm around his shoulders.

"Jordan, babe, this is Isaiah, a good friend. He's been in Africa for a couple of years with Doctors Without Borders."

"And South America too," Isaiah added with a smile, extending his hand. "Nice to meet you, Jordan."

Jordan shook it, giving as firm a grip as he got, and Isaiah's gorgeous amber eyes raked over him with a little more intense scrutiny. Russ's touch steadied him, and the green monster inside him at least stopped growling, even if it didn't slip completely back under the rock from whence it came.

Before the moment could become awkward—or any more awkward—Phyllis clapped her hands and said, "Well, why don't we all go inside. I'll get us somethin' to drink, and you can tell us about what you've been up to, Isaiah."

Jordan saw Isaiah's gaze shoot sideways to Russ, like he'd had other plans, but he smiled and bowed to Phyl. "Lead the way. I've been dreaming about your lemonade for three years now, Phyl. Please tell me you can put me out of my misery."

"I'll do better than that, hon. I made a full pitcher just this morning, and it's just waitin' for ya."

AFTER WHAT felt like the longest lunch in the history of mankind, Jordan scurried to the barn to sulk while Russ walked Mr. Perfect to his car. Car wasn't exactly the right word to describe the enormous gleaming black Expedition that dwarfed Jordan's red convertible in the parking area. It served as the perfect metaphor for the way he was feeling at that moment.

That's me, small and shiny but not particularly practical, next to that behemoth that could carry a family of six and all their gear through rough country and smooth, plus tow a horse trailer if need be.

At least neither one of the vehicles looked particularly at home on the ranch. He had that bit of consolation to hold on to.

The long and short of the conversation around the kitchen table had been that Isaiah Green was *practically perfect in every way*. Not only was the man a doctor who'd passed on a lucrative residency to do charity work in underdeveloped countries for the last two-plus years, but he was a self-made man who'd worked his way up from a disadvantaged childhood. And now he was back in the area indefinitely, a gleaming addition to a prestigious hospital in Houston, come home to help take care of his aging parents.

"A paragon. A fucking saint," Jordan groaned.

And Russ had been in love with him before Isaiah had gone off to save the world. It was written all over Russ's face every time he looked at Isaiah. Jordan had actually thrown up what little he'd eaten at lunch before coming outside with everyone else to say goodbye. Now he was hiding in the back of the barn with his face pressed into Marina's neck, wondering how in the hell he was supposed to compete with that.

"Why did he have to be a fucking god?" he murmured miserably into Marina's shoulder. "I mean, come on. How is that even fair?"

"Jordan? You in here?" Russ called from the door.

With a groan, Jordan patted Marina's neck one more time and stepped away. By the time Russ reached him, Jordan had composed himself enough that he hoped the sick feeling in his stomach didn't show.

"There you are. Wow. That was somethin', huh?" Russ blew out a breath, his cheeks still flushed and his eyes a bit wide. "I haven't seen him in three years and up he pops, no call or nothin'."

"You didn't know he was back?"

"Nope. He said he wanted to surprise me. That was some surprise."

Russ's smile seemed forced. Jordan supposed he was trying to look reassuring, trying to hide that he was rattled, but Russ sucked at hiding. If he wasn't blustering and grouching or teasing and laughing, his mask didn't cover his feelings for shit.

"He should have called," Jordan grumbled.

"Yeah, probably," Russ replied absently.

If he'd been hoping for any indignation or criticism of Isaiah, apparently he was going to be disappointed. Unsure how to proceed, he worried his lower lip and studied the man he thought he knew so well.

"Still, it's great he can come back to help his parents," Jordan offered when he couldn't take the silence anymore. "I'm sure they're very happy to have him home, safe and sound, after traveling all over the world like that."

"Yeah. Yeah. Rita and Kenneth will be ecstatic to have him home, though they were really proud of him for going." Russ gave Jordan another absent smile before turning his attention to Marina. "How's our girl today? Is she ready for a little workout?"

With equal parts guilt and relief, Jordan jumped at the change of subject, and before too long, Russ was leading Marina out into the paddock for a little one-on-one time while Jordan set to his tasks with the same feverish intensity he'd given them his first days on the ranch.

He could not afford to think too much right now, or he really might lose his shit.

One thing was certain, now was not the time to try to have that talk with Russ. At least not until Russ stopped walking around looking like someone had just smacked him in the head with a board or he'd been struck by lightning.

Jordan might be overreacting. He didn't know the particulars of their relationship or their breakup. There could be absolutely nothing to worry about. But he'd never seen Russ thrown for a loop before, and that queasy feeling in his stomach wasn't going away until Russ started acting like his old self again.

CHAPTER TWENTY-THREE

ISAIAH "IZZY" Green was back to stay.

Russ couldn't quite wrap his head around it. He walked the ranch in a daze all afternoon and barely slept that night. At four in the morning, he'd finally given up and snuck out of bed so at least Jordan could get a few hours of undisturbed sleep.

"Good morning," Phyl said as she settled in her rocker next to him.

A slash of orange had just erupted along the horizon, so at least someone in the house was able to sleep to her usual time.

"Mornin'."

"Coffeepot was almost empty. How long have you been up?"

He shrugged. "A couple hours."

She took a sip of her coffee and eyed him for a bit. "You know, if that boy weren't such a good person and a pillar of the community, I'd be tempted to put my boot in his ass until he never came back."

"What?" He gaped at her.

"What?" she threw right back at him. "Isaiah. That's what. Ain't never seen anyone that can tie you in a bigger knot than that man. He's not back in your life a day and you're already not sleeping and brooding on the front porch... when everything was just fine, better than fine, not twenty-four hours ago."

"He just caught me by surprise. That's all. I need a minute to wrap my head around the fact that he's back."

"Uh-huh."

Russ's lips twisted sullenly. "We left it as friends, Phyl. You know that. We've traded emails over the years. We're good."

"But it's different seein' him in the flesh, knowing he's going to be an hour or so away. Isn't it? You may have parted as friends, but that wasn't what you really wanted. You were being noble and letting someone you loved follow his dreams and his passion. He left you hurtin', even if he didn't mean to. You can't lie to me about that, 'cause I was here to watch you put the pieces back together."

With a sigh, Russ let his head *thunk* back against the rocker and closed his eyes. "It was almost three years ago. And as you said, I put the pieces back together. I'm okay."

"No, you're not. Not yet anyway. You've obviously still got some things to work through in your head. Otherwise you'd have been tucked up with that lovely boy upstairs instead of brooding on the front porch in the dark."

"Before, you were warning me against Jordan. Now he's a 'lovely boy'?" he said, giving her a pointed look.

With a wave of her hand, she rolled her eyes. "That was weeks ago. Besides, I warned you to be careful, not to stay away from him. And if you remember correctly, it was because of Isaiah that I felt I needed to butt my nose in and give you that warning... and I never said Jordan wasn't a sweet boy."

Holding up his hands in surrender, he said, "Okay. Okay. You made your point. Maybe I have a few unresolved issues with Izzy, but I'll work 'em out. I promise. I'm not gonna dump Jordan like a hot rock just because Izzy's back in town. You know me better than that... or you should."

"Of course you won't. All I'm sayin' is don't just remember the good times with Isaiah and forget everything else you went through. That man could charm the hair off a frog's ass. I won't deny it. He and our Jordan got a little bit in common there, I think."

"*Our* Jordan?"

She smacked him lightly on the arm. "Don't change the subject."

"And what is the subject again?"

She huffed. "Don't let him and all that unfinished business rattle your cage so much you do something stupid and forget what you've already got in front of you. And that's all I'm gonna say on it."

With that, she stood and strode back into the house, leaving Russ with a headache starting behind his right eye. He rocked for a while, not really thinking about anything, until his phone buzzed in his pocket. Grateful for the distraction, he pulled it out and read the text.

Morning, Russ. I figured you'd be up with the dawn, as always. It's Izzy. This is my new number. I forgot to give it to you yesterday. Things were a little crazy, huh?

Russ blinked at the screen for a few seconds, and before he could think of a proper response, it flashed with a new message.

BTW, I know I said it yesterday, but it was really good to see you. I missed you.

It was good to see you too, he typed back after blowing out a breath.

I gotta go. Shift starts in an hour. But we should get together soon. Just the two of us, and really catch up.

"Shit."

"Everything okay?" Jordan asked as he pushed open the screen door and stepped onto the porch.

"Yeah. It's fine," Russ said, shoving his phone back into his pocket.

Jordan frowned as his eyes tracked the movement. "Okay. Phyl says breakfast is almost ready."

"Okay, I'm comin'."

EVEN AFTER breakfast, Russ was still so distracted he decided to take a ride to clear his head. Jordan and Phyl had eyed him strangely the entire time he'd been eating, and Ernie and Jon joined in as soon as they arrived for the day. The scrutiny made him itchy and irritable. The way they were watching him, you'd have thought someone died.

It was Friday, so the early weekenders would be arriving soon, and Russ was likely to bite some unsuspecting volunteer's head off if he didn't have some time to himself.

On the ridge above the ranch, where he'd first kissed Jordan, he dismounted and plunked his ass on the ground under the dubious shade of the live oak, while Archer, a big gray that was close to being ready to be adopted, grazed on the sparse vegetation.

Phyl was right. He was rattled. He didn't want to admit it to anyone, especially not Jordan, but he and Izzy did have a lot of unfinished business. Russ had given his heart completely to that man. Three years ago, he'd even had dreams of a little house somewhere close to the ranch, or halfway between the ranch and the hospital, where he and Izzy would raise a couple of kids together. He hadn't exactly been clear on the details of how that was going to work with him working full-time on the ranch and Izzy pulling crazy shifts at his job, but the dream had been there—however unrealistic.

Then Izzy had been offered the opportunity to travel the world, and Russ had learned that the selflessness and civic-mindedness he'd admired so much in Izzy was also what would be taking him away. Healing the sick in Texas was no longer enough to satisfy Izzy's humanitarian passion. He needed more. How the hell could Russ have said no to that?

"And now he's back."

Archer twitched his ears in Russ's direction and lifted his head a little, but when Russ didn't say anything else, he went back to grazing. Despite the early hour, the Texas heat rose off the dusty turf in shimmering waves as he watched people moving about their business down below. He could just make out Jordan's blond head by the barn.

Did he still have feelings for Izzy?

Of course he did. He didn't just stop loving someone because they'd gone away for a few years. They'd agreed to stay friends, but Russ had assumed Izzy would find someplace more exciting to settle down—and someone more exciting to settle down with. Russ had thought he might see Izzy once a year or so when he came to visit his folks, never that he'd come home to stay.

Russ pulled his phone out of his pocket and read the messages again.

If they really were friends, like he'd promised they would be, one dinner would be harmless enough. He'd be wrong to refuse such a simple request from a friend. He doubted Phyl and Jordan would see it that way, though.

Jordan.

Resting his head back against the trunk, he stared up at the clear blue sky above. Jordan had been unusually quiet since yesterday, despite Russ's efforts to hide how unsettled he was. He was pretty sure Jordan would not understand him wanting to have dinner with his ex to work some of this out in his head, which left him in a damned-if-he-did, damned-if-he-didn't situation.

It wasn't as if Jordan intended to stay on permanently anyway. Jordan had made that clear from the get-go. What they had was only temporary, and Russ had accepted that. He was a grown-up. He knew he couldn't ask more of anyone than they were willing or able to give, especially someone who'd just had his whole life ripped out from under him.

"I sure can pick 'em, can't I?" he said to Archer, who twitched his ears but didn't bother lifting his head. "You're not much help."

With a sigh, he stood up and dusted off his jeans. The weekend was coming, and he couldn't afford to spend all day sitting on his ass. He needed to check on their newest additions before Tish arrived that afternoon, and he needed to make sure the horses closest to being ready for adoption were cleaned up and looking pretty. He had a job to do. The question of Izzy could wait.

ANOTHER WEEK went by with Russ feeling as off-balance and out of sorts as he had the day Izzy surprised him on the ranch. Izzy kept texting him, here and there, subtly pushing for a get-together, but luckily he was too busy with his work, his parents, and finding a place to live to pay another visit, and he was easily put off when it came to deciding on an actual date for dinner.

Jordan was as edgy as a wet hen all week, but Russ had issues of his own to deal with, in addition to their four newest fosters that needed practically round-the-clock care. He and Jordan slept in the same bed each night, but the ease, tenderness, and teasing they'd had before was strained. Russ should have taken the time to ferret out whatever bug crawled up Jordan's butt, but he didn't. Jordan was avoiding him, and he didn't have the emotional energy to chase him down right then. Phyl was right. No one could tie him in knots like Izzy, and he needed a breather to wrestle with those knots, so he pushed his guilt aside and let things go on as they were, despite knowing he'd probably pay for it later.

IN KEEPING with this trend, he rode out by himself every day for at least an hour to give himself someplace quiet to think, where no one needed anything from him or constantly jawed at him. He didn't exactly make much progress on these trips, but the respite was nice.

That was where he was on Friday when a flash of light drew his attention to the long drive up to the house in time to see Jordan's red sports car headed for the main road, kicking up a cloud of dust as it went. Feeling a sudden twist in his gut, Russ mounted his horse and nudged him into a canter back to the barn.

Phyl was talking to Michelle by the donkey pen, so he dismounted and walked Archer the rest of the way over to her. "Where's Jordan going?" he asked when the ladies turned to greet him.

"He said he had some errands to run in the city," Phyl answered, her expression inscrutable.

"He didn't say anything about it to me," Russ grumbled, some of the tightness in his chest easing. "He does know today's Friday, right?"

"I didn't ask him, but I imagine he knows what day of the week it is," Phyl replied blithely.

Russ narrowed his eyes as irritation took the place of his earlier anxiety, and Phyl rolled hers. Placing one hand on her hip, she wagged a finger at him. "Don't get your panties in a bunch. We have plenty of people to help get ready for the weekend. If the boy wants a day off, he can have a day off. I think he's earned it and then some. It's not like we're paying him, in case you forgot."

"Still, he could've asked. I got Tish coming in a couple of hours. I have Red and Archer here that need a bath, in addition to everything else that needs doing," he defended crossly.

"Well, we managed all right before he got here. We'll manage today too, I expect. Might do you some good, actually. Remind you of what you might have taken for granted."

A quick side glance at Michelle reminded him they weren't alone, so he bit back asking her what the hell that was supposed to mean, spun on his heel, and led Archer back to a pen where he could get someone to give him a good grooming and possibly a wash if they had time.

After making sure Archer had water and giving him a little treat for being such a good boy under the saddle, he stomped off to the barn to check his to-do list for the day and make adjustments for Jordan's absence. He was still glaring at the seemingly endless list of chores when he heard a shout from the yard. Poking his head out the door, he saw Jon and Ernie running for the house. Russ started running too before he even got a good look at what they were racing toward, or who.

"Phyl!" Russ shouted as soon as he saw her on the ground.

She had a gash on her forehead that was bleeding heavily and dripping down over one eye. Her face was scrunched up with pain as she held her right wrist gingerly to her chest.

"What happened?" Russ demanded of the others as he dropped down next to her.

"I don't know," Ernie answered anxiously. "She was just climbing the stairs to go inside and she fell, I think."

"Shit. Jon, go inside and get a towel," Russ ordered harshly.

There was a lot of blood.

"Say something, Phyl. Is anything else hurt?"

"Nope," she gritted out through her teeth. "Don't think so."

Her voice was threadier than Russ liked, and her deeply tanned skin looked a little gray.

"You're gonna be okay, Phyl. We're gonna take care of you."

"Everybody stop fussing. I just got a little bump on the head and hurt my wrist. I'm not dyin'," she grumbled.

When she moved to get up, Russ put a hand on her shoulder and smiled in relief. "Don't you dare. Just sit still for a second, stubborn woman."

Jon returned and handed over two towels. Russ used the first to mop up some of the blood so he could get a look at the wound on her head. It wasn't big, despite all the blood—a small, rapidly swelling gash through her eyebrow—but it meant she'd hit her head pretty hard on something, and Russ's stomach twisted.

"Can you move your wrist?" he asked.

Phyl winced and shook her head.

"Okay," he said, placing the second towel Jon had dampened with cold water to her forehead. "Jon, will you go back and grab us a bag of ice and meet us at the truck. It'll be faster if I just drive her to Lake Granbury myself instead of waiting on an ambulance."

Ernie stepped forward, and the two of them gently helped Phyl to her feet. She didn't seem all that steady, so Russ picked her up and carried her to the truck.

"If I'd known I could get carried around by a handsome man like a princess, I'd have fallen down the stairs years ago," Phyl teased weakly.

"Stop jawin' and save your strength for the ride," he said as he strapped her in.

Jon returned with a bag of ice wrapped in another towel, and Russ gently placed it over Phyl's wrist in her lap. Turning to the others, he said, "You guys got everything covered here? Tish is supposed to be here soon."

"Go," Ernie ordered, shooing him toward the driver's side. "We know what we're doing, and so does the doc. We'll check the board. Don't worry."

Russ's hands shook, and he gripped the steering wheel harder as he pulled out onto the main road. He'd tried to drive as carefully as possible, but the bumping and jostling had left Phyl looking grayer than ever, though she didn't make a peep.

"Let me know if you need to puke, and I'll pull over," he said.

She threw him a scathing look. "Don't get cheeky. I can still whoop your ass left-handed."

Russ's answering grin died when she hissed in pain at another bump in the road.

At the ER, they took her back right away, probably because of her age and the blow to her head, and Russ was left to worry in the waiting room. The smells, the sounds, the people bustling here and there were all too familiar. Memories of the hours he'd spent holding Phyl's hand in waiting rooms when Sean had gotten sick—hours sitting next to the once strong man's bedside, watching him waste away—came flooding back, and Russ felt ill. For the life of him, no amount of talking to himself would let his heartbeat slow or the sick knot in his belly loosen.

He tried Jordan's cell phone three times before he gave up. He texted Jon and Ernie to let them know he and Phyl had made it, and he'd call them later when he knew something. Then he was left to twiddle his thumbs and pace until a woman in a dark ponytail and white lab coat approached him.

"Are you Russ?"

"Yeah. That's me," he replied, hurrying over to her.

"I'm Dr. Woolsey. Phyllis asked me to come out. So far, we know she has a broken wrist, and we think only a mild concussion. She's resting a little more comfortably, now that we gave her something for the pain, but we're going to take her back for an MRI in just a little bit. She's awake and engaged, which is a good sign, but because she felt dizzy and faint right before her fall, I'm a bit concerned, so we're running some other tests as well."

"She what?"

Dr. Woolsey's thin sculpted eyebrows lifted. "She didn't tell you that," she guessed with a small smile.

Russ growled. "No, she did not."

"Has she complained of any tiredness, weakness, or dizziness at all recently?"

"She's been tired a bit, but running a ranch will do that to you."

The doctor nodded. "I have a call in to her regular GP. Once I talk to him and get some of her tests back, I'm sure we'll know more. We're just waiting on the machine to free up right now, and after her scan is done, I'll send someone to take you back to her, okay?"

After blowing out a breath, Russ thanked her, and she gave him a sympathetic smile. "She's in good hands. It may just be that she got a little dehydrated or overheated and tried to do too much, but with a head injury at her age, we just want to make sure."

If the doctor's intent was to reassure him, she'd failed miserably. What else had Phyl neglected to tell him concerning her health? He'd been so caught up in his own bullshit, he hadn't been paying attention. He'd promised Sean to take care of her, and he'd been doing a piss-poor job of it lately.

Agitated, frustrated, and worried, Russ pulled his cell out again and texted Jordan.

Where are you?

When he still received no reply, he growled and scrolled through to the last text Izzy had sent and tapped to call him.

"Hey, Russ!"

"You busy?"

"Not really. I just got off shift. What's up?"

Russ started to relate what had happened, but Izzy cut him off only a few words in. "What hospital?"

"Lake Granbury."

"I'll be there as soon as I can."

Russ slumped into one of the waiting room chairs and sighed. "Thanks, Izzy."

"Be there soon, babe," Izzy replied before hanging up.

Just knowing someone was coming and he didn't have to do this alone eased some of the ache in his chest. Sean's passing had been too soon for the echoes to fade, and all that remembered fear and dread was making him queasy.

He called Ernie to let everyone back at the ranch know what the doctor had said. Apparently Phyl hadn't confided any health concerns to anyone there either, which made him feel a little less guilty. By the time Izzy walked into the waiting room, a nurse was ready to take him back to see Phyl, and Izzy took his hand and they followed the nurse back. Russ gave him a smile and squeezed his hand in gratitude.

Phyl looked pale and ten years older lying in the hospital bed. They'd given her an IV. Her wrist had been put in a temporary brace, and they'd bandaged her forehead.

"Look that bad, do I?" she slurred with a goofy smile.

"Guess they gave you the good drugs, huh?" Russ teased, trying to school his expression into something a little less pained.

"It's sweet of you to stop by, Izzy. Thank you, hon," she said, turning her head and smiling at him.

"Anything for you, Phyl. How are they treating you?" Izzy asked, taking her good hand and giving it a gentle squeeze.

"I've been poked and prodded every which way, but I guess I can't complain."

"Has your doctor been back in yet?"

"No, not yet."

"Okay, good. I'd like to hear what she has to say."

When Dr. Woolsey returned, Izzy introduced himself, and she smiled.

"It's a pleasure. Well, I won't keep you in suspense. We can go over the specifics in a bit, if you like, but what we think is going on here is that you're on too high a dosage with your blood pressure medication, Phyllis. I've spoken to your doctor, and he'll get a copy of the bloodwork we've done. The MRI showed you do indeed have a mild concussion, but with a few days' rest, you should be fine. We'll give you a prescription for painkillers, and obviously, you're going to have to take it easy. Dr. Trent, our orthopedist, will be here in a little while to do your cast, and you'll be able to go home after that. So, until then, try to get some rest."

The flood of relief made Russ's knees weak as he smiled at Phyl and took her good hand. Dr. Woolsey and Izzy stepped to the side to talk in medical-ese, but Russ ignored them. He knew what he needed to, and he trusted Izzy to tell him anything important later. It wasn't long before Phyl closed her eyes and dropped off to sleep—as if she had just been waiting for permission to do it—and Russ, Izzy, and Dr. Woolsey crept out of the room.

After saying goodbye to the doctor, Izzy grabbed Russ's wrist and led him down a series of hallways until he pulled him into an empty room.

"You okay?" he asked as soon as the door closed behind them. His gorgeous amber eyes were filled with concern, and Russ blew out a breath and slumped against the wall.

"Yeah. Just flashbacks getting the better of me, I guess. I really don't like hospitals. No offense."

Izzy's full lips curved, and he nodded. "None taken. You're thinking about Sean, right? I know that had to have been hard. I'm sorry I wasn't here for you."

"It's okay. You called when you found out. It helped. Thanks for coming today."

"Of course. Anytime. You know that."

Izzy dragged his fingers through Russ's hair before resting his palm on the side of Russ's neck and squeezing. "I really missed you, Russ."

He held Russ's gaze as he leaned in close, and Russ was just needy and confused enough not to stop him. Izzy's lips were as warm, lush, and soft as Russ remembered. The familiarity was comforting. He'd kissed those lips thousands of times before, felt the strength in that body wrapped around him. Still shaky from an emotional day, he longed to lose himself in that comforting familiarity, but guilt needled him, and he put a hand to Izzy's chest and pushed.

"I can't," he sighed.

"The blond? Jerry? Jory?"

"Jordan," Russ corrected.

"Is it serious?" Izzy asked, absently caressing Russ's jaw and throat.

Russ's entire body was starting to tingle, so he wrapped his hand around Izzy's to stop him and cleared his throat. "Yes… and no. It's complicated."

Izzy smiled and took a step back. "It doesn't have to be complicated, you know."

With a grimace, Izzy straightened and adjusted himself. After studying Russ for a second, he cleared his throat and smiled sheepishly. "I know I can't just come blazing back into town and expect you to upend your life for me. You know I'm not that guy. But if things aren't serious with this kid—"

"He's only a couple of years younger than you are," Russ pointed out with a wry smile.

Izzy shrugged. "Still, if they aren't serious, or they're *complicated*, all I'm saying is I'd like to toss my hat in the ring. But if you tell me it's serious, I'll back off."

Russ would have been lying if he said he wasn't tempted. When things had been good with Izzy, they'd been *really* good. But he wasn't as tempted as he might have been only a few weeks before, even knowing what he had with Jordan wouldn't last, and that surprised him. Knowing something and feeling it were two different things, he supposed, even if he was pissed at the bastard for not responding to his calls. This was too much for him to deal with at the moment, though. Especially on top of worrying about Phyl.

With another sigh, he pushed himself off the wall and headed for the door. "Come on. We need to go someplace a little more public before I get myself in real trouble here. I want to be there when Phyl wakes up, and I've already got something I'm going to need to confess and grovel over."

Izzy's chuckle followed him out the door.

CHAPTER TWENTY-FOUR

IZZY STAYED with him until Phyl was released. They parted with a hug in the parking lot, and Izzy gave him a pointed look before sauntering off to find his truck.

Back at the ranch, Jon and Ernie had stayed late to see Phyl for themselves. They helped Russ put Phyl to bed before heading out, leaving him to sit by himself in the living room and wait for Jordan to return, if he planned to return. The tension and distancing Russ had felt from him over the last week could have been Jordan's way of trying to tell him something. But Jordan had promised not to play stupid games. He'd promised to speak up if he had something to say.

Of course, so had Russ.

Except Russ didn't know what he wanted to say. He was already in deeper with Jordan than he should have been. Despite all his bluster to the contrary, he wasn't going to be just fine when Jordan left. Jordan had a place at the ranch now, and that space would be empty when he was gone, like the hole in the air where Sean used to be.

But Jordan hadn't been there when Russ needed him, and Izzy had. Jordan wouldn't be there in the future, he reminded himself, but Izzy would.

Growling in frustration, Russ threw open the refrigerator and grabbed a beer. His head had been going around in circles all week with no real clarity on the horizon. After collapsing on the couch, Russ took a swig from his bottle and glared out the windows at the fading sunset.

Why did life have to get so complicated all the time? And where the hell was Jordan?

Full dark had fallen before Russ heard tires on gravel and saw the flash of headlights outside. By that point, he'd had a few beers and plenty of time to build up a full head of steam over Jordan's disappearance. Right or not, the stresses of the day, the tension of the last week, worry over everything that wasn't ready for the influx tomorrow, burgeoning worry over Jordan, and a little guilt thrown in for good measure, had him spoiling for a fight.

"Where the hell have you been?" he growled as soon as Jordan walked into the room, after studying every inch of him and finding no sign of injury or distress.

Jordan blinked at his tone and frowned. "I told Phyllis I had a few errands to run in Dallas… and hello to you too."

"So why didn't you answer your phone when I called?"

He wouldn't meet Russ's gaze, but he folded his arms across his chest and said defensively, "I forgot to plug it in last night, so it died partway through the day, and I didn't notice. I didn't see the notifications until late, after I found a charger, and the only message you left was to tell me to call you. I was almost back here, so I figured I'd see you when I got home. What's the big deal?"

"It never occurred to you that it might be important?"

Jordan rolled his eyes. "I needed to get away for a few hours. Sue me."

He turned to climb the stairs, but Russ chased after him and blocked his way. "I'm not done talkin' to you," he said, wagging a finger in Jordan's face.

"You're drunk and pissed off, so I think maybe I'm done talking to you."

Russ narrowed his eyes and clenched his jaw, but he didn't move out of the way, and Jordan glared right back at him. "You're acting like I committed some crime when I just decided to take a day off for once. Jesus. You know, you've been disappearing in the middle of the day all week too, and nobody's snarling at you for it," he huffed.

"I ride out for an hour, tops, not all damned day. I'm still on the ranch, and I'm giving the horses exercise while I'm at it. That's still working."

Jordan threw his arms out to the sides. "Well, I'm sorry, okay? Maybe I am just as spoiled and useless as you used to think, huh? You know, not everyone can be a saint like your ex. Some of us are just human," he shouted.

"Keep your voice down," Russ hissed. "Phyl needs her rest. She got hurt today while you were out running your *errands*."

That drew Jordan up short, and he gaped. "What?"

"She fell down the stairs, and I had to take her to the hospital."

"Oh God. Is she okay?"

A little mollified at Jordan's reaction, Russ took a step back and said, "Broken wrist. Bump on the head. Doc says she'll be fine, though she'll be in a world of hurt for the next few days."

"I'm sorry, Russ. I didn't know," Jordan murmured, his face etched with regret.

"You would've known if you'd bothered to call me back. You've got responsibilities here now, you know, people who depend on you."

Jordan hung his head. "Yeah, I forgot that. I'm sorry. It won't happen again."

He looked miserable enough that, of all the emotions swirling inside Russ, guilt started to take the lead. It niggled at him, making him feel his justifiable anger wasn't quite as justified as it should be. He hadn't exactly been a saint that day either. He had some apologizing of his own to do, and he'd best get it out of the way or it'd keep him up all night.

He cleared his throat and said, "When I couldn't get hold of you, I called Izzy, and he stayed with me at the hospital until they let Phyl go."

Russ was prepared for suspicion, jealousy, or maybe a little hurt. He was even prepared for anger or disbelief. But Jordan's face went completely blank.

"Oh," Jordan said tonelessly.

"He was a big help with talking to the doctor and stuff. He was a good friend."

"Okay."

Russ worked his jaw for a second, took a deep breath, and plowed on. "Things got a bit emotional for me. After everything that happened with Sean, hospitals are not one of my favorite places. I was worried about Phyl and dealing with old ghosts, and he was kind, just like the old days, and I got a little carried away when I shouldn't have, and, uh… we kissed."

"Oh."

Russ frowned. "Oh? That's all you got to say? You're not mad?"

Jordan shrugged.

"You don't even seem surprised." Russ had no right to be, but he was kind of offended by that.

"I'm not," Jordan replied, his tone still dull and a little cold. "I saw how you looked at him."

"Jordan—"

Jordan held up a hand. "Would you excuse me for a second, please?"

Without another word, Jordan moved past him and up the stairs. Russ watched in disbelief until he heard a door quietly close upstairs.

"What the hell?"

His temper spiking again, he raced up the stairs after him. The only closed door he found was the one to the bathroom. He charged over to it and knocked. "Jordan?"

He wanted to pound on the wood, but Phyl was sleeping just below them.

"Jordan, open the door."

"No."

Russ gritted his teeth. "Open this goddamned door and talk to me," he hissed. "Don't pull this immature bullshit with me and hide behind a door. If you're pissed, come out here and tell me to my face. Punch me. Do something!"

The sound of the toilet flushing shut him up for a few seconds. Water splashed in the sink a moment before Jordan yanked open the door, still patting his face with a towel.

His blue eyes flashed over sallow-looking cheeks. "You know what?" he said, tossing the towel angrily aside. "You're right. I am immature. I'm unreliable and a drama queen. I'm a fucking mess, actually. I'm sure this is only making your decision that much easier."

Rearing back in confusion, Russ asked, "What decision?"

Jordan rolled his eyes. "Oh come *on*. I get it. I do. I was okay in the short-term, but long-term would be a joke, right? It's the story of my life, really. I'm good, just never good enough. Not when you've got Dr. Perfect waiting for you, and you can't tell me he's not. I've seen you looking at your phone all week, and I bet he came running the second you called."

Russ winced. "Look. I'm sorry I kissed him. I really am. It was a mistake. But it was just one kiss. I put a stop to it and told him I was in a relationship. I'm telling you now because I don't want to lie to you. I promised you that at the start, and I meant it." He blew out a breath and grimaced. "Yes, he's texted me a couple of times this week, but he was just asking if we could get together to catch up. That's all. I wasn't going to meet him without talking it out with you first. You gotta know that." He pursed his lips and studied Jordan's face, looking for answers. "I don't know where you're getting all this other stuff from, so you're going to have to help me here, okay? As far as I knew, the words 'long-term' were never brought up between us before... at least this is the first I'm hearing it. If that's changed, you haven't told me. You can be mad at me for the kiss and for being a bit of a jerk this past week. I deserve it. But you can't be mad at me for something we haven't even discussed."

The fire in Jordan's eyes went out, leaving only defeat behind as he slumped against the doorjamb. "What does it matter now?" he murmured dejectedly.

"It matters to me," Russ prodded. He'd rather have Jordan spitting mad at him than this. This was breaking his heart. "You gotta let me in on what's going on in that head of yours or I can't help. Tell me to get my head out of my ass. Say *something*."

After a quick breath, Jordan lifted pain-filled eyes to Russ and said, "So what? You want me to throw my heart out there, spill my guts so you can tell me you're still in love with your perfect ex and you're going to give it another try with him? Is that really what you want?" Without giving Russ time to answer, Jordan pushed off the wall and stepped close. "Okay. Fine. Have it your way."

Jordan shoved past him and continued to the stairs. "Come on. I'll show you."

Confused and a little overwhelmed, Russ followed Jordan down the stairs and out the front door.

Jesus, what a day... hell, what a week, for that matter.

Jordan swept a dramatic arm toward the parking area, and in the spotlight from the barn, Russ saw a shabby little blue sedan parked where Jordan's convertible usually sat.

"Whose is that?"

"It's mine. That's what I was doing in Dallas. I traded in the convertible for a crappy little car I can afford, and I pawned everything else I had that was worth anything." Jordan tucked his hands into his pockets and gazed off into the darkness, not looking at Russ. "I talked to Phyl a week ago about staying on the ranch on a more permanent basis, and I was digging up the courage to talk to you about it when Dr. Perfect rolled up." With a bitter laugh, Jordan shot a look at him over his shoulder. "Clearly someone out there wanted to remind me of just how little I actually had to offer you before I humiliated myself. I suppose I should thank them." When Russ just blinked at him, speechless, Jordan grimaced and wrapped his arms around himself. "Yeah, so my plan's kind of fucked, and I'm not sure what the hell I'm going to do now, but I figured I couldn't put it off any longer. I needed to start adulting at some point, even if it isn't going to be what I'd hoped."

Russ moved closer to him, but Jordan's posture didn't exactly seem welcoming, so he stopped before touching him. "What were you going to offer?"

"Russ—"

"Tell me," he whispered gently.

Jordan turned to face him, his expression wounded. "Me. Okay? I was going to offer me… which seems really stupid and pathetic now. I mean seriously, look at me. I'm a mess." Throwing his arms wide, he paced the length of the deck as he continued, "I'm unemployed and virtually homeless. Only one person in my family is actually speaking to me. I'm well-educated, but I have no real-world skills to speak of, because I've never really had to take care of myself before." He stopped dead a few feet away and spun around. "I'm wearing your goddamned clothes, for Christ's sake!"

"I think you look pretty good in my clothes," Russ murmured.

"Don't. Please don't," Jordan whispered, shrinking in on himself. "I've made it this far without crying. I'm not sure I'm going to make it much further."

"Come here," Russ ordered gruffly, closing the distance between them.

Jordan wouldn't look at him. He stood stiffly when Russ pulled him close, but Russ held on.

"Look at me," Russ murmured, but Jordan shook his head and tried to pull away. "Please?"

After another long pause, Jordan blew out a breath and shrugged out of Russ's embrace. He turned away from Russ, braced his palms on the railing, and spoke out into the night. "I'm not stupid. I know you care about me. I know you don't want to hurt me. But we've barely been together a month at this point. You loved him way before you ever met me. I get that. He's got everything going for him, and I don't. Despite my best efforts to hide from reality, being here these last few weeks has taught me some things about myself. I've got a long way to go, obviously, but I'd like to think I've grown up a little. I'd like to think I'm less selfish and self-involved than I used to be." He cleared his throat and straightened his shoulders. "The new, improved adult me wants to be mature about this. I want you to be happy—apparently even more than I want myself to be happy, which is weird. But you deserve it. I know you never really needed me as much as I needed you, so I'm trying to do the right thing here." Glancing over his shoulder, he gave Russ a wry smile. "This is new for me, and I don't know how long it'll last, so you better quit dragging this out and take advantage of it before I totally go drama queen on your ass."

Russ closed the distance between them one more time and wrapped a hand around the back of Jordan's neck. Jordan shivered and barked out a laugh that sounded painful. "I'm serious about the not being sure how long I'm going to be able to stay mature about this. Stick around much longer and you'll get to see just how much of an immature diva I can be."

"I don't mind. But I'm feeling a little slow, and I need some clarification, okay?" Russ said carefully.

"Okay."

"If I'm understanding you correctly, you're saying you want to stay here on the ranch with me long-term, but you're willing to sacrifice that because you think I'll be happier with Izzy. Is that about right?"

"Yes."

"Because you love me?"

Jordan swallowed visibly and whispered, "Yes."

"But somehow you think you don't have anything to offer me?"

"He loves you too. I could tell by the way he looked at you… and you know it. You've been thinking about it ever since he got back. I'm not blind." Jordan straightened his shoulders, and this time he looked Russ straight in the eye. "I'm just trying to be the bigger man here and tell you that I understand. I get it." With a shrug, Jordan's lips curved in the mockery of a smile. "Like I said before, it's always been like this for me. I'm good, just never quite good enough. Bad timing. Fate. Poor character. Who knows? I'm getting there, though, one small step at a time. Improvements have been made… I think."

"You're too hard on yourself."

"Says the man who thought I was a spoiled brat from day one."

Russ rolled his eyes. "I can admit to being wrong every once in a while. In fact, I seem to remember admitting to it several times where you're concerned." He pulled Jordan close, caging him against the railing. "But," he whispered against Jordan's lips, "I learn from my mistakes."

He sealed their lips together despite Jordan's gasp and shiver, and he didn't let up until Jordan melted against him. Drawing away only enough for both of them to catch their breath, he pressed his forehead to Jordan's and simply held him as a cool breeze ghosted across the yard and crickets sang their nightly serenade to the moon.

"You're not making this easier," Jordan teased breathlessly.

"I'm not trying to."

"What about Dr. Perfect?"

With a sigh, Russ pulled back enough to look Jordan in the eye. Brushing the soft blond waves off Jordan's forehead, he said, "You can't make up my mind for me, darlin'. You know that, right? If this thing between us is going to last, you're gonna have to stop jumpin' to conclusions every time I go quiet for a few days, okay? I warned you I'm not always the best with words."

"And is it... going to last?"

"I want it to."

"Really?"

Russ chuckled. "Don't look so surprised. I would have thought the couple of weeks before this mess might've given you a clue that I liked being with you, just a little bit. Didn't I say so? Apparently, I've been fallin' down on the job."

Jordan rolled his eyes and gave Russ a little shove. "It isn't that. Believe me, I have no complaints there. You're the best boyfriend a guy could ask for. I just... this is so new, and he's so fucking perfect."

"He ain't perfect. Nobody is perfect. I won't say he doesn't have his fine points, but you've got quite a few yourself."

"But what you had with him—"

"Is over," Russ clarified.

"Is it?"

"Yes. You're right. I was messed-up for a bit, and I'm sorry if I hurt you by not talking to you about it, but I honestly didn't know what to say. I thought I'd put all that behind me."

He read concern and curiosity in Jordan's face, but no understanding. With a sigh, he took Jordan's hand and led him to the two rockers. After they both sat, he took Jordan's hand again and said, "I was head over heels for him when Izzy came to tell me that he wanted to go to Africa. I made the choice not to try to stop him for a lot of reasons, but that didn't make letting him go any easier. Phyl was here; she could tell you. I was a mess for a long time and hiding it from him. But I did work through it eventually... or at least I thought I did."

"But then he came back," Jordan prodded.

"Yes, and the tangled mess was there again, not so sorted as I'd believed, I guess. The truth is, what tied me up in knots was that neither one of us had changed or done anything wrong. He was still the guy I loved. He just wanted something very badly that I couldn't be a part of, not and follow my own dreams. He hadn't done anything that I could get mad over. He wasn't... *isn't* a bad person, and neither am I. I hurt, but I had no outlet for it. I *was* mad, but I had no right to be."

"But he's back to stay now, isn't he? And obviously he's hoping to pick up where you left off."

"Maybe, but I'm already with someone else."

Jordan frowned at him. "If it were that cut and dried, his coming back wouldn't have thrown you for a loop."

"I didn't know where we stood. Now I do."

"That simple?"

Russ shrugged and smiled. "I'm a simple man."

With a snort, Jordan shook his head. "Bullshit."

Russ grinned and stood up. Kneeling between Jordan's thighs with his hands resting on Jordan's knees, he said, "Then how about, I'm a man of my word. If you want to make a go of this…. If you want to stay here with me and Phyl and do whatever it is you agreed to with her, I'm all in. No more questioning or worryin'—"

"Or kissing ex-boyfriends?"

"None of that either."

"That simple?"

"Yup."

"Why?"

Russ's eyebrows drew down. "What do mean, why?"

"Why me when you could have Dr. Perfect?"

With a sigh, Russ shook his head. "I already told you he ain't perfect. I'm not gonna sit around and list his faults, 'cause that ain't me, but I've already got a guy. He's sittin' right here in front of me, and I love him."

"You do?" Jordan's eyebrows shot to his hairline, and the wary hope in his eyes nearly broke Russ's heart.

"Yeah, I do."

"I can't think why."

"Guess I'm gonna have to get better at tellin' ya, then, aren't I?"

Jordan hung his head and blew out a shaky breath. "I'm sorry, but yeah. Every once in a while, I'm going to need the words… even though I shouldn't with how good you are to me."

"There's no should or shouldn't. You need what you need. As long as you tell me what that is and don't get too mad when I forget sometimes, we're good. You put up with my cranky ass, don't you? I should have talked to you. I made a promise to be all in with you, and then the first time something rattled my cage, I stepped back. You were braver than me, coming out with all that even though you were afraid of losing me. I didn't want to hold you back, though, if you wanted bigger and better things."

"I as much as told you I didn't intend to stay. I could hardly blame you if you wanted to be with someone who did."

"What changed your mind?"

"You, Phyl, this place. I had certain ideas ingrained in me about what a life was supposed to look like, and even though I thought I'd left all that behind, I hadn't. I've never been happier than I've been here. I love horses. I love how helping them and the other animals makes me feel. I love being here with everyone. I love you."

"I love you too."

Jordan gave him a watery smile and a weak chuckle. They made goo-goo eyes at each other for a while before Jordan bit his lip and said, "Russ?"

"Yeah?"

"Can we go fuck now? I'm a needy bitch. I know. But I want the words and all the rest of it too, particularly the hot sex."

With an exaggerated sigh, Russ climbed to his feet and offered Jordan a hand up. "I suppose I can manage that, if you twist my arm."

Jordan gave him a playful shove. "I'll twist more than that if you don't get your cranky ass upstairs."

What followed was the quietest pushing, groping, heavy-petting wrestling match in the history of time as they tried to beat each other up the stairs to Russ's bedroom without waking Phyl.

CHAPTER TWENTY-FIVE

JORDAN STRETCHED out in Russ's bed like a cat, luxuriating in the aches and pains from a thorough night of fucking. Russ had already slipped out of bed before dawn, but he'd planted a kiss on Jordan's forehead and murmured an "I love you" before he went, so Jordan didn't mind so much.

A beep sounded from his phone, and he snagged it off the nightstand.

At airport. Headed to Key West with Britney. Will cont mission Pride when I get back. Mom's melting. She misses you. Hugs.

Jordan's chest tightened, and he set the phone aside. Gemma had decided to become his champion with the family since her visit. What that would accomplish exactly, he wasn't sure, but he was grateful, if only because it meant she cared that much for him. The pain had finally faded a bit from those first weeks, but it was still there when he chose to prod it, like a sore tooth.

With a groan, he rolled to an upright position and swung his feet over the side of the bed. It was Saturday, Phyl was laid up, and someone had to get the place ready for the weekenders. He couldn't wallow in the past all day. Thank God, Phyl hadn't mentioned any scout troop or other groups coming in, because he really didn't think he could handle it without her. Not yet anyway.

Despite the text and the busy day looming ahead, he had a spring in his step as he went to take a shower. It would take a lot more to get him down that day.

He loves me.

Russ would have to say it a few hundred more times before it sank in, but every time the thought ran through Jordan's head it put a smile on his face and a shivery feeling in his stomach.

Fuck you, Dr. Perfect. He's mine.

Jordan would kick the guy's ass for putting the moves on his man if Izzy didn't outweigh him by a good fifty pounds of solid muscle. He could probably crumple Jordan like a soda can, so a throw-down was not going to be in the cards. Jordan wasn't that stupid.

Still, he wanted to.

After peeking in on a still-sleeping Phyl and see-ing someone had already left water, some fruit, and a prescription bottle on her nightstand, he wandered to the kitchen for a cup of coffee. Russ had already started the pot, of course, and Jordan sighed into his first cup.

"Hey," Russ said from the doorway.

"Hey," Jordan replied with a giddy smile.

"I've just come in to check on Phyl again, see if she needs anything else."

"I just checked on her. She's still asleep."

"Okay. I suppose you and me are gonna have to figure out something for breakfast."

"I got mine," Jordan responded, lifting his coffee cup, and Russ frowned.

Jordan rolled his eyes, sauntered over to Russ, and gave him a peck on the lips to ease that frown. "Okay. Okay. I know. You'll pitch a fit if I don't eat enough for a small army. After last night, I will admit to being a little hungry."

Russ's lips quirked, and he pulled Jordan close and kissed him again. "If that's what it takes, I suppose I can rustle up a repeat any time you need it."

Jordan shivered and pressed himself closer for a second before pushing away with a groan. "It's Saturday," he reminded them both. "You go check out Phyl's calendar to see what's on for today while I grab my tablet and watch some YouTube videos on how to make breakfast that won't kill either of us or burn the house down."

With a grin, Russ swatted him on the ass and headed for Phyl's office. "Thank God," Russ threw over his shoulder as he sauntered away. "I was afraid you were gonna make me cook breakfast."

"God no. You're the one who says he hates hospitals," Jordan teased back.

At the stove, after replaying a few short videos three or four times, Jordan thought he might just be able to handle some scrambled eggs, bacon, and toast. He'd watched Phyl enough times, and it didn't look that complicated. He might have burned a few things around the edges, but he blamed that on Russ, who kept coming up behind him and nibbling on his neck, distracting him.

He had to give it to Russ, though, the man choked down every last bit without complaint. And he didn't even give Jordan shit for not eating the burned parts of his own food.

"Should we save some for Phyl?"

"Naw. We'll have volunteers here most of the day, and I think Jon and Ernie plan to come in on their day off to check on her. If I know their wives, we'll be knee-deep in casseroles before noon."

Russ's grin fell away as his phone buzzed, and Jordan's stomach lurched. "Is it him?" Jordan asked.

"Yeah," Russ sighed. "He texted me earlier this morning too."

Forcing himself not to crane his neck so he could see the screen, Jordan said, "What does he want? Or is that a stupid question?"

Russ gave him a soft smile and took his hand. "He wants us to catch up over dinner, just the two of us."

"And what did you say?"

"Not much yet. I wanted to talk to you first."

"'Cause that's what boyfriends do?"

Russ's smile widened. "Yes. That's what they do." With a sigh, Russ held Jordan's gaze. "I will need to see him face-to-face at some point. I don't feel right sayin' what I have to say over the phone. Are you okay with that?"

No.

"Sure."

Russ's eyebrows lifted, and he chuckled. "Sure?"

Rolling his eyes, Jordan got up from the table and carried his dishes to the sink. After rinsing them off and setting them in the dishwasher, he turned around and leaned back against the counter. "This adulting shit is hard. You know that, right?"

Russ brought his dishes over, set them on the counter, and took Jordan's hands. "I know."

"I really don't want to be fair and let you see that man alone, but I know I shouldn't stop you from what you feel is right either."

"You trust me?"

"Yes… mostly."

"I gave you my word, and I'm a man of my word, right?"

"Yes," Jordan reluctantly agreed.

"It's you and me now, not me and him. I just want to tell him that to his face, the right way. Me and him are done. I promise. We were done almost three years ago, when he left to follow his dreams…. You see, I'm a selfish man, deep down. I want the man I love to include me in those dreams. I want to be one of those dreams, not the one standing in the way of them."

"Okay." Jordan nodded and blew out a breath. "You are, you know… one of my dreams. I didn't have any when I got here. I'd been so busy before, trying and failing to be someone I wasn't, that I hadn't taken any time to make dreams. But I have now. I love this ranch. I love the horses and the work we do. I love Phyl. I love you. This is what I want."

Russ's deep brown eyes got all soft and shiny as he pulled Jordan in closer. "Then we're family now—you, me, Phyl, Jon and Ernie, the ranch, and all the animals we save. This is a family. If you tell me that's enough for you, you'll make me the happiest man in Texas."

"It is."

"And if it ain't at some point, you'll tell me, right?"

"Yes. But I don't think I'll ever dream of anything that doesn't include you beside me."

"That's good enough for me."

Jordan kissed him, long and sweet. He clung to Russ's hard, wiry shoulders, wanting to wrap the man around him like a blanket and just wallow in him, but a throat clearing from the doorway and a set of tires on the gravel drive ended the moment.

"Sorry to interrupt," Phyl said, and they both rushed to help her to the table while Russ scolded her for being out of bed. She shooed him away. "I'll go back soon. I just heard doves cooing in my kitchen and figured I needed to check on things."

Jordan flushed and Russ rolled his eyes. "Stubborn woman."

She grinned as car doors slammed outside. "I'm gonna guess that's the cavalry."

Jon and Ernie came through the door, both carrying aluminum-foil-covered casserole dishes, and Russ threw Jordan a grin.

Watching the three men fuss over Phyl and her grumble and grouse at them while trying to hide her smile, Jordan couldn't help but go a little doe-eyed.

"I can hear your gears turning from all the way over there," Russ murmured as he set the casseroles on the counter and dished up a couple of plates for the guys and Phyl.

Jordan bit his lip and cast a quick sideways glance at Russ as he moved to help. "Russ, you know I'm still a mess, right? I mean, I'm working on it. I'm happy… ecstatic really, that you and Phyl want me as part of your family, but I'm still kind of a mess."

"We all are sometimes. Nobody's perfect. The B STAR's here to help, if we're willing to put the work in." He grabbed the plates and threw a wink over his shoulder. "Besides, I told you I'd be the happiest man in Texas to call you my mess."

Not quite sure whether he liked that, Jordan stood frozen at the stove frowning until Russ threw him another grin and said, "Come on, slowpoke. We got work to do."

In Victorian London, during a prolonged and pernicious fog, fantasy and reality are about to collide—at least in one man's troubled mind.

A childhood fever left Arthur Middleton, Viscount Campden, seeing and hearing things no one else does, afraid of the world outside, and unable to function as a true peer of the realm. To protect him from himself—and to protect others from him—he spends his days heavily medicated and locked in his rooms, and his nights in darkness and solitude, tormented by visions, until a stranger appears.

This apparition is different. Fox says he's a thief and not an entirely good sort of man, yet he returns night after night to ease Arthur's loneliness without asking for anything in return. Fox might be the key that sets Arthur free, or he might deliver the final blow to Arthur's tenuous grasp on sanity. Either way, real or imaginary, Arthur needs him too much to care.

Fox is only one of the many secrets and specters haunting Campden House, and Arthur will have to face them all in order to live the life of his dreams.

www.dreamspinnerpress.com

CHAPTER ONE

A LOUD clatter and frightened shout from beyond my door jolted me out of a fitful doze and left my heart hammering in my chest. Nestled in my warm cocoon of blankets on the floor, frozen with my heart still in my throat, I blindly searched the darkness until my mind at last supplied a name for that voice. It was only Tom, the footman my uncle had hired last year to replace John.... At least I was fairly certain the previous footman had been John, although that could have been Henry. I couldn't quite remember, because neither John nor Henry had lasted long. Tom had made it almost an entire year thus far. He must've been made of sterner stuff than the others... or my uncle had offered him a higher wage.

Fully awake, I frowned into the darkness around me and pulled my blankets higher atop my shoulders.

What is Tom doing in the upstairs hall at this time of night?

I strained to hear more but was rewarded with only the creaks and pops of the house and the rattle of shutters from an errant breeze outside my window. Perhaps I had imagined it, after all.

Still curious but no longer alarmed, I slipped from the comfortable nest of blankets I'd made in front of the hearth and crept to my door. I had nothing better to do. My fire had died too low to read by, but perhaps I might have a bit of a diversion yet.

Placing my ear to the heavy wood, I caught the sound of hushed whispers some distance away, but I couldn't quite make out the words. Relieved I wouldn't be subjected to another round of the pitiful moans and tortured wailings that often plagued me at night, I strained against the door until I felt sure my cheek would bear the impression of its carved surface. The voices were familiar and comforting, even if the words were unclear.

Then the whispers stopped abruptly, and the silence was broken by the quiet rattling of doors being opened and shut and the scuffle of hurried footsteps up and down the hall. I felt the vibrations through my cheek and hands as each door was opened and closed, and I huffed in frustration at not knowing what was going on. The light from a lamp grew through the gap beneath my door, only to fade away again shortly after. Then the sounds and vibrations ceased entirely, and all was still and dark again.

I waited, but when nothing else happened, I sighed and straightened. With only a token glare for the ever-present lock on my door, I shivered and shuffled back to my little nest. The novel I'd been reading before I fell asleep tumbled free as I tugged the blankets about me again, and I tucked it close to my chest and settled in for another long night. I was awake now, with no fire to read by and nothing but my thoughts to keep me company. That usually boded ill for my state of mind.

As the supposed master of the house, I could've kicked up a fuss and demanded to know what had occurred outside my door. I could've pulled the bell rope and forced Pendel, my butler, to return and explain his and Tom's presence abovestairs at this hour. But, as always, I hated to be a bother. If the disturbance had been of any real import, I trusted Pendel would have come to me on his own. A little mild irritation over my curiosity going unsatisfied wasn't worth all that. And besides, the chill January air had crept beneath my nightshirt and dressing gown after only that brief excursion outside the warmth of my nest—despite my nightcap, mittens, and wool stockings—and I was loathe to leave it again.

Running my fingers over the cloth binding of my novel, I turned from the dull orange glow of the dying coals in the stove and peered forlornly through the darkness toward the heavily curtained alcove hiding my window seat. Regardless of the cold, I might have been tempted to move my nest there if even a scrap of moonlight were to be had, but I knew I would find only a deeper darkness beyond the thick green velvet brocade. For months, everything outside the rippled glass of my windows had been draped in a fog so dense and unending, I feared—in my darker moments—that the world beyond might have disappeared entirely, save the odd laborer or tradesman who would suddenly appear on the grounds beneath my rooms as if conjured out of the mist.

The newspapers had commented almost daily on the pernicious fog that had shrouded all of London, so I knew it wasn't just our little corner of Kensington that suffered. But as the bleak months dragged on, the dense fog and cold were taking their toll on my spirits, and I ached for even a glimpse of sunlight or moonlight to cut through the unending gray beyond my prison.

Hissing in disgust, I turned away from the thick darkness behind me and returned my gaze to the coals in my hearth. I couldn't allow myself to think like that. This was not a prison but a haven to keep me safe and to keep others safe from me. I belonged here. I was well taken care of. This was my home.

I took a deep breath of frigid air and blew it out forcefully, counting to three on the inhale and another three on the exhale, as I'd been taught. I flexed my frozen fingers in my mittens to get the blood flowing, drew my shoulders back, and lifted my chin. I was a Middleton, heir to a long and illustrious line, and I could not allow myself to be beaten by melancholia or any other manifestation of my illness.

The voices in the hall had been real. I'd recognized the footman, and I would know Pendel's gruff whisper anywhere. I could still tell the difference between reality and those other sounds and voices that plagued me. Someday soon the sun would return, and I would shake off this new and unwelcome addition to my troubles, just as I did the rest. Someday I would be well and no longer need these rooms. I had to persist in that belief.

I held my rigid posture for only a few moments before I shivered and wrapped my arms more tightly around myself as a wave of hopelessness threatened to crash over me again. I was so weary of fighting. The melancholia, the visions, the voices, all of it was that much harder to overcome when the world seemed determined to keep me in the dark and dreary gray forever.

Agitated and unable to distract myself with my novel, I tossed the volume on the nearby chair, collected the blankets around me like a cloak, and moved to my pianoforte. I could play by feel in the darkness, after countless nights of practice, and music often soothed me when the forced confinement and solitude of my existence became too much to bear. If I played quietly, I would not disturb anyone's slumber. The servants' hall was too far away for them to hear me unless I truly made an effort.

I had just reached the bench and was fussing with my blankets so I could settle comfortably, when another sound reached my ears, this time from the stairwell leading up to my rooftop conservatory. My uncle had commissioned the conservatory for me so I might have the fresh air and sunshine Dr. Payne recommended without having to leave my house. I barely had to leave my rooms, in truth. No expense had been spared for my convenience. The finest of materials and skilled craftsmen had been hired to construct it, but the staircase just on the other side of the wall my pianoforte rested against still creaked whenever someone trod upon it.

Tom used a second door from the hall to access those stairs daily, stocking the coal stove up there so the more delicate of my plants wouldn't suffer too badly in the bitter cold. But he'd already seen to that duty before the rest of the house turned in for the night, and I hadn't heard a key rattle in the lock on the hall door. I couldn't imagine Pendel allowing him to have the key on his own, at any rate. Perhaps Pendel was the one using the stairs after whatever the disturbance in the hall had been.

I froze, straining for more, and heard two more quiet creaks as someone ascended the stairs. My heart racing despite the myriad explanations for the sound, I crept on slippered feet to the door that separated my rooms from the stairwell, drew the heavy insulating velvet drapes aside, and pressed my ear to the wood. A slight draft brushed my cheek from the gap between the door and its frame, as if the outer door at the top of the stairs had been opened, but no lamplight penetrated those spaces. I couldn't imagine any of the servants taking the stairs in the dark, particularly not Pendel, now that he was getting on in years.

Holding my breath, I carefully turned the knob and poked my head through the opening. I saw nothing as I squinted into the deeper darkness, and no more stairs creaked or latches rattled no matter how hard I listened. The air was still and cold, and I shivered in my dressing gown. But I'd already stirred myself, and, my curiosity piqued for the second time that night, I crept up the stairs and eased the outer door open.

An inky gray-black, barely lighter than the darkness behind me, stared back at me as I searched in vain for the source of the sounds. The glass walls and roof of the conservatory were of little help due to the thick fog outside. I gripped the doorframe and strained but saw and heard nothing. I was on the verge of dismissing the whole thing as another trick of my mind when the faint tinkle of something metal falling to the stone tiles and a muffled curse stopped me.

"Hello? Is someone there?" I asked breathlessly.

My words were met with silence, but a spot of darkness, deeper than the rest, detached itself from the far end of the conservatory and moved toward me. Instinctively I retreated.

"Hello? Who is it? Who are you?" I croaked.

The shadow said nothing, only continued to follow me as I retreated down the stairs and through the door to my rooms. I stopped in front of my hearth, still cloaked in my ridiculous mound of blankets, and waited with my heart beating frantically. Then my heart stopped altogether when I heard the rustle of the thick curtains being pushed aside and saw the faint outline of the shadow as it stepped into my rooms.

I had to swallow against a sudden dryness in my throat before I whispered, "Say something. Please."

The shadow finally halted its silent advance. This close, in the faint light of the coals, the dark shape resolved itself into a man, looming over me. I was about to repeat my somewhat shaky demand, when the shadow finally spoke.

"Don' cry out. I mean ye no 'arm."

His accent was strange to me. I couldn't place it, but that was hardly surprising, given the limited number of people I'd been allowed to interact with in my life. His speech lacked the elocution of a gentleman, but he spoke in a pleasant baritone I found quite soothing to my nerves nevertheless. My anxiety melted by slow degrees as I let his voice wash over me, and I forced myself to think the situation through instead of giving in to my fear.

I had never heard that voice before. He was a stranger. A stranger could not possibly have just appeared in my conservatory in the middle of the night. Campden House resided in a respectable neighborhood surrounded by a large park that rarely ever received visitors beyond tradesmen. My rooms were on the third floor. No one but Pendel, Tom, Sarah the maid, the doctor, and on the rare occasion, my uncle ever came to the third floor or into the house at all. And Pendel kept the place locked up tight at all times. Surely if that little disturbance in the hall a few moments ago had been about an intruder, Pendel would have notified me.

These were all things I knew to be true. Because of my illness, I could trust in those facts better than I could trust my own senses. Therefore, I could only conclude that this shadow was not real. It was simply another creation of my illness, another vision sent to plague me in the dark of night when I was unable to sufficiently distract myself or too weak to fight.

"Have ye nothin' to say?" the shadow asked, and I smiled for the first time in weeks.

It seemed this hallucination might be different from the others—the ones that hovered silently and menacingly over me until I was fit to scream or pull my hair out. This one almost sounded put out that I hadn't spoken again. I couldn't remember the last time I'd had a vision I could talk to.

I worried my lip as I pondered the shape in front of me. Dr. Payne would doubtless see the appearance of another hallucination as very concerning—and perhaps I should as well—but I had to admit I was relieved more than anything. This one seemed like it might just be amusing. I was so very tired of being alone and fighting my illness day after day. One night of surrender would not be so bad, particularly if I remained fully cognizant of the fact that he was not real.

What harm could it do to talk to it just this once?

I turned my back on it and made my way to my bed. The fire no longer gave enough warmth to offset suffering the hardness of the floor, and if my hallucination were going to bless me with some conversation, I could at least make myself comfortable.

After settling my blankets over the bed, I crawled beneath them, relaxed against the stack of pillows, and waited. The apparition had been silent and still through all of this. If it had a face, I could not see it, but it shifted slightly, giving it an air of puzzlement before it spoke.

"Ye're not gonna bring the 'ouse down on me 'ead?"

I chuckled. "Why would I do a thing like that?"

"'Twould seem the natural thing to do... under the circumstances."

I frowned at it in suspicion. "Is that what you want, for me to bring the whole house down on us? To shout them awake from their beds?"

"O'course not. I'm just surprised, is all."

Its rather peeved grumble made me smile again. "The days of me making a spectacle of myself over my visions are long gone," I said loftily, "at least as long as I can help it. You've no need to worry about that."

"Yer visions?"

I rolled my eyes. "Yes. My visions, my fancies, my hallucinations. You are not the first, nor will you be the last, I fear. But I've learned to live with you. And if you're actually willing to talk, then I am more than willing to listen and while away the hours until I fall asleep again. I could use the distraction, since I've no light to continue reading my novel and the winter nights are so damnably long."

Silence fell as the shadow seemed to ponder my words.

"Are ye sayin' ye think I'm not real, then?" it asked, hesitating as if it were choosing its words carefully.

I laughed. "Of course you aren't. You arrive in my rooms in the middle of the night, a dark specter in the heart of winter, without so much as a cloak or a hat to shield you from the cold—without even a jacket, as far as I can see in this blasted darkness. My rooms are on the top floor of the house, and Pendel checks the locks on all the doors and windows every night as part of his routine. Has done for ages. What else could you be?"

This time the vision chuckled too. "I s'pose that makes as much sense as any. So what are ye gonna do, then, if not call down the guards?"

"I'm going to sit here comfortably and listen to whatever it is you've come to tell me, obviously."

The silence that fell after my proclamation was soon broken by the sound of footsteps in the hall. A quick glance in that direction revealed the flickering light of a lamp beneath my door. The added light revealed more of the shape of the man before me but still no detail and no face.

"My lord?" Pendel called quietly from the hall. "My lord?"

"Yes, Pendel," I answered, turning my attention to the door again.

"Forgive the disturbance, but I happened to be on the stairs, and I thought I heard you speaking. Are you well? Is anything amiss?"

I glanced toward the apparition, but the shadow had vanished.

Damn.

Sighing in disappointment but not surprise, I answered, "All is well here. Is there something wrong?"

"No, my lord. So very sorry to disturb you at this hour."

"But I thought I heard you in the hall earlier."

"Yes, my lord. The footman, Tom, thought he saw someone, but we've searched the rooms and found no sign of any disturbance and all the doors and windows remain locked. I will check them again, to be sure, but I expect he saw only his shadow or a trick of the light."

"Perhaps he saw the headless spirit of the first Viscount Campden," I teased as I scanned my rooms for my visitor.

"Perhaps, my lord."

I could almost see Pendel's frown of disapproval from his tone, and I hung my head. I had to find humor in such things as visions and specters or I might have collapsed under the weight of my illness long ago, but poor Pendel had enough of a burden caring for me without me making light of such things. I cleared my throat and asked, "Did Tom say why he was up here in the first place?"

My question was met with a brief silence in which I could almost see the stern twist of Pendel's lips. "No, my lord. But that is a question I will have answered soon. I promise you."

Pendel had been with my family since my father was a lad. Loyal to his core, no matter how unhinged I might be, Pendel would not stand for anyone treating me as some sort of carnival attraction to be gawked at or whispered about. Campden House would need a new footman in short order if Tom couldn't provide a more convincing story for his presence where he should not have been.

"I'll leave you to it, then. Good night, Pendel."

"Good night, my lord."

His footsteps receded, along with the light, and I was left to my solitude again, wishing I could have had some excuse to keep him there longer.

"Is he another of your visions?"

The softly spoken words from close beside my bed nearly made me jump out of my skin, despite the veiled humor in them. I'd thought my visitor had dissolved into the ether, as they so often did when the real world intruded, but perhaps this one was more real than the others. Tom had heard something. But if all the doors and windows were still locked, a stranger couldn't have entered the house.

Wrapping my arms around myself, I frowned at the shadow. "No. No. Pendel is real. He's been with my family for years."

"Perhaps he is, and perhaps he isn't," the voice teased.

"He is," I insisted.

"But if you can see and hear me, as you can see and hear him, how is he real when I am not?"

Before I realized what I was doing, I reached beneath my cap and pulled a few hairs from my scalp. I could feel them in my palm, along with the slight sting, and I gritted my teeth. A real intruder would hardly hang about simply to tease and torment me. He had to be another vision conjured by my own mind to make me miserable. I rubbed my temple seeking to ease the growing ache behind my eyes as anxiety and frustration formed a vise around my chest. When I caught myself reaching for my hair again, I fisted my hands and forced them beneath the covers, keeping them firmly in my lap so I wouldn't do my scalp any more damage.

"I know the difference between what is real and what isn't. *I know it*," I asserted, mostly for my benefit. "If you've only come to upset me, I want you to leave. Leave now, please."

I clamped my lips shut against their trembling and breathed deeply as Dr. Payne had taught me. The icy air hurt my nose and throat, but it was good for the body.

"Fresh air, quiet, and exercise are the keys to continued good health," Dr. Payne always intoned.

I closed my eyes to blot out what little I could see of the shadow in the darkness and continued my breathing exercises, hoping it would go away.

"Wait. Forgive me. I didn't mean to upset you so. I'm very sorry. Please, don't cry." The words came at me in a rush, almost desperate in their pleading as I heard him move closer to me.

"I'm not crying," I insisted between labored breaths. "I'm breathing."

"Oh. Well. Good, then."

The hints of confusion and amusement in his voice didn't startle me as much as the change in his accent. Earlier, despite my not being able to place it, his accent had been undeniably working class. Now, his English was crisp and proper as any gentleman's. The change was enough to startle me out of my attack of nerves, and I stopped my exercises and frowned at him.

Did I alter his speech to ease my distress or so I would put a higher value on his words?

I'd never considered myself so much the snob before. I was hardly one to cast stones on what was right and proper in this world—wretched creature that I was. But I learned things about myself from my visions, after the trauma of their presence receded and I had hours and hours alone to reflect.

"Can you forgive me?" the shadow asked into the silence. "Truly, I did not mean to upset you."

With effort, I unclenched my palms and allowed the rest of my body to relax against the pillows again. A flicker of movement and flash of murky white light in a far corner to my right tried to distract me, but I ignored it in favor of the more solid and unfamiliar vision at the foot of my bed. "Yes, I can forgive you. Only please don't ask me such things again. It's upsetting enough to have you here, without my own hallucinations questioning my sanity."

The shadow chuckled, but the flicker and flash to my right caught my eye again, and I couldn't help but turn toward it. The hazy apparition I'd seen so many times before struggled to take shape in the corner by my window seat. It glowed with an eerie light, though that light didn't touch anything around it. It writhed in place, almost taking a form reminiscent of a woman in a diaphanous gown, but it never quite solidified. Like the darker shadows that plagued me, this vision never spoke, only hovered for a while before fading away again. It wasn't as bad as some of the others, but her appearance often preceded worse.

"What's wrong?" the shadow asked, and I chuckled helplessly at the lunacy of it all.

Perhaps there was some harm in not rejecting this new vision, after all. Perhaps it only opened the door to more.

"Someone else is competing for my attention, I'm afraid," I said, forcing a laugh. "I'd be flattered at my popularity, if I weren't merely flattering myself."

I heard the faint rustling of cloth as the shadow turned this way and that. "You see them now?"

"Yes." I sighed tiredly. "My visions always get worse the more unsettled or distressed I become. I'd take another dose of my medicine, but I don't wish to disturb Pendel again, and I really do hate the stuff. Besides, if I took it, I'd probably fall asleep and you'd disappear again, and then where would we be?"

"I see."

His tone said clearly he did not, in fact, see, but he was no longer baiting me like before, and the nervous ache in my head and chest lessened.

"Is the other vision still there? Where is it?" he asked.

I glanced toward my window seat, but the apparition had disappeared along with the worst of my anxiety. "No. She's gone."

"She?"

"She, it, I don't know." I sighed my irritation. "It reminds me sometimes of a woman in a flowing gown, but mostly it's just a floating kind of mist."

"Do you see her often?"

"Not so very often of late. I see her more when I'm feeling unwell, either in body or spirit."

"And you are feeling unwell now?"

I rolled my eyes, though I knew he could not see it in the dark. "Perhaps," I hedged, wishing he'd change the subject.

"Is there anything I might do? Would a lamp help? I could light one for you if you tell me where it is."

"No. I'm not allowed a lamp or a candle."

"Why?"

"For fear I may set the house ablaze and burn everyone in their beds, of course," I bit out irritably.

"And would you?"

"Of course not, at least not intentionally."

"And yet someone thinks you might?"

"No—I mean yes." I growled in frustration. "I don't know. I suppose they must, at least a little."

"How about a gas lamp? Surely such a grand house as this should have had them installed by now."

I lifted my chin. "Of course. After the fire several years ago, my uncle had them installed, but none in here, I'm afraid. I think they fear I might have another bad spell and blow the house up for good and all." I forced a chuckle.

"But I can see the faint glow from the hearth," the shadow argued. "You're allowed that obviously."

This subject had been done to death already, long before tonight. If the damned vision was going to quibble with me all night about things that hadn't changed in over ten years, then he could bloody well be on his way.

"The stove is filled and locked before the servants go to bed and then refilled in the morning when they wake," I explained through clenched teeth. "But really, this conversation is becoming tiresome. The least you could do is talk of something interesting, if you are going to plague me in the middle of the night." I sounded haughty and peevish, but I didn't care. This wasn't the kind of distraction I wanted.

The shadow let out a bark of laughter. "Of course, *my lord*. Forgive me, *my lord*. I should hate to think you aren't being sufficiently entertained."

"I thank you, good sir. It *is* a terrible tragedy to be without proper diversions," I threw back at him, choosing to ignore the acid in his tone, and I was gratified to hear him chuckle again.

He had a nice laugh, a laugh that warmed me and made me smile. Perhaps I could allow myself to be teased a little, after all, if it meant I could hear him laugh again.

No one else ever dared tease me. Pendel loved me in his own way, but he would be scandalized if I were to suggest a greater intimacy than we already shared as master and servant. The underservants rarely spoke a single word to me, let alone in jest. And my uncle and

I talked on his monthly visits, but he was always so careful with me—as if I were made of spun glass—hesitant to speak of anything beyond estate business and the exchange of the usual pleasantries for fear of upsetting me. I'd read so many books and plays where the characters traded witty barbs and dueled with words, the results quite hilarious, but I'd never had the chance myself.

I liked this vision, despite his annoying propensity to discomfit me. For once, I found myself wishing I knew how to make him stay, rather than begging him to leave me in peace. If only my traitorous mind had given a face along with that laugh.

My mattress shifted under me as the shadow settled on the end of my bed, startling me a little. He was not the first of my visions to have substance, though I shivered at the memories of the others. During the worst of my spells, early in my illness, my visions had terrified me. Phantom hands had held me down, their weight smothering me until I fainted dead away in my fear. I hadn't had such an episode in many years, and I hoped to never experience that again.

I caught my hand reaching for my hair, but forced it down and bit my lip instead. Such thoughts could twist my visions into something ugly and fearful if I dwelled too long in the past.

"If I am to amuse you, I will require amusement in kind," the shadow said, his voice thankfully teasing and light as he broke in on my dark thoughts.

"What kind of amusement?" I croaked gratefully.

"Satisfaction of my curiosity, I think—an answer for an answer. I will answer your questions, if you will do the same for mine."

"What kind of questions?"

"Impertinent ones, I'm sure."

"How impertinent?" I asked, tensing again.

The shadow shifted on the bed and chuckled. "Oh no. I've answered one for you. It's my turn now. What is your name?"

Whether I agreed that I owed him an answer or not, at least the question was an easy one, and one I wasn't at all ashamed of. Without even thinking about it, I sat up straighter, lifted my chin, and drew my shoulders back. "I am Arthur Phillip James Baptist Middleton, Viscount Campden."

"My word, that's certainly a mouthful. I think I'll call you Arthur, then."

I felt a brief jab of pique at such familiarity, before I was reminded that I was speaking to a creature of my own creation and to demand it use my title seemed the height of absurdity.

"And what is your name, pray?" I asked wryly.

"Hmmm. I feel I should not reveal too many of my secrets, lest you lose interest too quickly. You may call me Fox."

I frowned at him. "That hardly seems an answer. I feel I'm being cheated somehow."

"I said I would give you an answer for an answer. I didn't say it would be a good one." He laughed, and I couldn't help but join him. His laugh did strange things to my stomach.

"I like you," I blurted out before clamping a hand over my mouth and blushing in mortification.

How ridiculous. I was in my own rooms, with only an apparition for company. I should not have been embarrassed. But years of always saying the wrong thing at the wrong time and shaming myself and my uncle in the few social situations I'd been allowed as a youth—before we'd given up and had to lock me away completely—had taken their toll.

Fox's laughter died, and he was quiet for a time before he said, with mild surprise in his voice, "I like you as well, Arthur."

"Well... good," I replied stupidly, shifting uncomfortably but unable to stifle a smile. If anything, my blush deepened under the warmth in his voice, and I thanked the darkness that he could not see. I cleared my throat. "I suppose with that out of the way, we could continue our question and answer, then?"

"We could," Fox agreed hesitantly. "But I fear my time here grows short. It won't be long before the sun rises, and though the fog still seems thick enough to cut, I'd rather not risk discovery. I'll need to leave before dawn to avoid being seen."

I lurched forward, clutching blindly for his sleeve. My grasping hand encountered smooth, padded silk, and I twisted a desperate fist in it, grateful his substance didn't dissolve beneath my grasp.

"Don't go, please. I'm the only one who can see you. There's no need."

Realizing again that my reaction was wholly inappropriate to the circumstance, I released his sleeve as if it had burned me and shrank back again. "Forgive me. I—it's just... we've only begun talking."

How pathetic was I that I was willing to get on my knees and beg a figment of my own imagination not to leave me alone?

Fox sighed as I began my breathing exercises again and clenched my fists in my lap.

"I can spare a few minutes," he replied, "but not much more. I'm sorry."

Other shadows skittered and writhed around the edges of my vision, but I kept my gaze focused on the dark outline at the end of my bed. "At least tell me a little about yourself," I pleaded quietly trying to regain my calm.

Fox chuckled. "If I am indeed merely a product of your fancy, shouldn't you be the one to tell me who I am?"

"It doesn't work like that. My mind has a way of surprising me. You might be a character from a novel or a play I've read. You might be one of the infamous ghosts that local gossip claims haunts this house. You might be someone barely remembered from my childhood, before…. Well, you might be a combination of people or things really. I never know."

Fox was silent for a few moments before he leaned back against the post at the foot of my bed. The wood creaked quietly under his weight, and the heavy bed-curtains rustled in the darkness. "All right. If I can be anyone, then, I will entertain you with my tale… which may or may not be the truth."

His teasing tone had returned, and I smiled as I felt my desperation ease. If I could keep him talking, perhaps he would forget this nonsense about leaving.

"I am a thief," he began. "But no lowly brute on the smash-and-grab am I, for I am also a gentleman… well, *mostly*. I slipped into your beautiful and grand house this night, fully intending to slip out again with as much treasure as I could carry, but instead of the upper halls being dark and empty—as they had been every night for the past week—I nearly tripped over a great lumbering oaf in your hall and had to dash into what I thought might be a bedroom before I was seen. I tried to wait him out, but the oaf and another man blocked the stairs, so I had to think of some other way to get out of the house. I believed God had smiled on me when I discovered the bedchamber I'd hidden in was in actuality a stairwell. The stairs led up instead of down, but I still counted myself lucky. Except the fog that was supposed to obscure my departure made it near impossible for me to see my own hand in front of my face, let alone the locks I needed to pick to carry out my escape. I was fumbling with my tools when a quiet voice called to me. I thought I was done for, but the owner of that voice simply backed down the stairs, climbed into bed, and ordered me to tell him a tale, as if thieves in his house were an everyday occurrence. Apparently my luck held true, after all." Fox's arm moved in the darkness in what I thought might have been a dramatic flourish, and then he chuckled. "So what do you think about that, Lord Campden? Entertaining enough for you?"

Smiling, I clapped my hands vigorously. "Yes, very much so. I suppose I should be flattered you chose to sit and chat with me during all that excitement. I truly had no idea."

"You should be flattered. I wouldn't do such a thing for just anyone. In fact, you're lucky I didn't simply bash you on the head and make a run for it."

"Oh yes, I'm very lucky," I teased back a little breathlessly.

The slightest edge to his voice sent a thrill through me, but whether of fear or excitement, I refused to name it. An apparition Fox might be, but he was solid enough to my fractured mind, and I had made him several inches taller than myself, perhaps to add to that delicious hint of danger I must somehow be craving.

I was not a large man, but I was no milksop either. Though I never left the confines of my rooms and rooftop conservatory, I kept myself fit with the forms the doctor had taught me. Compared to the laborers and deliverymen I'd seen from my windows, I thought I measured up well enough. Fox had to be larger than myself to give him any of the deliciously menacing qualities I'd read about in my novels. A gentleman thief indeed—what on earth could I be thinking? Perhaps Dr. Payne had been right to caution against the influences of such stories. Still, boredom and loneliness could lead to their own kind of madness in time. I was very grateful Pendel chose to not look too closely at the packets of books Wallace Fuller, the bookseller, sent me every two weeks.

Fox cleared his throat, drawing my wandering thoughts back to him. "So now I have answered you. I believe it is your turn to tell me a story."

"What kind of story?"

"Tell me about yourself, of course. Quid pro quo. Tell me how is it that the Viscount Campden came to be locked in a room in his own home with no light to see by and a dying fire he's not even allowed to stoke with his own coal?"

I shifted uneasily at the edge in his voice, my discomfort returning. "I already told you that."

"Not really," he pushed. "You said you are ill, but not how. Have you always been ill? How long have you been confined to these rooms? Where is the rest of your family? You spoke of an uncle making decisions for you, but why is he not here in this enormous house with you? I watched the house for days and only saw a few servants moving about. That's why I picked it. I assumed the family was away."

"I don't wish to speak of it. Not now, please," I replied quietly, twisting my hands in my lap.

After a pause, Fox sighed and stood. "Perhaps that should be all for tonight, then. I should go."

I ruthlessly smothered my first inclination to grab for him again. My pride wouldn't allow another lapse in dignity, even if I feared he'd never return. "If you must," I murmured. And even though I knew it to be pointless, I couldn't help but add, "But you will come back, won't you?"

"I don't know," he replied. "It seems I upset you more than I entertained you. I can't think why you'd want me to call on you again."

"But I do… please." I didn't bother concealing the need in my voice this time.

"Well, if all you've said is true, and I am a thing of your creation, then that is entirely up to you now, isn't it?" he asked teasingly, his voice receding as he moved away from me.

I stuck my tongue out at him. He couldn't see that brief lapse in decorum, but it made me feel better nonetheless. "Possibly," I replied with as much hauteur as I could manage. "But it is only polite to ask." When he made no reply, I grew nervous again. "Will you?" I pleaded.

I heard the distinct click of a door latch, and a slight draft of colder air rustled my bed-curtains. "I will try. Good night, Arthur."

I had to swallow a slight lump in my throat before I could reply. "Good night, Fox."

After a brief moment of silence, I assumed he'd gone, evaporated into the ether like the others, but then his voice drifted to me again, quiet and hollow, as if from a long way off. "Arthur, if I do come again, I should like to be able to see your face when we talk. No matter your illness or the story behind it, the lord and master of the manor should not be kept in the dark in his own house, particularly if he does not wish to be."

ROWAN MCALLISTER is a woman who doesn't so much create as recreate, taking things ignored and overlooked and hopefully making them into something magical and mortal. She believes it's all in how you look at it. In addition to a continuing love affair with words, she creates art out of fabric, metal, wood, stone, and any other interesting scraps of life she can get her hands on. Everything is simply one perspective change and a little bit of effort away from becoming a work of art that is both beautiful and functional. She lives in the woods, on the very edge of suburbia—where civilization drops off and nature takes over—sharing her home with her patient, loving, and grounded husband, her super sweet hairball of a cat, and a mythological beast masquerading as a dog. Her chosen family is made up of a madcap collection of people from many different walks of life, all of whom act as her muses in so many ways, and she would be lost without them.

Email: rowanmcallister10@gmail.com

Facebook: www.facebook.com/rowanmcallister10

Twitter: @RowanMcallister

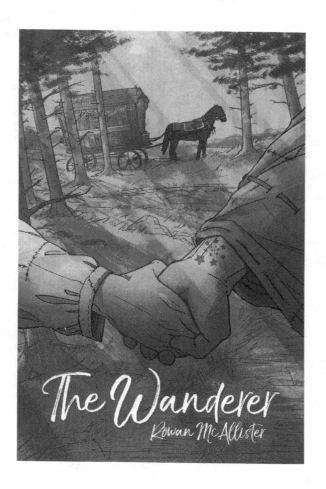

The Wanderer

Rowan McAllister

Chronicles of the Riftlands: Book One

After centuries of traveling the continent of Kita and fighting the extradimensional monsters known as Riftspawn, mage Lyuc is tired and ready to back away from the concerns of humanity.

But the world isn't done with him yet.

While traveling with a merchant caravan, Lyuc encounters Yan, an Unnamed, the lowest caste in society. Though Yan has nothing but his determination and spirit, he reminds Lyuc what passion and desire feel like. While wild magic, a snarky, shapeshifting, genderfluid companion, and the plots of men and monsters seem determined to keep Lyuc from laying down his burden, only Yan's inimitable spirit tempts him to hang on for another lifetime or so.

All Yan wants is to earn the sponsorship of a guild so he can rise above his station, claim a place in society, and build the family he never had.

After hundreds of years of self-imposed penance, all Lyuc wants is Yan.

If they can survive prejudice, bandits, mercenaries, monsters, and nature itself, they might both get their wish… and maybe even their happily ever after.

www.dreamspinnerpress.com

AIR AND EARTH

ROWAN MCALLISTER

Elemental Harmony: Book One

When absentminded video game developer Jay Thurson impulsively follows his intuition westward, he never expects his rideshare to turn out to be a gun-toting madman. In an act of desperation, Jay turns to the gift he's long neglected and feared for help and leaps from the moving car on a dark and deserted back country road.

Running for his life leads him to the doorstep of Adam Grauwacke, a roadside nursery owner and sometime vegetable farmer, whose affinity for the earth goes far beyond having a green thumb. Adam's world is ordered and predictable, dependable and safe, but despite having his dream farm and business, he's always felt something's missing. When he welcomes Jay into his home, life seems to click for both men, and together they explore their gifts and their attraction.

But harmony has no value if it is easily won, and a crazed gunman and volatile ex might be their end if Jay and Adam can't learn to trust the strength of their bond.

www.dreamspinnerpress.com

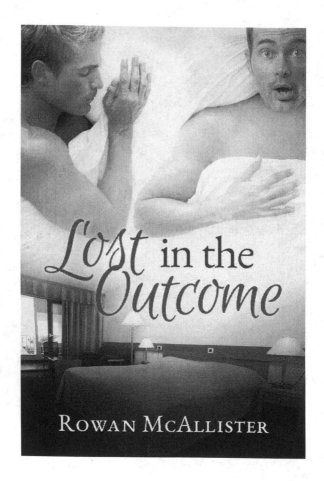

Lost in the Outcome

Rowan McAllister

When Nathan Seward wakes up in a cheap hotel with a stranger, unable to remember the night before, unscrupulous plots and clandestine schemes are the furthest thing from his mind. True, he's in Houston to bid on his biggest contract yet, one that will put his software development company on the map, but he's the underdog at the table, not one of the big players. Unfortunately someone out there sees him as a threat and isn't above drugging and blackmailing him to put him out of the running. Luckily for Nathan, the man in bed next to him couldn't be further removed from the corporate world.

Tim Conrad is scraping the bottom of the barrel. He left college during his freshman year to take care of his dying mother, and life and lack of money prevented him going back. Now twenty-seven, his dreams are long buried, and he's scraping by with dead-end jobs and couch surfing because he can't afford a place of his own.

As Nathan tries to run damage control and figure out what the hell happened to him, he and Tim discover a connection neither was looking for, as well as dreams they've both forgotten.

www.dreamspinnerpress.com

William Carey has played many roles in his thirty-two years of life. Though born to privilege, he fled his disapproving family and, purely out of spite, devoted himself to a life of danger and infamy. William never thought twice about his self-destructive behavior until he met a passionate woman who showed him how to harness his rebellious nature and return to London, his family, and society as a respectable gentleman of fortune. But William's beloved wife is six years gone, and with her his joie de vivre.

William devotes his days to the pursuit of empty pleasure until the night William's brother asks a small favor by which William meets a young man who ignites a spark in him he'd thought long extinguished. Stephen is fiery and passionate, handsome and mysterious—exactly what a fallen devil needs to stir the ashes of his heart. Unwilling to lose that spark now that he has found it again, William devises a scheme to claim Stephen for his own, but Stephen is beyond reluctant, with another benefactor and secrets he will not share. William will need more than cunning to win Stephen's trust and love. He'll need all the luck he can get.

www.dreamspinnerpress.com

MY ONLY
SUNSHINE

ROWAN
McALLISTER

Tanner Wallis is nearly at the end of his rope the night Mason Seidel finds him lying next to the mangled body of a cow on the back pastures of the Seidel family's Wyoming ranch. Recently out of the hospital after he and his boyfriend were brutally beaten, Tanner is jobless, homeless, and almost penniless. His desperate hope is that Mason will believe he's innocent of the senseless crime and give him a place to heal, both physically and emotionally, until he can get on his feet again.

But Mason already has enough on his plate. He's only been back on the ranch a few months, ten years after his father kicked him out for being gay, and only because his sister begged him to come help after the man's disabling stroke. With all his responsibilities—running the struggling ranch and keeping his sister and father off his back—Mason can't really afford the distraction Tanner represents. But he can't just abandon the attractive young man either. There's trouble in spades on the ranch, but if they face it together, Mason and Tanner might find a future with a little sunshine.

www.dreamspinnerpress.com